Jack Batten, after a brief and unhappy career as a lawyer, has been a very happy Toronto freelance writer for many years. He has written thirty-five books, including four crime novels featuring Crang, the unorthodox criminal lawyer who has a bad habit of stumbling on murders that need his personal attention. Batten reviewed jazz for the *Globe and Mail* for several years, reviewed movies on CBC Radio for twenty-five-years, and now reviews crime novels for the *Toronto Star*. Not surprisingly, jazz, movies, and crime turn up frequently in Crang's life.

Books of Merit

STRAIGHT NO CHASER

STRAIGHT NO

A Crang Mystery

CHASER

Jack Batten

THOMAS ALLEN PUBLISHERS
TORONTO

Library and Archives Canada Cataloguing in Publication

Batten, Jack, 1932–
       Straight no chaser : a Crang mystery / by Jack Batten.

First published: Toronto : Macmillan of Canada, 1989.
ISBN 978-0-88762-747-7

I. Title.

PS8553.A833S8   2011   C813'.54   C2010-908132-3

Cover design: Sputnik Design
Cover image: Steve Buchanan/Getty Images

Published by Thomas Allen Publishers,
a division of Thomas Allen & Son Limited,
390 Steelcase Road East,
Markham, Ontario L3R 1G2 Canada

www.thomasallen.ca

ONTARIO ARTS COUNCIL
CONSEIL DES ARTS DE L'ONTARIO

Canada Council
for the Arts

The publisher gratefully acknowledges the support of
The Ontario Arts Council for its publishing program.

We acknowledge the support of the Canada Council for the Arts, which
last year invested $20.1 million in writing and publishing throughout Canada.

We acknowledge the Government of Ontario through the
Ontario Media Development Corporation's Ontario Book Initiative.

We acknowledge the financial support of the Government of Canada
through the Canada Book Fund for our publishing activities.

11 12 13 14 15   5 4 3 2 1

Text printed on 100% PCW recycled stock
Printed and bound in Canada

For
Howard Engel
and
Eric Wright

STRAIGHT NO CHASER

1

DAVE GODDARD was asking me to tail a guy he said was tailing him.

I said, "At law school, Dave, when I went, I don't recall they taught a course in close and surreptitious pursuit."

"The reason I flashed on you for the gig, man, you're a criminal lawyer."

"You got that part right, Dave."

"So dig this, you're a criminal lawyer, and the thing going down, this dude on my case, it's a crime."

"Watching and besetting maybe."

"That's no jive, man."

"Dave, when I said watching and besetting, that's what we lawyers call legal wit."

Dave wasn't in the mood for legal wit. He had a cup of coffee in front of him. I was drinking vodka on the rocks. It was a few minutes after midnight, and we were sitting at the table in Chase's Club reserved for musicians. The table was next to the door into the kitchen.

"Here's the deal, man." Dave leaned six inches over the table. "The dude follows me to my pad. You follow the dude. I fall into bed."

Dave stopped talking. He was still leaning.

I said, "That seems to leave me and your alleged tail all by ourselves on the street."

"Wait for it, man," Dave said. "What this dude's gonna do, me down for the night, you dig, he's gonna head back to his own pad. You with me, man?"

I said, "And I keep him company at a discreet distance. Which gets us the gentleman's address and eventually his name."

Dave signified his pleasure.

"Solid," he said.

"I'm a quick study, Dave."

I let a beat of silence go by. Dave swallowed from his cup of coffee. Black with enough sugar to give an ordinary man diabetes.

"What if I have a doubt or two?" I said.

Dave put down his coffee cup.

He said, "Crang, the dude's not how you said. Alleged? Last two days, he's right there. I look, dude's back there. Yesterday afternoon, I'm in my room at the hotel, TV's on, I'm laid out on the bed watching my soaps, somebody starts working on the lock from out in the hall. 'Hey', I holler. Whoever's out there splits. It had to be the same dude."

"Sounds persuasive, Dave."

I lied. Dave wasn't persuading me to take part in his dingbat enterprise. But just because it was Dave, I was willing to sit at the table in Chase's while he tried more persuading.

Dave was a tall, reedy guy in his late fifties, about fifteen years older than me. His face was oval-shaped, the kind you usually see on a woman. It looked fine on Dave. He had a head of hair that was still dark, still full. One of his eyes was a fraction off-centre. I think it was the right. When he talked to me, the left was the eye that seemed to be staring into mine. Dave had on a lightweight brown sports jacket and a pale-brown shirt. The jacket had no lapels, and the shirt had a roll collar like the kind Billy Eckstine used to wear. Maybe Mr. B still wears them. A thin leather strap was looped around Dave's neck and hung almost to his waist. A metal clip was fixed to the end of the strap. It held Dave's tenor saxophone when he played. Dave was a jazz musician. In my value system, that gave Dave a status close to heroic. Should a grown man have a hero? Soft spot maybe. I had a soft spot for Dave, and it made me more patient than I'd otherwise be with the talk about trailing a stranger who was trailing Dave.

I said, "Let me suggest something else, Dave, an alternate plan."

Dave focussed his left eye on me.

I said, "Why not step up to the gent and ask how come the fascination with you?"

Dave raised both hands and made shooing motions.

"Definitely no eyes for that, man," he said.

"Understand, Dave, I'm doing what a lawyer's supposed to do."

"Man?"

"Ask questions."

"I'm hip."

"So what's wrong with the frontal approach?" I asked. "The guy may be about as threatening as a shy fan."

"Not this dude." Dave went into his leaning routine. "See, the amount of years I been on the scene, I can suss when a cat's not cool. This dude isn't. Maybe I crossed him somewhere a long time back. You remember what I was like ten, fifteen years ago, juicing, sticking needles in my arm, all that shit. I did far-out numbers I didn't know I was doing. Maybe this dude, he's somebody I ripped off. Who knows? Cat could be pissed at me from way back."

"Getting even?" I said. "That's what you think the guy doing the following is all about?"

Dave shrugged.

A waiter in a black bow tie and a red jacket with stains down the front put a tray of drinks on the table at my elbow. I moved my elbow. It was a protective measure. I was wearing my Cy Mann navy blue. Twelve hundred dollars of suit, the most extravagant garment in my wardrobe. The waiter mused over the tray and selected a glass from the collection. He placed it in front of me. I hoped it was vodka and ice. The waiter performed his duties in slow motion. Probably didn't want to get more stains on the jacket. I tasted the drink. The vodka was the bar variety, sweet and lacking in punch. The ice was the genuine article.

"How I read it," I said to Dave, "you may have things wrong way round."

"You don't want another vodka?" the waiter said to me.

"Not you," I said to the waiter. "Fine with the drink."

"First was a vodka. You ask for another, I figure you mean same as before."

"I was talking to the other gentleman."

"Something wrong with the coffee, Mr. Dave?" the waiter asked Dave.

Dave said, "Kinda chilled out now you mention it, man."

The conversation was getting away from me. Not that I had much grip on it from the time I arrived at Chase's to keep the appointment with Dave Goddard.

"You want me to top it up?" the waiter asked Dave.

"You don't mind, man?"

"A pleasure."

The waiter needed twenty seconds of slow-mo lifting to reclaim the tray of drinks and amble in search of fresh coffee.

"You were laying something on me back there, man?" Dave said to me.

"I was."

I intended to offer Dave a couple of reasons for excluding me from his scheme. Dignity, for one reason. It wouldn't be dignified for a lawyer like me, not precisely a pillar of the bar but still a criminal counsel with eighteen years' worth of plucky service in the courtrooms of Toronto, to do a Philip Marlowe. That's what I intended to say. But I couldn't get the words out, not with Dave Goddard the jazz musician asking me for this favour. The hell with dignity.

"Okay, Dave," I said, "what's the gent on your case look like when he's on your case?"

"Man, I'm sitting here rapping with you and he's making the scene."

"He's in the club now?"

"Would I shuck you?"

"Suppose not."

I started to turn my head for a survey of the room.

"Don't avert your eyes, man," Dave said.

Avert? Was that a piece of hip phraseology I'd missed out on? I left my eyes on Dave.

"The dude's sitting at the bar," Dave said. "I'll give you the word when to peek. Far end of the bar."

Dave's off-centre eye alignment must have yielded an edge in the vision department. He didn't have to avert his eyes to sneak a peek.

"Go, man," Dave said.

I turned my head. The bar ran along the back of Chase's. Photographs of musicians who'd worked the room over the years hung on the wall behind the bar. The club was three-quarters full, a very good house for a Wednesday night. I glanced to the end of the bar long enough to register the man sitting on the last stool. He had on a beige jacket and was drinking a glass of beer. He was looking straight ahead toward the bandstand. Not for long. His head twitched in the direction of Dave and me. I turned back to Dave. The beige jacket I was sure of. The guy may also have had thinning hair and a small moustache.

"Man in the beige jacket," I said to Dave.

"Bald dude," Dave said.

Ah.

"Got a moustache," Dave said.

Double ah. The powers of observation remained intact.

"The jacket," I said, "with it, he'll stand out in a crowd."

Dave's expression didn't change, but his voice edged up a notch in volume. "This mean you're in, man?" he said.

"I'll follow your buddy, Dave. But before we decide the next move from there, we regroup for further strategy."

"Mellow."

"Right, Dave."

Dave Goddard was a man locked into the late 1940s. His language. His clothes. His music. He blew the tenor saxophone the way Stan Getz and Zoot Sims blew theirs in Woody Herman's orchestra when it

5

was called the Four Brothers Band. That was 1948. Getz and Sims let their styles evolve over the years. Dave held firm with his. His sound was light and feathery, and he shaped his solos in graceful little arcs. Dave hadn't seemed to notice the passing of the last four decades. But his playing kept him employed. Maybe it was his Canadian origins. That was quaint for a jazz musician.

When I was a kid, I heard Dave play at concerts and clubs around town. Dave was a Toronto guy. His playing used to send little thrills through me. It still did. When Montreal was the hot Canadian jazz city, Dave lived there. All the clubs booked him. Same with Vancouver. Sometimes things broke exactly right for Dave and he toured Europe and Japan, played clubs in California and Manhattan. Usually he went as a sideman in somebody else's group, somebody with a big name. Dave could always fit in.

He wasn't an anachronism, more like a man who'd found the perfect year and decided to cling to it. Dave's year happened to be 1948. I'd have to ask him where he found the Mr. B shirts in 1989.

"Hold tight till one bell, man," Dave said.

He wanted me to wait until one o'clock.

It was time for the last set of the night. Dave stood up and walked toward Chase's tiny bandstand. When Dave walked, he took long, deliberate strides. His body moved in sections.

The waiter in the stained red jacket chugged back to the table. He was carrying a glass Silex coffee pot.

"Too late for Mr. Dave?" he asked.

"Beats me."

2

THE QUINTET played "Milestones" first, then a ballad, "I Remember Clifford".

Dave Goddard wasn't the leader on the job. Harp Manley was. Harp was a short rotund man in his mid-sixties. He had skin the colour of a football, and he was experiencing a renaissance. He played trumpet in the manner of the man remembered in the ballad, Clifford Brown. Harp blew fast and fat. That took technique. Most bebop trumpet players, which was what Harp was, had small tones and spattered notes like pellets from a BB gun. There were exceptions. Clifford Brown, Fats Navarro, Harp Manley. Clifford and Fats died young. Harp was still with us and recently prospering.

He'd sunk from view for most of the 1960s and 1970s. He lived in Amsterdam and worked the clubs and festivals in Europe, the odd date back home in New York. Bebop always had a small audience. It changed for Harp when Martin Scorsese cast him in a movie. Harp played a retired Harlem pimp. He turned out to be as controlled an actor as he was a jazz musician, and he won an Academy Award nomination as Best Supporting Actor. He didn't get the Oscar, but the attention put his musical career in the hot category. Harp probably didn't think of it that way. He was blowing the way he'd always blown. The difference was more people were paying to listen.

Harp made another movie. It was set for a world premiere in Toronto during the week he was at Chase's Club. I read about the movie in a profile of Harp in that morning's *Globe and Mail*. Mark Miller wrote the profile, best jazz critic in the city. He didn't have a lot of competition. Harp played a Philadelphia cop in the movie. According to Mark Miller, advance word had it that Harp established himself as more than a one-role wonder.

In the meantime, he was touring with a small band that had three young black guys from New York in the rhythm section. In Toronto, Harp added an extra horn to the group's front line. The extra horn was Dave Goddard on tenor saxophone.

The quintet finished the set with a Thelonious Monk tune, "Well You Needn't". Dave's solo was a marvel of gentle curves.

"Lovely stuff, Dave," I said when he came back to the table next to the door into the kitchen.

"You ready, man?"

I guessed Dave was too distracted to absorb the compliment.

"More or less," I said.

Dave had his tenor saxophone in his right hand, its case in his left. He sat down across the table from me. The saxophone was a Selmer and looked like it had been with Dave for all his years in the jazz life. Its brass colour was dull and scuffed, and elastic bands were wrapped around four or five of the valves. The case was a different proposition. It was spiffy and gleaming black, fresh from the store. Dave fitted the saxophone into the case. He took the strap from around his neck, draped it over the saxophone, and snapped shut the case.

"This shadow job," I said, "where's the first stop?"

I felt like an idiot talking about shadow jobs. More G. Gordon Liddy than Philip Marlowe.

Dave said, "Place where I'm staying? That part's a touch, man. Six, seven blocks down the street. We can stroll it. Me, the dude, and you."

"In that order."

"To the Cameron."

"The Cameron House's where you have a room?"

I went into my astonished expression. It involved a drooping of the lower lip.

"I hadda let my old place go, the apartment," Dave said. "Been on the road is why."

"But the Cameron, Dave?"

I was still wearing the astonished expression. The Cameron House was home to the chic young musical crowd. Electric pianos, synthesizers, fusion. To the Cameron bunch, fusion meant mixing jazz with rock, folk, salsa, other musical detritus. To me, it meant dilution of the only music that counted. Jazz. Scornful me.

"Give it a chance, man," Dave said. "The kids over there, they dig what I'm laying down."

"See you as an elder statesman maybe."

"Whatever," Dave said. "A young cat fixed me with a freebie room for the week."

"On the House?"

"On the young cat."

"The kids may be salt of the earth, Dave. Forgive me if I don't get excited about their music."

Harp Manley's voice drifted over from a table near the bandstand. Harp had a high-pitched voice. It made an odd match with his portly body. He was sitting with a group of middle-aged fans who appeared delighted to be in Harp's presence. Bet they were as narrow-minded about jazz as I was. Around the rest of the room, patrons were taking care of essential business, ordering the last drink, paying the bill, heading for the door. The man in the beige jacket was holding steady at the end of the bar.

Dave said to me, "Your chorus, man."

He meant that I should take up position for my tailing operation. I was a whiz at interpreting Dave's messages. Twenty-five bucks seemed enough to deal with two vodkas, the cover charge, and a tip for Speedy Gonzales. I dropped two tens and a five on the table, and squeezed my way through chairs and tables and people toward the door. While squeezing, I affected an air of nonchalance. It was designed to throw

Beige Jacket off the scent. Never would he suspect the intrepid Crang had his number.

Outside Chase's, the air was windless and dulcet and had the soft feel you sometimes get in early September. A Department of Public Works truck had passed a few minutes earlier and done a wash job on the pavement. Toronto the Scrubbed. The street was Queen, and I crossed it, over the streetcar tracks, and stood deep in the doorway of a second-hand paperback store.

Chase's Club was on the north side of Queen two blocks and a bit west of University Avenue. The place was owned by a canny gent named Abner Chase who was fond enough of jazz that he'd kept his club in musical business for thirty years, even when jazz slumped as a consistent drawing card. Abner did a brisk lunch trade that offset the slow jazz nights. The major attraction at noon was the salad bar. It was fifty feet long and currently featured arugula.

I waited ten minutes. It was one-thirty. Three streetcars swayed by, one eastbound, two westbound. Clumps of people left the club. I recognized the jolly group that had been at Harp Manley's feet. The neon sign over the door into the club blinked off. It spelled Chase's minus the apostrophe. Without the neon, the street turned marginally darker.

Dave Goddard came out of the club five minutes later. He had the shiny saxophone case in his right hand. I tensed for action. Dave paused, pivoted to the right, and set off along Queen to the west at his gait of the long lopes. He got two dozen lopes down the street and the man in the beige jacket emerged from Chase's. He too hove to the right and travelled west about twenty yards back of Dave. I waited a few seconds and enlisted in the migration. Westward ho.

Beige Jacket looked more formidable standing up and moving than sitting down and drinking. He was about my height, just under six feet, but had me beat in the tonnage department. I weighed one-seventy. Beige Jacket would clock in at fifty pounds over that. Most of the weight was concentrated in his upper body. He had a stiff, squared-off look, like Raymond Burr when he played Perry Mason.

Dave crossed Beverley Street and passed the Bakka science-fiction bookstore. Beige Jacket did likewise. On my side of the street, the south, it was restaurant row. Le Marais. Chicago's. Le Bistingo. I'd dined in all. Some of their maîtres d' knew me by name. Gave me a table in the window. All that heady stuff. I was a neighbour. When I got out of law school, I opened a practice in an office on Queen over a Czech ma-and-pa hardware store. That was before the street changed in the direction of gentrification. Now it was trendy restaurants and medium-couture shoppes. The Czech ma and pa were squeezed out by a boutique called Trapezoid that offered a line in leatherware to all sexes. Only two establishments remained from the Queen West of eighteen years earlier, a branch of the Legion and my office. A sturdy duo.

Dave's stride was deceptive, much faster than it looked. It meant he, Beige Jacket, and I were covering the sidewalks at a lively clip, each of us holding at the distances we set at the beginning of the adventure. Beige Jacket was twenty yards behind Dave, and I was ten yards and the width of Queen to the rear of Beige Jacket. Apart from us, the street was sparsely populated. A bunch of kids were yakking it up outside the Bamboo Club on the north side. Dave passed them, passed Trapezoid and my office, and stopped for the red light at Queen and Spadina.

I dropped into the shadows of the entrance to Makos Furs at the southeast corner of the intersection and watched Dave and Beige Jacket cross Spadina Avenue. Spadina is as wide as the Gobi, and all the lurking in the Makos entrance opened the gap between me and Beige Jacket to fifty yards. The lights changed again, red to green, and I took up the trip across Spadina at something between a trot and a scuttle.

The Cameron House is a short block west of Spadina at the corner of Queen and a street called Cameron Avenue. Hence the hotel's name. By the time I crossed Spadina, Dave and Beige Jacket had turned the corner at Cameron and disappeared from sight. I escalated my speed from trot and scuttle to sprint.

The Cameron is four storeys of brick that someone decided would look good in black paint. On its Cameron Avenue side, gaudy murals that reach as high as the second floor interrupt the black. The entrance door to the hotel is positioned mid-mural about halfway up the street. Dave was standing outside the door when my sprint brought him back into sight, and he seemed to be in distress.

Beige Jacket had caught up to Dave, and the two were performing a bizarre fandango. Beige Jacket was trying to yank the saxophone case from Dave's grasp. Dave was resisting mightily.

I was still on the south side of Queen. A passing streetcar blocked my view of the tussle over the saxophone for five seconds.

The streetcar got by. Beige Jacket had the case in his hands and was running north on Cameron. Dave was in pursuit. Beige Jacket had impressive speed for a top-heavy guy. He was ten yards up on Dave.

I jogged to the centre of Queen. Beige Jacket rounded the north corner of the Cameron House. Dave followed. I waited for a Weston Foods transport trailer to rumble by in the north lane.

I ran up Cameron past the murals. No time to admire art. There seemed to be an alley running behind the Cameron House where Beige Jacket and Dave had turned in. I reached the north corner of the Cameron House. There was an alley, but there was no Beige Jacket, no Dave.

I checked out the terrain. The alley had three or four faint overhead lights that broke dim holes in the darkness. There was a pickup truck parked against the back wall of the Cameron. It had tires that a Brobdingnagian must have ordered. There were no other vehicles further down the alley. Nothing stirred. All I had to contend with was silence. For a semi-brave chap, that seemed sufficient.

I walked deeper into the alley until I was even with the pickup. Its huge tires lifted the back of the truck a couple of feet over my head. I counted my footsteps. Eight of them took me past the truck. The ground under my shoes made a light crunching noise. The alley was paved but covered in a coating of sand and grit.

I stopped.

There was nothing that caught my eye.

But something caught my ear.

It was more of the light crunching sound. And it didn't come from under my shoes. It came from behind me.

I started to turn my head. It didn't get far. A very hard object struck the back of it with a purposeful force.

The alley rose up to smack my face. Or my face fell down to hit the alley. Either way, there was nothing behind my eyeballs except a black abyss.

3

THE WORST PART was I had on the Cy Mann navy blue.

Most days I go casual to the office. Jeans, work shirt, Rockport Walkers on my feet. Days I'm in court, I wear the Cy Mann. This had been one of those days, and with me spread out in the alley behind the Cameron House, the suit was bound to be losing its flare.

"Shit," I said, not to myself. Out loud.

I opened my eyes. My line of vision was aimed at a garage on the south side of the alley. There was a sentence spray-painted on the garage door. "The moon is full of roses and bum cheese." How enigmatic. How ridiculous. What did it mean? I pondered the question with a clear head. That surprised me. I'd been KO'd, and my head was clear. No buzzing, no ache, no dizzy spell.

I stood up and felt a tad light-headed. Nothing more life-threatening. The damage was to the suit. I brushed at the grey dust that covered my jacket and pants. The dust was stubborn, and all that my brushing accomplished was to blend the grey of the dust more intrinsically with the blue of the fabric.

My watch said it was exactly two o'clock. I couldn't have been unconscious for more than a minute, not long enough to destroy many brain cells but long enough for the alley to empty of friend and foe. There was nothing back there except me and the graffiti.

I walked past the pickup truck with the oversized tires, out of the alley, and back down the street to the door into the Cameron. A sticker on the door said "Pull". I pulled. The hall inside was narrow, and a mad muralist had wreaked his artistic will on its walls. Green fish with bulging eyes swam in a sea of vibrant pink. At the end of the hall, another corridor, equally narrow, branched left and right. I chose left and stepped into the Cameron's bar. It was almost empty.

The room's only occupant was a woman sitting at one of the small round tables that lined both walls. She was drinking from a can of Diet Coke and reading the personals section of *Now*.

It's the weekly that caters to what passes for the Toronto counter-culture these days. The woman was in her late twenties and had pale skin, frizzed brown hair, and a figure that in polite circles is generally called full. She was wearing a peasant blouse that scooped low across her breasts. *Now*'s personals must have been juicy. The woman didn't look up from them until I spoke.

I said, "Wonder if you could help me?"

The woman let her eyes run up my suit to my face. It took five seconds.

"I would," she said, "except I don't do dry cleaning."

She had a light voice.

"A man stays here named Dave Goddard," I said. "You happen to know did he come through here the last ten minutes?"

"Guy talks like a Jack Kerouac novel?" the woman asked. She kept her finger on a *Now* ad.

I said, "That'd be Dave."

"Got funny eyes?"

"Those too."

"Collars on his shirt the same size as lapels on a jacket?"

"Right again."

"Which he hasn't got anyway, the lapels."

"I think we've got the identity problem licked."

"Right now," the woman said, triumphantly I thought, "he's at work down the street, the guy you're looking for."

I had a feeling I wasn't going to locate Dave in the very immediate future. I had another feeling. Exasperation. Two in the morning was a dumb hour for a lawyer who'd been bopped on the bean to be gadding about the bohemian byways of the city.

"Well, no," I said to the woman. "When last seen, a few minutes ago, Dave Goddard was outside this very hotel."

"Who last saw him?"

"I."

"That gives you the edge on me."

The bar was no bigger than my living room and not as cunningly furnished. Everything looked like it'd come from a basic-black sale, the small round tables, the leather banquettes. The air was an advertisement for black-lung disease.

I gave the woman one more shot.

I said, "Correct me if I've got it wrong. Dave Goddard, the man I'm trying to locate, he's staying here, far as you know?"

"Jim Kirk lent the guy his room while he's doing places up north with his band. Timmins. Sudbury. Jim's got two-nighters each place."

"Jim Kirk?"

"Keyboard man."

She would say keyboard man. What happened to pianist?

I said, "Which would Jim's room be?"

"Top floor, very front," the woman said. "I'm on the second at the back."

"You live here too?"

"I'm a singer." The young woman took her finger from its place on the *Now* ad. "I do kind of an Ella Fitzgerald act. Scat on 'Lady Be Good', cover the Duke Ellington songbook, material like that, you know? I got a special arrangement on 'A-tisket, A-tasket'."

This was musical progress. On the other hand, Linda Ronstadt recorded albums that destroyed the works of Porter, Arlen, and Rodgers and Hart. I elected not to pursue the subject of Ella Fitzgerald.

"When it's slow with the act," the young woman said, "I waitress."

I couldn't help myself.

I said, "Oh my, the terrible things happening to verbs."

"Say what?"

"Access. Impact. It's computers. Inducing illiteracy."

"What's the story, guy?"

"To waitress isn't a verb."

"For a person looks like he's been rolling in the sandbox," the young woman said, "you're talking awful picky."

I was in danger of losing her to *Now*.

"Sorry," I said, and meant it. "It's been an awkward evening."

The young woman's finger was back on the ads. Her eyes were sure to follow.

I said, "Be a problem about me tapping on Dave's door?"

"Fine by me," the young woman said. Her head had dropped down. "One thing, that's the wrong possessive."

"How so?" I asked the top of her frizz.

"It's Jim's door."

The stairway was narrow all the way to the top, four flights up. Sounds of television sets and record players came faintly from behind the doors. Inside, the rooms may have been heavenly little oases. Out in the hall, it felt like the Gulag Archipelago.

Jim Kirk's door had an advertisement for Yamaha Pianos pasted in the centre with Kirk's own name neatly printed in block letters along the top of the ad.

I knocked softly on the door.

Nothing stirred inside.

I knocked more vigorously.

A door opened behind me, and I looked back. A man was leaning out of a room halfway between me and the stairs. He was Oriental and didn't have a shirt on.

"Nobody's home down there," the man said.

"What about the temporary tenant? Dave Goddard?"

"Still working up the street."

That made it unanimous.

I went down the stairs. The Ella Fitzgerald act was still analyzing *Now*'s personals. With her brand of respect for the printed word, she might be able to decipher the graffiti on the garage door out back. I left the Cameron and walked home.

It wasn't far, east on Queen to Beverley Street, left turn, and north for three and a quarter blocks. I own a duplex that looks across Beverley to the orderly park behind the Art Gallery of Ontario. Two gay chaps named Ian and Alex and their Irish setter rent the apartment downstairs. I live upstairs. The setter's name is Genet.

In the kitchen, I took the bottle of Wyborowa out of the freezer and poured an inch and a half into an old-fashioned glass without ice. When I raised the glass to my mouth, I felt nauseated. That wasn't the reaction Polish vodka customarily induced in me. The bang on the head must have been kicking in on a delayed reaction. I poured the Wyborowa back in the bottle without losing a drop and switched to milk.

I drank two glasses and took my nausea to bed.

4

IT WAS LATER than it was supposed to be.

I switched on the small black Sony radio on the table beside the bed and heard Peter Gzowski's voice. Peter Gzowski's program comes on the CBC at 9:05. My usual waking hour is seven-thirty. I looked at the small black Sony clock behind the radio. It said nine-fifty. Something else was different. I had a headache.

I put on my maroon cotton dressing gown, a birthday present from Annie B. Cooke, and carried the radio into the bathroom. Gzowski was interviewing a Hungarian movie director who was in town for the Festival of Festivals. Whatever pain reliever nine out of ten doctors would take to a desert island wasn't in my bathroom cabinet. I filled the sink with cold water and held my face in it. Gzowski thanked the Hungarian movie director and took a break for the ten o'clock news. Who would trust a doctor who'd pack a pain reliever on a trip to a desert island?

In the kitchen, I got three oranges out of the refrigerator and pressed them in an electric squeezer. The squeezer was neither small nor black nor Sony. Large, white, and German. I patronize all the old Axis powers. There was a pair of Gucci loafers on the floor of my closet. I drank the juice with two vitamin C tablets. It didn't do much for my headache, but it made me feel the model of healthy virtue.

I started up the Mr. Coffee and went downstairs to fetch the *Globe and Mail.* The entertainment section had a long article on the prospects for the Festival of Festivals. It was starting that night, the third- or fourth-hottest film festival in the world measured in commerce, number of movie luminaries on site, and other such criteria. There was Cannes and New York and then probably the Festival of Festivals. Or maybe Berlin snuck into third place.

There was a small mirror, antique with a carved wooden frame, hanging on the wall inside the kitchen door. I unhooked it and took it to the bathroom. By standing with my back to the mirror on the cabinet, tilting my head, and holding the antique mirror at about two o'clock, I could conduct an examination of the crown of my head.

Didn't seem to be anything back there except hair. No cut, no blood, nothing of a foreign nature. A check with my fingers didn't reveal a bump. The dastardly attack from behind had left me with not much more than a headache and an extra two hours of sleep. I spent another minute on the crown. It looked fit to present in public.

I got busy. Shower. Shave. Two cups of coffee. A perusal of the *Globe*'s sports pages. National Hockey League teams were in training camp. I looked out the kitchen window. The sun was shining, and a slim woman in shorts and a halter was picking flowers from her garden two houses up from mine. Why didn't the NHL wait till the ponds froze over before they started training camp? I reloaded the Mr. Coffee and put on clean jeans, a long-sleeved shirt with a lot of vertical stripes in different shades of blue, and the Rockport Walkers. Not many ponds left around Toronto to freeze over.

Peter Gzowski was delivering a little essay on the radio. It was about the Labour Day weekend he'd spent up north with the woman in his life. That was his expression, "the woman in my life". As descriptions of female persons one isn't necessarily married to but to whom one is committed, it beat "the girlfriend" or "my old lady". Most of the time on Gzowski's program, three hours of it, he interviews people. Occasionally he serves up essays he writes in the spirit of a latter-day E. B. White. Except E. B. White probably wouldn't have said a phrase like "the woman in my life" out loud. Neither would I, come to think of it. The woman in my life was Annie B. Cooke.

I turned off the radio and looked up the number for the Cameron House in the telephone book. The man who answered my call was polite and of minimal assistance.

No, he hadn't seen Dave Goddard that morning, and, no, there wasn't a phone in Dave's room. Correction. Jim Kirk's room. I asked if he'd mind hiking up to the fourth floor and tapping on Jim or Dave's door, and he said, no, he wouldn't mind. Five minutes later he was back on the phone and said, no, nobody was at home in the Jim Kirk room. I thanked him for the nos, and poured my third cup of coffee.

The day stretched empty in front of me, and I liked the sensation. Nothing like a dash of sloth to comfort a man. The day before, I ended a preliminary hearing that went two weeks in Provincial Court. My client was charged with fraud in big numbers, and the Provincial Court judge had to decide if he should commit my guy for trial in a higher court. The way the crown attorney spelled out the case, my guy bought an apartment building for one million bucks. That's how much the building apparently commanded on the market, one million, but my guy sold it to a pal of his for five million. The five million never changed hands. But the pal got a trust company to advance him a mortgage loan for seventy-five per cent of the apartment building's value, which the pal said was the five million he was supposed to have paid my guy. Seventy-five per cent of five million works out to $3,750,000. Subtract the one million my guy paid for the building in the first place, and there's $2,750,000 in spoils. My guy and the pal split the money and went around smiling widely. There were also allegations of a fifty-thousand-dollar payoff to a loan officer at the trust company that granted the mortgage. I spent the two weeks trying to convince the judge in Provincial Court that the crown didn't have enough evidence to send my guy on for trial. The judge said he'd take a few days to think it over. That freed up my schedule. People in the fraud business call the kind of deal my guy and the pal allegedly pulled an Oklahoma Scheme.

I walked into the living room and looked across Beverley Street into the park. The leaves on the trees were still green, and so was the grass. Verdant, I thought. A teenage girl in white painter pants and a white sleeveless blouse was perched on one of the picnic tables gently rocking a baby carriage. Two old geezers were sitting at another table playing cards. I watched the game for a few minutes. Gin rummy, it looked like.

My headache was beginning to recede. Should I interrupt the torpor of the day by chasing after Dave Goddard? What was my obligation to Dave? Was he a client? Or a friend in need? Had I botched the tailing operation? Should I make it up to Dave? Who was the guy in the beige jacket? Many more questions like those and the headache might stage a return.

I elected to postpone all decisions until after lunch and left the house on foot. My destination was the Belair Café. Annie B. Cooke was sure to be there. I'd give odds.

5

ANNIE HAD A NOTEBOOK laid flat on the table in front of her. Her dark head was bent low, and she was writing very quickly in the notebook.

A woman I recognized, Helga Stephenson, was taking care of the talking. Helga Stephenson had lips like Sophia Loren's, high cheekbones, a face of kinetic force. Plenty of guys must have cracked up on the shoals around Ms. Stephenson. Annie had introduced me to her a couple of times over the years. Helga Stephenson was the executive director of the Festival of Festivals.

Eleven-thirty in the morning, and the Belair was abustle. I got a table against the wall. It left a wide but mostly unobstructed space between me and Annie. I ordered a vodka and soda with a wedge of lime.

The third person in Annie's group was an overweight guy in a checked sweater and thick glasses. He looked familiar. He had a notebook too but wasn't writing. He was waiting, and not patiently. His legs jiggled under the table.

"I told you it was too early," the kid at the table next to mine said to his friend. The kid was about seventeen, and he was twisting in his seat to look around the room.

"Last year, right over there, I saw Bertolucci drinking Perrier water," the friend answered the kid. The friend was a girl the same age. "That table second from where the waiter's standing."

"Could you tell who he was with? Bertolucci?" the kid asked. He had fuzz on his upper lip and scarlet acne streaked across his forehead.

"Press I suppose," the girl answered. "Somebody boring like that."

I squeezed the lime into my drink and prepared to sip. If the vodka gave me nausea, I might have to throw a tantrum.

"We still haven't decided about Sunday morning," the girl at the next table said. She had skin without flaw. Life was unfair.

"Why do they make such dumb schedules?" the boy said. "The David Lynch on practically the same time as one of the Truffauts, that's maximum dumb."

"Not as if the tickets are exactly cheap or anything," the girl said.

"Your father paid for yours," the boy said with the disdain only an adolescent can summon.

"It's still money, Don."

I was a quarter of the way into the vodka and soda. Not a hint of upset tummy. All seemed copacetic with my gastric world. Annie was still writing in her notebook and still oblivious of my manly presence in the restaurant. Would she have sensed the aura of Dennis Quaid?

"We've already seen *Stolen Kisses* on TV about three times, Karen," Don said to the girl with the perfect complexion. She had blonde hair and a little bow mouth to go with the skin.

"Plus it's on VCR," Karen said.

"The only thing—"

Karen talked over Don. She said, her turn for disdain, "I know what you're going to say, Don. It's not the same on small screen."

"The values, Karen," Don said. "You have to admit."

"I still think it's ridiculous to miss a new David Lynch," Karen said. "There's probably going to be a hundred more Truffaut retrospectives besides this one. He is dead after all."

Don and Karen were scrutinizing their Festival of Festivals schedule. The schedule folded accordion-style. Open, it covered most of Don and Karen's table. The Festival ran eleven days and screened maybe two hundred movies. Don and Karen may have been going for the all-time, all-world attendance record. On their schedule, there were tick marks beside four or five movies on each day. The theatres the Festival used were in midtown, an easy hike from the Belair, and Helga Stephenson's offices were around the corner on Yorkville Avenue. Proximity qualified the Belair as the Festival's unofficial watering hole. It was done in peach and grey and ficus plants and had a pianist in the bar who didn't gag at playing "Feelings" half a dozen times an evening. Bernardo Bertolucci once took Perrier at the Belair. I had Karen's word for it.

Across the room, Helga Stephenson talked, Annie wrote, and fatso jiggled. Don and Karen stewed over the Sunday-morning blank space. I willed them to take the old François Truffaut instead of the new Dave Lynch. When I saw *Blue Velvet*, I came down with a severe case of the heebie-jeebies. To celebrate my recovery from the Wyborowa trauma of the night before, I asked the waiter for another vodka and soda.

Don cranked his head around the room and turned back to Karen in high excitement.

"Roger Ebert," he said. His voice cracked.

"Oh wild," Karen said. Her voice didn't crack. "With those two women in the corner."

Don and Karen had it right. Roger Ebert was the jiggler with Annie and Helga Stephenson. Could Gene Siskel be far behind?

Annie folded her notebook, stood up, and smiled at Helga and Roger. Annie had a sneaky smile. She turned it on, and you felt select. She turned it off, and you noticed an ache in your heart that didn't use to be there. Annie was petite, as they would say in *Vogue*. No bigger than a minute, as my old mother would have said. Her hair was black like midnight is black, and she wore it cut in a tight cap around her head. She had on a pale-blue denim dress that buttoned down the front and stopped within hailing distance of her knees. Her leather shoes, flats, were the same pale-blue, and the only jewellery that adorned her person was a small gold pocket watch on a gold chain around her neck. Annie saw me, and I got the smile. I knew all about the ache in the heart. So far, two years of Annie and me, the ache hadn't come close to permanent.

"Aren't you just full of surprises," Annie said. She leaned over my table and kissed me lightly on the lips. "You're supposed to be in court. Your Arizona man."

"The judge gave us a holiday," I said. "You were in swift company over there."

"Roger? He and Gene Siskel come up for the Chicago papers every year."

Silence emanated from the next table. Don was tilting in Annie's direction. Karen, more subtle in the arts of eavesdropping, sat upright and stared straight ahead.

I said to Annie, "It's Oklahoma, by the way, the scheme my guy's charged with."

"Sweetie pie, is the state relevant?"

"It could be Delaware, in your view, and my guy'd still be guilty?"

"I couldn't have phrased it more cogently."

Annie didn't disapprove of all my clients. Ninety-nine per cent of them.

"Your pal Roger seemed antsy," I said. Don and Karen would be grateful for the change in topic back to movie personnel.

"He thought he'd scare me off with his big rep," Annie said. "It was my appointment with Helga, and dammit, I needed every second."

"Fill your notebook?"

"Crang, this year, seriously, it's freelance heaven." Annie's deep-brown eyes shone. "I've got *Metro Morning* same as usual, but it's stepped up to five minutes every single day of the Festival. Television, *The Journal*'s having me on for a wrap-up panel a week from Friday. And last night I get a call from San Francisco, the *Chronicle*. Their regular guy's all of a sudden sick, and would I file two big pieces? You impressed?"

"Pauline Kael, step aside."

Annie reviewed movies. She had one steady gig. It was radio, twice-a-week commentaries on the local CBC wake-up program. For the rest, she scrambled. Articles in *Premiere Magazine*, sometimes a radio documentary, guest spots on TV. It made for a precarious career.

"Helga's setting me up for the major leagues," Annie said. "Get this, a half-hour interview Tuesday night with Daniel Day-Lewis."

Don made motions like he might fall out of his chair.

I said, "The English guy, that Daniel Day-Lewis? Handsome, young, talented, probably articulate?"

"The material I can get," Annie said, "all the radio producers, newspaper editors, they'll be kissing me on both cheeks."

"Daniel Day-Lewis, the guy the two women in the movie you took me to year before last went crazy over?"

"*The Unbearable Lightness of Being.*"

"The same reaction to Daniel Day-Lewis among women, I imagine, applies off the screen."

Karen's head made a nod that I assumed to be of enthusiastic affirmation.

Annie said, "If this is jealousy, Crang, put a sock in it. I need you for something else."

"My charm?"

"Later," Annie said. "Right now, it's information."

"Charm comes free. Information, I turn the meter on."

"Suppose I ask my questions, and you answer charmingly."

"You want to order an expensive lunch while we talk?"

"Just a spritzer," Annie said. "We'll eat at the press conference."

"What press conference?"

"The one I need the information for."

A waiter sauntered by to bring Coke refills for Don and Karen. I asked for Annie's spritzer. Was Don unaware of the red horrors the sugar was wreaking on his forehead?

Annie flipped through her notebook to a blank page.

She said to me, "A man in your racket, criminal lawyer by the name of F. Cameron Charles."

"Sure," I said. "Classmate of mine at law school, and today the Clarence Darrow of his time and place."

"He's that good?"

"According to Cam he is."

"I see," Annie said. "We're dealing with an ego."

"Like the CN Tower."

Annie's spritzer arrived.

"Maybe I'm ahead of you on this, kiddo," I said. "Cam's on the Festival of Festivals board. That's the reason for the questions?"

"Him on the board is last year's news."

"Yeah? What's the latest poop?"

Annie held her wine glass by the stem and took a tiny sip.

She said, "Charles's fronting a counter-festival. I don't know who's actually booking the films. Guess we'll find out more at the press conference. Anyway, Charles's name is on top of the information releases, and his office is listed as the festival's headquarters. He resigned from the Festival of Festivals board in the spring and started this new deal. The Alternate Film Festival it's called."

"Cam, it sounds like, is going head to head with Helga Stephenson."

"Almost," Annie said. "The Alternate starts Sunday night and runs to Saturday. That makes a fairly consistent overlap with the Festival of Festivals."

"Enterprise like that, it doesn't strike me as one of the great and wise commercial decisions."

"Helga isn't particularly bothered," Annie said. "Actually, Charles is going at it pretty intelligently. Keeping everything small-scale but quite interesting. He's using one theatre only, the Eglinton, which is the nicest in the city if you ask me, and he's got a festival theme of sorts."

"What sort?"

"Mildly radical, I guess you could say," Annie said. "Movies from Third World countries, movies black people made in Chicago on small budgets. Minorities stuff. Chicanos in New Mexico, like that."

I said, "Right up Cam's alley."

"Well, tell me. What I need's background. How come a criminal lawyer's doing a movie festival?"

Don and Karen didn't care to know the answer to Annie's question. They checked out of our conversation and returned to the dilemma of their Sunday-morning movie. Annie took another miniature taste from her spritzer. She'd made a half-dozen passes at the drink, and the level of wine, soda and melting ice hadn't dropped a quarter-inch. She was thirty-five years old and hadn't learned to drink like a man.

I said, "Cam's speciality is minorities. In his law practice I'm talking about. People he acts for, they're, oh, Jamaican guys charged in stick-ups. Hong Kong kids doing extortion over in Chinatown. What else? Sikh bombers. Those are Cam's clients. He defended the Moonies last year."

"Moonies?" Annie said. "They don't go with the rest."

"Just because a group is rich and diabolical doesn't mean it can't be a minority."

"The Reverend Sun Myung Moon aside," Annie said, "your friend Cam sounds okay. Altruistic I might describe him."

"Some of my colleagues at the criminal bar say Cam's the only lawyer in town can afford his clientele."

"Well, well, aren't we snide at the criminal bar."

"Cam isn't, by the way," I said, "my friend."

"No?"

"He thinks I'm frivolous."

"Now I'm really panting to meet Cameron Charles."

I said, "The point about Cam affording the Jamaicans and the Sikhs and the Hong Kong kids, it's usually Legal Aid pays their bills. Pays little, I probably told you before, and pays late. And Cam—here's the real point—he's conspicuously wealthy."

"Not from the law, I take it."

"From Dad and Granddad. Those signs on construction sites all over the city are theirs. CharlesCorp. They build condos."

Annie jotted a couple of lines on the notebook's blank pages. The ice was melting more rapidly in her glass, and the level of liquid was approaching the overflow mark.

I said, "This is probably totally unfair to Cam, but I think of him and I think of the magazine piece Tom Wolfe wrote a lot of years ago, the article about Leonard Bernstein and all the New York people with the money that took up the Black Panthers."

"I didn't get to Tom Wolfe till *Bonfire of the Vanities*."

"Radical chic, Wolfe called it," I said. "These upper-class Manhattan liberals—this is how it goes—they had so much money they could afford to feel guilty about how lousy it is to be black in America. So who do they identify themselves in public with? The most radical and maybe violent edge of the black movement. The Panthers. But it was their money that made the posture possible."

"The way you're putting it, that comparison, Cameron Charles sounds like a dabbler."

"I don't know," I said. "He's consistent, give Cam that. His clients, for one thing, and a couple of years back, he went on some kind of task force to El Salvador. And he's in the *Globe* every five minutes with letters about the Palestinians, the Tamils, black South Africans. All of a piece, the minority thing."

"That makes the Alternate Festival make sense."

"There you go, honeybun," I said. "That the background stuff you were looking for?"

"And so charmingly done."

Annie's drink was trickling down the sides of her wine glass and soaking the paper coaster underneath. She looked at the pocket watch on the chain around her neck and read the time.

She said, "Charles's press conference and lunch is getting going about now."

"Beats me how you can read that thing upside down."

"Practice," Annie said. "First couple of months I had it, I used to turn up an hour early or an hour late for appointments."

"Where's the lunch?"

"It's a press conference too."

"Matter of priorities."

"Both are steps from here."

Annie dropped her notebook into a cloth shoulder bag knitted in greens and blues. The notebook disappeared. Prince Edward Island would have disappeared into the shoulder bag.

I said, "Whole world's steps from here. You have that impression?"

Don and Karen had attained the moment of decision.

"No changing at the last moment," Karen said to Don. "Once I mark it, this is final. The David Lynch, okay?"

Annie looked at the two kids.

"Are you talking about Sunday morning?" she asked. "David Lynch's new movie's on when the Truffaut series is running?"

"It's *Stolen Kisses* on then," Karen said, a little tremor in her voice. She seemed awed to be addressed by the woman who had sat with Roger Ebert. Guess she'd changed her mind about the boring press.

"And you guys are choosing the Lynch?" Annie said.

"Well, yes," Karen answered. "But, like, there's arguments on both sides."

"Stick to Lynch," Annie said. "Good choice."

I paid the bill and kept my mouth shut.

6

ANNIE SAID, "Cameron Charles goes first cabin."

The long tables in front of us had starched white cloths that were covered in goodies fit for kings and press. Platters of fat oysters in crushed ice. Little squares of quiche in chafing dishes, smoked salmon. Three or four salads, one with hefty chunks of avocado. Two guys in tall white chef's hats and long white chef's aprons were standing behind the tables. One was slicing a roast of beef cooked rare, and the other was slicing a roast turkey cooked tender. The champagne wasn't domestic and it wasn't the ersatz Spanish bubbly. It was Veuve Clicquot.

Forty or fifty invitees were munching and slurping and milling around the room. It was the largest of the conference rooms that open off the west corridor in the Park Plaza Hotel. There was thick green carpeting on the floor, and down at the far end of the room, a lectern and a microphone waited for someone's use, probably Cam Charles's. Cam was nowhere in sight, but a sextet of tall and immensely chic young women seemed to be handling the role of hostesses more than capably. They circulated, made introductions, and bestowed dazzling smiles at random.

"The ladies have PR firm stamped all over their silk Saint-Laurents," Annie said.

"Ladies?" I said. "What ladies? Don't notice any ladies."

"Tell your eyeballs to stop spinning."

I dipped one of my shrimp into a tomato-and-horseradish sauce of surpassing richness.

"Job like yours," I said, "a person could blow their cholesterol level off the scale."

"Don't kid yourself, sweetie," Annie said. "This event is the exception."

"You telling me life isn't a regular round of wining, dining, and other bribery for you swells on the movie beat?"

"Free coffee at advance screenings," Annie said. "In styrofoam cups."

I was making inroads on a little silver dish of macadamia nuts when someone slapped me cheerily on the shoulder. I turned and found Trevor Dalgleish on my flank. The slap, for all its cheeriness, gave my equilibrium a shake. Trevor packed some heft.

"Well, well, Crang," he said, "the movies bring all sorts together."

"At this shindig, Trev, I'm an appendage," I said. "Annie here's the main act."

I made the introductions, and Trevor lathered the charm on Annie.

"I'm a *fan*," he said to her. "Wouldn't miss you on that morning show. Wednesdays, isn't it, and Fridays?"

Annie answered in words that were suitably grateful and humble, and Trevor followed up with more commentary that proved he really did listen to Annie's reviews.

Trevor Dalgleish was handsome in a beefy, Teddy Kennedy style. He looked older than his age, which was early thirties, a little grey around the temples, a bracket of deepening lines in the cheeks. But he exuded vigour. The vigour was of an upper-crust sort that usually comes from riding horses and hitting squash balls. Trevor had a faint sound of hoity-toity in his voice.

"Trev's another one of us," I said to Annie when Trevor's gushing wound down. "Criminal lawyer."

"An associate of our host's," Trevor elaborated.

"Of Cameron Charles's?" Annie said, perking up, maybe scenting some inside dope for her coverage of the Alternate Festival. "Really? And are you involved in the movie end too?"

Trevor assumed a modified aw-shucks look.

"Cam's assigned me to book a handful of the festival's films," he said. "Fascinating to see the movie business from a different perspective."

Trevor didn't get any further with his perspective. One of the tall, chic visions interrupted him. She was standing at the fringe of the crowd, waving one arm in the air, and she was asking us in her loudest voice if we'd care to bring our champagne glasses and coffee cups to the other end of the room.

"Showtime," Annie said.

Three guys who looked more rugged and sweaty than the rest of us guests peeled off and strapped themselves into television cameras that had been resting on the floor behind the serving tables. A dozen others, radio types, got out pocket-sized tape recorders. Annie had a notebook and pen in her hands, and so did everyone else around me. I was the only stiff in the room who wasn't working.

Cam Charles looked sleek. He made his entrance from a door in the wall on the right side of the room and walked to the lectern. Cam had olive skin and black hair that was combed back flat from his forehead. His face and body showed a bit of excess weight, but if he was plump, it was a firm variety of plump. Dark and sleek and plump. Cam looked like he should be mated to an otter. He had on a light grey double-breasted suit, a darker grey shirt with a white collar and white french cuffs, and a blue tie with a delicate pattern. Cam tapped his finger on the microphone and got back a satisfying bump on the sound system.

"Welcome to the first annual Alternate Film Festival," he said into the mike. "I'm Cameron Charles."

The guys with the TV cameras switched on their lights, and the radio people held their tape recorders in the air.

"I'm only going to take a few minutes of your valuable time," Cam said. "The young ladies will have printed material for you as you leave, schedules and so on. What I have for you in my short time is an announcement of a purpose."

Cam paused. It was for one of his dramatic effects. I'd seen him do it a hundred times in court. I hated it all one hundred times.

"And an announcement of a very important surprise," Cam said.

The sophisticated press got scribbling. Cam the silver-tongued devil had done it again.

"As many of you will know," Cam said, "I chose to leave the other film festival in town"—that drew a small snicker, Cam's emphasis on "other"—"and my reason had to do with purpose. The Festival of Festivals has no purpose beyond simple entertainment. Mindless entertainment in too many instances of the films they choose to offer the public. At the Alternate Festival, my associates and I do have a purpose, and it is this: simply put, we will show films that, through theme or story line or character, through attitude, through the intent of the filmmakers themselves, make a statement about the reality of power and politics in the world today."

More people were filtering quietly through the door on the right side of the room. There were twelve or fourteen men and women, mostly men, and they gathered congenially a few steps back of Cam. They must have been the associates he was talking about in his speech. The man immediately behind Cam made an odd associate. He was Harp Manley, veteran bebop trumpet player and recent movie actor.

"We have secured a film from South America that I assure you is stunning," Cam was saying into the mike. "It was made inside Chile, unknown to the Pinochet regime, and smuggled out of the country and into our hands. And I tell you, ladies and gentlemen, it is a devastating delineation of oppression under a military government."

One more man joined the clump of associates ranged back of Cam. I recognized him too. It was Beige Jacket. Different jacket, something in lightweight plaid this time, but it was the same moustache, same thinning hair, same Perry Mason build.

"That guy over there," I said to Annie in a low voice. "In the plaid jacket. He mean anything to you?"

"From the neck down, he could stand in for Raymond Burr."

"It's said if people spend long enough in one another's company, they begin to think alike."

"I've heard that."

"With us," I said, "I think the process is in an advanced stage."

"I still don't know who the man in the plaid jacket is."

"Excuse me," I said. "I have business to attend to."

Annie and I were standing about dead centre of the crowd of reporters in front of Cam. I edged to the back of the pack, circled one of the TV cameramen who was shooting from an outer angle, and approached the man in the plaid jacket on his right side.

"Hi, there," I said. "I believe we share a mutual affection for jazz."

The man kept his face a blank, but his eyes shifted over me and opened fractionally wider. He remembered.

"Get lost, Jack," he said. He had a rumble for a voice.

I said, "More specifically, a mutual affection for one jazz musician. Who could forget Dave Goddard?"

"You deaf or what?" the man said. His hair and moustache were dark-brown, and his face had a Slavic cast. "Take a hike."

A pair of festival associates made shushing noises at us, and I could hear Cam Charles raise his voice at the microphone to keep the crowd's attention from wandering to the exchange between me and the man in the plaid jacket.

I said to him, "The three of us got together last night, you, me, Dave, in the alley behind the Cameron."

"One more time, Mac," the man said. "Hit the road."

"Is that who I think it is? Crang?" Cam Charles said, turning in my direction. He had his left hand covering the microphone, but his voice leaked over the sound system. "This is a press conference, Crang, and whatever you are, God knows you aren't press."

I said to the man in the plaid jacket, "Any second now, you're going to run out of similes for go away, and we can start talking."

The man planted his hands on my chest and shoved. I sat down hard on the thick green carpeting and heard the crowd of reporters go *ohhhhh* and *ahhhhh.*

"Get him out of here," Cam said from the lectern.

Cam meant me. The man in the plaid jacket was already on his way through the door. I pushed off the floor.

Annie had her hand on my arm.

"Anything hurt?" she asked.

Trevor Dalgleish was right behind her, wearing a stern look.

"God's sake, Crang," he said, not as chummy as he'd been earlier. "That man was a guest here."

"I assure you, ladies and gentlemen," Cam was announcing into the microphone, "this little scene was not part of our presentation."

"Do me a favour, honeybunch," I said to Annie. "Find out from Cam or someone, maybe Trev here, who the bully in plaid is."

"Never mind him, Crang," Trevor snapped at me. "Just do what Cam asked. Get out of here and stop interrupting the press conference."

"Now for the very important surprise I mentioned earlier," Cam said to the press. "I'd like to ask Mr. Harp Manley to step forward."

"*Crang,*" Trevor hissed at me.

"What're you going to do?" Annie asked me.

"Follow the bully," I said.

7

THE BULLY didn't look behind all the way to the Silverdore Hotel. His wide plaid shoulders made him a stickout in the pedestrian parade along Bloor Street. Bloor is prime for people-watching. Fresh-faced kids from the university a block to the south. Splendidly shaped, coiffed, and groomed young matrons conducting raids on Creed's and Holt Renfrew. I only had eyes for my bully. How come he didn't examine his rear? Didn't he suppose I'd chase after him? Or didn't he care? That struck me as humiliating, the not-caring possibility.

The bully marched resolutely along the south side of Bloor, crossed at Yonge, went three blocks south to Charles, turned east, then into the Silverdore. As Toronto hotels go, the Silverdore is middle-class tourist trade. It has a utilitarian look, fifteen storeys of pale-brown brick straight up and five flags flying from the marquee over the entrance. The Stars and Stripes occupies the middle pole.

I hung back of the Silverdore's glass doors and watched my quarry. He didn't head for the front desk. He was pulling a key from his jacket pocket as he stepped toward the elevators. Must be a Silverdore guest. Crang, the master of deduction.

I walked to the other side of Charles and leaned my hip against a phone booth.

Now what?

I knew the guy had a room at the Silverdore. I knew, or suspected on reasonable grounds, that he'd knocked me out in the Cameron alley and had probably made Dave Goddard disappear. I knew he was connected with Cam Charles's Alternate Film Festival. And I knew he had a wardrobe of two or more summer jackets.

The question facing the house, how did I organize this dazzling array of facts?

I went up to the subway station on Bloor, rode a train and a Queen streetcar to my office, and got on the phone.

Abner Chase was at his club.

"I been telling you at least ten years, Crang," he said after I identified myself. "There's no sense me stocking the Polish vodka. You're the only customer asks for it."

Abner Chase always went to the point, whatever point was on his mind.

"This time I'm trying to do you a favour, Abner," I said. "I think we might have a problem with Dave Goddard."

"There's a problem with the guy, I won't know it till nine tonight."

"That's the thing. Dave may be among the missing."

"Missing?" Abner said into the phone. "He don't show bang on time the first set, Harper Manley'll have his balls in a vice. Or I might do his balls myself."

"Dave hasn't called you today?"

"No reason to."

"Harp hasn't heard either?"

"You jokin' me? The guy's all over the place—TV interviews, personal appearances, record stores. Dave'd never get ahold of Harper. He's a goddamn genuine celebrity. That's why I'm doing this fantastic business at the club, on account of Harper's getting known from the movies. You gotta've heard about that."

"Hard to miss it, Abner," I said. "Why have I always thought Harp is a nickname? Like Bird was for Charlie Parker."

"Wrong. It's short for Harper."

"Probably you and his mother are the only people who call him Harper."

"His mother, nice old lady, she's dead."

I was sitting in the swivel chair behind my desk. I swivelled sideways to look down into the wide sidewalk on Queen Street. A man in black pants held up by loose red suspenders was banging on a conga drum. A blonde woman who had the moves of someone on speed was twirling two large fans in time to the conga beat. People stopped to catch the show and drop coins into an upside-down grey fedora beside the drum.

I said to Abner Chase, "About Dave, anybody else you can think of he might be in regular touch with?"

"Ralph Goddard. You met Dave's brother? He's been getting Dave's act together the last couple years."

"He hasn't done much to update Dave's style in clothes."

"The business side I'm telling you about. Dave's a helluva musician, I don't need to remind anyone knows these things like you. He's just never acted like an Einstein with the dollars and cents."

"I'll try Ralph."

"Out in the sticks somewhere," Abner said. "You better be wrong about Dave. He's a reliable guy, freaky but reliable."

"Which part of the sticks?"

"Don Mills, I think. Look it up in the fuckin' phone book. Ralph's the kind of guy, you first talk to him, you think he's got mud on his shoes or something. But I dealt with him a bit now, and he's a pretty astute guy."

Abner hung up, and I found Ralph Goddard's number in the phone book. I dialled. Ralph answered. He didn't sound astute on the phone. He sounded like a pussycat. Or a cocker spaniel. He wanted me to trot right over to his place.

"Crang, well, sir, I always meant to meet up with you," he said on the phone. "Ever since you got Dave out of the scrape way back there."

Dave had almost lost his musicians' union card over a fracas in a club. It seemed the manager refused to turn off the TV set while Dave's quartet was playing. Dave put a gin bottle through the screen in the middle of *The Beverly Hillbillies.* That was in Dave's drinking and drugging period. I argued his suspension before a union disciplinary hearing and, by and large, won. Dave's only punishment was the purchase of a thirty-inch Panasonic for the club.

I said to Ralph Goddard, "I hear you're managing your brother's career, Mr. Goddard."

"Mr. Goddard was my dad. Call me Ralph."

"Swell, Ralph."

"Smartest thing I ever did for Dave. I got him to sign me over power of attorney, and ever since I been running the whole shooting match from right here in my den. Negotiate the fees, deal with the bookers. Mean buggers, pardon the language, those bookers. I should've done this for Dave a long time ago. But you know how it is."

I said I did.

Ralph said, "I had to make my own pile. But now I'm retired, kids out in the world, and I'm doing for the baby brother. Get him something in the bank."

"Reason for my call," I said, "you happen to have heard from Dave this afternoon?"

"Not since Monday," Ralph answered. "The first of every week I give him an allowance. Mail it if he's out of town. This Monday, I took him a money order to Abner Chase's club. Didn't stay long. I'm more of a country-and-western man myself."

I said, "Dave may be in some difficulties, Ralph."

Ralph sounded like he was sighing.

"Not the drink again?" he said.

"Nor the drugs."

I gave Ralph a précis of the previous night's events.

"Well, that just bothers the dickens out of me," Ralph said when I finished.

"The big guy doesn't mean anything to you?" I asked. "The man Dave thinks was following him?"

"Dave used to run with some real characters. But that was all in the past. My brother's a reformed person, Crang."

"He drinks a lot of coffee all right."

"You don't think we might be jumping the gun? Why, heck, Dave is just as liable to walk into the club tonight like nothing happened."

"Apart from the boff I took on the head."

"I guess I like to look on the positive side of life," Ralph said.

I told Ralph I'd check at Chase's Club that night and let him know if Dave was absent. Ralph continued to look on the positive side of life. People who sound like pussycats and cocker spaniels tend to do that.

Down on the street, the conga drummer and his hopped-up fan twirler took a break to count their earnings. I swivelled back to the desk. The wits among my clients say my office looks like it's furnished in Early Salvation Army. I have a wooden desk as solid as the oak tree from which it came and badly chipped around the edges. There are four mismatched chairs, also wooden, also chipped, and there is a metal filing cabinet, which is green and chipped. I bought the desk, chairs, and filing cabinet at the Salvation Army depot on Richmond Street. I never reveal my secret to the wits among my clients. On the wall, I have a framed Henri Matisse poster. It's called *Jazz* and has a background of the loveliest blue I may ever have seen.

The phone rang, and I picked up the receiver.

"Fenk," the voice on the other end said. It was Annie's voice.

"What do I do with it?"

"Write it down, fella," Annie said. "It's the name you asked me to scout up."

I wrote it down.

"On paper," I said, "it looks like a typographical error."

"Raymond Fenk."

I wrote down the given name.

"He's a producer," Annie said. "From Hollywood. He's got a movie in the Alternate Festival about Mexican illegals in Los Angeles."

"You sure you're talking about the guy that floored me at the Park Plaza?" I said. "He doesn't look like a movie producer."

"He isn't," Annie said. "Not in the David O. Selznick tradition. The movie about the Mexican illegals seems to be the first legitimate thing he's got his name on. *Hell's Barrio* it's called. Imaginative, right? But get this, until now, Mr. Fenk's movies have been strictly for the porn market."

"Cam Charles fed you the hot stuff?"

"'Course not," Annie said. "This is original research. I got Fenk's name and the title of Fenk's movie from Mr. Charles. Cameron, I should tell you, is very distressed with you. The rest I just finished digging out of my library. I'm home right now, doing your legwork, planning on a soaky bath, putting on the finery."

Annie was covering the opening movie of the Festival of Festivals that night. The new Norman Jewison led things off.

"In your library," I said, "you've got books on pornographic movies?"

"Two reference works," Annie said. "I counted eight listings for Raymond Fenk before I quit. *Betty Blows Baltimore* is one of his."

"Alliterative."

"Okay, sugar," Annie said, "your turn."

"You're wondering what nature of bad guy I've hired on to defend this time."

"Something like that," Annie said. "In fact, exactly like that."

"Anybody's the bad guy, it's Raymond Fenk."

"He looks the part, I'll go that far."

"And I'm not acting for him."

"I didn't have the impression you were trying to collect a retainer from him this afternoon," Annie said. "So who is your client?"

"If I have a client, it's a man named Dave Goddard," I said. "Whatever he's involved in—Dave's a jazz musician—it may be troublesome. Other hand, it may be nothing."

"Oho, the familiar dichotomy," Annie said. "Knowing you, I pick troublesome."

"Dave, the history he's had, he doesn't deserve any grief," I said. "But he might've found it, and Raymond Fenk could be the one who made the grief. That's as far as events've gone."

Even to myself, I sounded defensive. I hadn't told Annie about the Cameron alley assault. I didn't want to get her worried. Or ticked off at my carelessness. No wonder I sounded defensive even to myself. Better to edge away from the subject.

"Annie?" I said.

"Uh-huh."

"When Fenk sat me down at the press conference, how silly did I look?"

Annie said, "Who was the American president who was always bumping his head and tripping whenever he got off Air Force One?"

"That silly?"

"'Fraid so."

Great line for an epitaph. Whom did the late Mr. Crang most remind you of, madame? Well, he had a touch of Gerald Ford.

8

HARP MANLEY was playing "Milestones" again. So were the three young black guys in the rhythm section. Dave Goddard wasn't playing "Milestones" or anything else.

I had a vodka on the rocks and a seat at the bar. Chase's was as crowded as it had been the night before, except two of the principal characters weren't centre stage. Raymond Fenk was probably at the Silverdore practising push and shove. It was Dave Goddard's no-show that bothered me. Not half as much as it seemed to be bothering Harp Manley.

He ended the first set early and abruptly, and ignored his adoring fans all the way to the bar. Manley pushed past a waiter into the bar's service area and spoke to the bartender. The bartender picked up a bottle of Johnnie Walker Black Label with a jigger on the end and held it over a tall glass until the jigger filled and emptied three times. The bartender didn't add water. I got out of my seat and carried my vodka with me.

"You mind we talk about Dave Goddard?" I said to Manley.

He was wrapping a small white cocktail napkin around the bottom of the glass. He finished the job and had a long pull from the drink. I wasn't sure he'd heard me.

"Dave Goddard?" I said. Alistair Cooke couldn't have enunciated more clearly.

"Damn," Manley said, "where's that kiddie at?"

His question was aimed at his drink.

"Let's discuss it," I said.

Manley swallowed more Scotch and used the swallowing time to give me a look of close inspection over his glass.

"Kiddie plays real pretty," he said. He spoke circumspectly.

"It's not Dave's musicianship I had in mind," I said.

"Thought you was a critic."

"A lawyer."

"Dress like a critic."

I followed Manley to the table beside the door into the kitchen. On the way, he drank the Johnnie Walker down to the middle of the glass.

"A lawyer, huh?" he said across the table. He had abandoned the circumspection. What I heard in his voice was the sound of a disgruntled boss.

"Yeah, and if you'll let me explain, I've got reason to think Dave Goddard may be in a piece of trouble."

"Trouble's the only time a lawyer comes round," Manley said. "Been my experience."

"Lot of people's experience, but okay with you we stick to Dave?"

"Trouble, huh?" Manley had a little ridge of tough hair under his lower lip. "That kiddie ain't seen trouble he don't get his sorry ass in here real fast. You understand what I'm saying, Mr. Lawyer. I need two horns, man my age. I can't do all the damn solos. Ain't got the lip like when I was young."

"Good point," I said. What should I call him? Harp seemed presumptuous, Mr. Manley too formal. Abner Chase had an exclusive on Harper.

"Does Raymond Fenk mean anything to you?" I said. "That name?"

Manley stared at me with an expression I read as incomprehension. His eyes were bloodshot, but apart from them and the patch of hair under the lip, Manley's face had a round and contained look. Symmetrical. No wonder the camera loved it. He had on a single-breasted suit jacket with three buttons. All three buttons were buttoned up. He wore a crisp blue shirt and a black knit tie that was knotted precisely dead centre of the shirt's wide collar. Short and rotund men don't always achieve the neat look. Harp Manley did. It was combined with an uncomprehending look.

I said to him, "Raymond Fenk was on stage same time as you at the Park Plaza this afternoon."

"You talking about the show for the TV people and the writers?" Manley said. "That was no Fenk. That was my man Cameron."

"He was in the group, Fenk was, with the rest of you behind Cam Charles."

"Nobody much back there except some fool slapping on another fool."

"I was the fool on the floor," I said. "Fenk was the fool on his feet."

Manley left his chair and walked to the bar. When he came back, his glass was full and darker than amber. He had a fresh cocktail napkin wrapped around the bottom. My glass could stand a recharge, but I didn't want to risk losing the audience with Manley.

"You're a lawyer for damn sure," he said to me. "First you say, hey, Harp, what about this kiddie plays in the band? Now you say, Harp, what about this other kiddie here? That's a lawyer's way of getting what you really got on your mind for Harp."

Was this an invitation to call him Harp?

"You're going to have to take my word on this, Harp," I said. "Some of it's conjecture. But I think the man I asked you about, Raymond Fenk, he's the heavy. He banged Dave over the head or something as bad, and that's why Dave isn't up there on the stand tonight."

"Conjecture, huh?" Manley said. "The kiddie send you down here with this conjecture?"

"My point, Harp, I'm trying to tell you I don't know where Dave is. Hurt some place. Worse maybe."

"Laying up with some woman more likely."

As skeptics went, Manley was making H. L. Mencken sound like a true believer.

He said, "The kiddies always got the stories when they don't make the job on time."

"Harp," I said, "the thing may be a story about Dave, but I'm an eyewitness, partly anyway. It happened."

"This the first time I remember a kiddie hired a lawyer to save his ass."

It seemed the moment for a switch in tactics.

I said, "May I ask how come you were the surprise package at Cam Charles's press conference?"

"You a movie man, Mr. Lawyer?" Manley asked.

"You should've won the Oscar, Harp."

"Saw me, huh?" Manley said. "Gonna see me again. What's it today? Thursday? All right, Mr. Lawyer, Sunday night, there's gonna be them long black stretch limousines, spotlights looking up in the sky, me in my tuxedo, all that fine shit. You hear what I'm saying? A world premiere."

He gave premiere the French pronunciation. Harp Manley hadn't come back from his years on the continent an unlettered man.

"Cam Charles?" I said. "He's got first dibs on your new movie?"

"You see that skinny little grey-haired kiddie beside me?" Manley asked.

"Where? At the press conference? Can't say I did."

"My man Cam and that kiddie did the deal," Manley said. "The skinny little kiddie owns the movie. Listen to this, Mr. Lawyer, he paid me cash money in my pocket. None of that, hey, Harp, we gonna be rich some day. He say, Harp, you take the cash money right now."

"Back up a couple of steps, Harp. You're talking about the producer of your new movie, and he's given Cam Charles rights to a first screening at the Alternate Festival. I'm with you?"

Manley nodded and drank some Scotch.

"The skinny kiddie wrote the movie," he said. "Then he got the cash money from the bank and he told me on the phone, Harp, you make this movie, you gonna be big as Clint Eastwood. Damn, I think that kiddie's right."

"Has he got a name? This paragon of a writer-producer?"

"Bobby."

I waited. Manley added no more names.

"Well, I asked, didn't I," I said.

"Huh?"

Manley swallowed more Johnnie Walker. I was stuck with an empty glass and a man whose narrative style fluctuated between convoluted and terse.

"Is Bobby a Hollywood guy?" I asked. Once again into the fray. Manley shook his head.

"New York," he said. "Bobby don't mess with them big California studios. He got his own cash money."

"From the bank. So you said."

Manley's drink had reached the level of the white paper napkin. How much of the stuff could he absorb before it fluffed his trumpet work?

I said, "I take it Bobby isn't likely to have connections in the business with Raymond Fenk?"

Manley frowned and gave me the same inspecting look he'd greeted me with earlier. The look must have been a specialty of his. Or else he saved it for people who roused the suspicious side of his nature. Me, for instance.

I said, "My thought is, Fenk's in movies, but he seems to be strictly Hollywood, and Bobby isn't."

"What's going on, Mr. Lawyer?" Manley said. He still had on the frown and the look of close scrutiny.

"Let's try to establish a small bond of trust, Harp," I said. "We're both interested in what's happened to Dave Goddard, you for business reasons, me for personal reasons."

"Personal, huh? You supposed to be the kiddie's lawyer."

"That too," I said. "The reason I'm asking the questions about Raymond Fenk, I'm sure he's got something to do with Dave's disappearance. Why and how, I don't know yet. You say you and your movie and good old Bobby have no tie-in to Fenk. That's a start. Negative, but a start."

JACK BATTEN

"This Fenk whapped the kiddie upside the head?"

"That's the assumption I'm going on."

Manley's eyes switched away from my face.

"I suppose I got to let that young kiddie I got on the piano stretch out some," he said.

"Take up the solo slack until Dave comes back?"

"Ain't worth shit."

"Who isn't?" I said. "You're not talking about Dave?"

"The young kiddie on the piano. Plays too many notes."

Manley finished the rest of his drink.

"All right if I ask something private, Harp?" I said. "How much Scotch can you hold when you're on the job?"

Manley looked at his empty glass.

"I don't hardly juice," he said. "Only time is if the kiddies get to acting bad on me."

"I'll alert Abner Chase," I said. "Get him to lay in an extra stock of Black Label for the rest of the week."

9

COMMUTERS call it the DVP. They say it with affection. It's the Don Valley Parkway. It's three lanes wide both ways, five lanes at the collector points, and it carries traffic from the centre of the city to the northern suburbs and beyond. A tractor-trailer passed me, and my car shimmied. A Tinker Toy could pass me and my car would shimmy. I drive a white Volkswagen Beetle convertible. I was on the inside lane of the Parkway and heading north. A grateful bank robber gave me the Beetle. A bonus, he said, for getting him an acquittal. The gift may reveal something about my clientele. If Cam Charles had a client overflowing in gratitude, the Reverend Moon maybe, he'd probably reward Cam with a Lamborghini.

On either side of the Parkway, tall dark trees stood on hills against the sky. The trees were all that was left of the old valley from the centuries before it was paved for the four lanes each way. Somewhere down below me to the left was the Don River. It had turned as grey and greasy as Mr. Kipling's Limpopo. I took the off ramp for Don Mills Road North and drove past a junior high school named after Marc Garneau. I had the top up on the Beetle, but the windows were open, and the air, away from the Parkway, felt damp and fresh. Marc Garneau was Canada's astronaut. Mission Control in Houston fired him into space and brought him back. Good for Marc. Were other schools named after living Canadians of renown? Deanna Durbin Collegiate Institute? Didn't seem likely.

On the north side of Eglinton Avenue, past the IBM complex, I took a right and got myself into the fringes of residential suburbia. The streets were laid out in loops and crescents that probably adhered to a master design. The design eluded me. I slowed and circled and watched for street signs. People who live in downtown Toronto look askance at people who live in the suburbs. The suburban dwellers drive into the city, take up parking space, talk noisy in restaurants, and go home to their crooked little streets on a highway they call by a pet name. Maybe it was just an image problem.

Ralph Goddard lived at 48 Hiawatha Crescent, and I was at the intersection of Tomahawk and Wigwam. Where was John Wayne when you needed him? I found Hiawatha and Number 48 on my own. Ralph's house was white stucco and two storeys. There was a Pontiac station wagon in the driveway, and the porch light was on. I parked in front of the house and walked up the sidewalk. It was made of rust-coloured bricks that had been fitted together in an intricate pattern. There was a birdbath on the lawn, and a sign by the door, raised black metal lettering on a light-brown plaque, announced "The Goddards". I didn't spot any pink flamingos.

Ralph Goddard answered the door after I pushed the bell a second time. He didn't look much like Dave.

"You must be the famous Mr. Crang," he said.

Ralph had a grin that would crack most men's cheeks.

"Any friend of Dave's," he said.

He gripped my elbow in his left fist and shook my hand with his right in a display of great conviviality. Ralph was taller, fatter, and greyer than his brother. He had on a short-sleeved white shirt, green gabardine slacks, and Hush Puppies. His eye alignment appeared to be in order.

"Come on up to the family room," Ralph said.

He led the way up a short flight of stairs carpeted in pink and into a room straight ahead. The pink carpet continued around to the left, presumably to the bedrooms.

"Get you a drink?" Ralph asked. "Something nice and cool?"

"Vodka'd taste good."

"One vodka coming up," Ralph said. He'd inherited the hearty genes in the Goddard family. "Anything with it? Tang?"

"Ice, just ice, Ralph."

He went back down the stairs. The family room had flocked wallpaper in a mustard shade. The shelves along one wall held a collection of china birds, and, on a low end-table, two marble bookends enclosed a short row of Louis L'Amour novels in hardcover. There was a set of a sofa and two armchairs covered in shiny material in browns and yellows that picked up the mustard on the walls. Another chair was aimed at the TV set. The chair had many movable parts, a headrest, a footrest, arms that raised up and down. You could buy chairs like that on your Visa card by dialling a toll-free number in Akron, Ohio. I'd seen the ads. Ralph's chair was in brown corduroy. He'd left the television on with the sound down low. It was tuned to the Blue Jays ball game.

Ralph came back to the room empty-handed.

"What's your second choice, Crang?" he said. "Doreen went to the booze store today and bought the place out, it looks like."

"Except no vodka."

"You got it."

"Why don't I have whatever you're drinking."

"That'll be two dark rum and Coke."

By the time I left the family room, I'd be on the road to gout. Why was it called the family room? If the kids were out in the world and Ralph and Doreen lived alone, wouldn't every room in the house qualify as family room? I'd ponder the question next time I strolled Philosopher's Walk.

The ice in the large glasses tinkled against the sides. Ralph carried a glass in each hand. He handed one to me and leaned over to turn off the television set.

"Top of the sixth," he said. "Jays in front by three. You a baseball fan, Crang?"

"You bet," I said. It was the second lie I'd told to a member of the Goddard family in twenty-four hours. Baseball makes me nod off, but there was no sense alienating Ralph at a time when I had more worrying matters for him.

"Dave didn't appear at Chase's tonight," I said.

"I thought that'd be it soon's I saw you standing at the door down there," Ralph said. He sat in the chair with the gadgets and touched something that swung it in my direction. I remembered the chair's brand. Motolounger. I was sitting on the sofa.

I said to Ralph, "I've got a name since I talked to you this afternoon. Raymond Fenk. He's the party seems to be responsible for all the rough stuff."

"The whole shebang buffaloes me," Ralph said. "Dave's been toeing the mark ever since I got him to let me look after things."

"Fenk's in the movie business. Might he have any business connection with Dave? Does the name mean something? Fenk?"

"I thought you told me Dave saw this bozo and didn't recognize him."

"The face registered nothing," I said. "Maybe the name does."

"Fenk?" Ralph rubbed his jaw and took his time over the name. "I got to tell you, Crang, there's a lot of people on a lot of contracts. But I don't recollect Fenk. I could look through the files. I keep Dave's records in apple-pie order. Nobody from Revenue Canada or any place else'd find a number out of place."

"Remind me to call you around income tax time, Ralph," I said. "Fenk is Hollywood. That's my information, and I know it's reliable. Let's suppose they had an encounter out there, Dave and Fenk. What do your records say about Dave in the neighbourhood of Hollywood?"

"How's that get Dave back on the job at Abner Chase's?" Ralph said. "He's lost a night's pay already, and I just know Harp Manley's bummed off, excuse my French. What we ought to be doing, my opinion, is beat the bushes for Dave right now. You sure he's not drunk or something? Had a relapse?"

"Fenk's the link. Let's go with that for the moment. If we can come up with a reason for Fenk's interest in Dave, maybe we stand a chance of locating Dave."

Ralph hadn't touched his dark rum and Coke. Neither had I. I was nervous about the taste. What was Ralph's excuse?

Ralph said, "Well, you're right about California. Dave was out there a couple of weeks ago on a tour. Dave Goddard and His Canadian All-Stars. I thought that one up. Dave's got a big underdog reputation, you know. Fans from way back still come out to hear him."

"Underground, Ralph. Dave's got an underground reputation."

"I'm not up on the jazz lingo," Ralph said. "All I know's I booked this band of Dave's into a bunch of clubs down the west coast. He was out there May to August."

"And at some point he hit Los Angeles?"

"Last stop on the tour. But I don't recall this what's-his-name had anything to do with the place Dave played at."

"Raymond Fenk."

"Off the top of my head, I couldn't tell you the name of the place either."

"Why not you get out the apple-pie records and we'll both take a look."

"Will do," Ralph said. He spun the Motolounger into the disembark position. "You sit there and enjoy the drink. I'll get the paperwork out of the den."

I sipped from the rum and Coke. It seemed short on rum and long on Coke. I sipped again. A few more sips and I'd have a personality as sugary as Bill Cosby's.

Ralph kept his brother's contracts, itineraries, and other documents in orderly six-by-twelve file folders. He had eight or nine of them stacked up. They were orange-coloured, and each was fat with forms held neatly together by paper clips.

"Four people were in the band besides Dave," Ralph said. He shuffled files as he spoke. "Dave rounded them up in Vancouver. I leave that end to him, the musicians. So, let's see, the band played the first two, three weeks right around Vancouver and after that, kept moving right on south."

"They reached Los Angeles in August?"

"Transportation's your biggest expense." Ralph stopped at one file, lifted out a sheaf of papers, and turned slowly through them. "Your other cost, it's the lay-over time. Some of these jazz clubs only run weekends. So what was I gonna do with Dave and the four other fellas Monday to Thursday? Ship them all the way back to Vancouver?"

Ralph raised his head from the papers and gave me the big grin.

"Not on your life," he said. "I just went on ahead and scouted through telephone books and whatnot for the areas out there, and I found universities, community colleges, the likes of them, places there was a lot of kids, and I sold them on a concert. Had to cut my price most times, but it paid the freight and some left over."

I said, "Abner Chase told me you were astute, Ralph."

"Did he now."

Ralph squared the sheaf of papers in his hand, returned them to their file, and resumed his shuffle through the other files. I leaned back in the sofa. This was going to take a while. I went at my drink very slowly. If I finished it, Ralph might offer me another.

"Portland, Oregon. Eugene, that's Oregon too," Ralph said, more to himself than to me. "All righty, now we're getting warmer. San Francisco. Dave did excellent there. Palo Alto is Stanford University." Ralph unclipped sheets of paper that looked like contracts.

"Here we go," he said, his voice louder. "Actual fact, it wasn't in Los Angeles Dave played."

Ralph separated out one contract.

"Culver City," he said. "I guess that's a Los Angeles neighbourhood or something, little town close by maybe."

"Like Anaheim, Azusa, and Cucamonga."

"It was the Alley Cat Bistro Dave worked at," Ralph said. "How in the world could a man forget a name like that? Alley Cat Bistro in Culver City."

Ralph handed me the contract. It was four pages long. Most of it was in printed clauses, standard boilerplate stuff, but there were dates and money amounts typed in. I flipped to the last page. Whoever signed for the Alley Cat had an illegible hand, but the name was too long to be Raymond Fenk's.

Ralph said, "Dave thought the audiences were hep at this Alley Cat. Couldn't have been a big place though, not according to what they paid."

"Did he play other jobs out there? A concert? Anything?"

"Not in L.A."

"What about a movie soundtrack?"

"A week at this Alley Cat and Dave flew straight home," Ralph said. "He was a pretty excited guy."

"How could you tell?"

Ralph performed the grin that lit up Don Mills.

"Oh sure, Dave's one for keeping the feelings to himself," he said. "But anybody could see the week with Harp Manley had him real pleased."

"He knew about that before he came back from the western tour?"

"Before he even went west," Ralph said. "I had the contracts signed up first of May."

"Signed with whom? Manley's people?"

"With everybody," Ralph said. "Abner Chase booked Manley into his club, and his agency in New York, Manley's agency, told Abner they needed another horn for Toronto. Abner asked if Dave was okay. Well, that needed backing and forthing because Manley had to give his personal stamp, which he did soon's he heard it was Dave. So, Bob's your uncle, the contract came from New York and Abner signed and I signed, and Dave felt real good about everything."

"Until Raymond Fenk arrived on the scene."

I gave the Alley Cat contract back to Ralph. He aligned the orange files so that their corners were exact and placed them on the floor beside the Motolounger.

Ralph said, "Where's all this get us?"

"Not far past square one."

"Don't think I don't appreciate your worry, Crang," Ralph said. "But I'm just thinking Dave'll walk in tomorrow, you know, sheepish, apologizing to all concerned. I'll read him the riot act, count on it, and we'll get back to business as usual."

No rum and Coke had passed Ralph's lips. Maybe Doreen was the drinker in the household. I finished my glass and told Ralph I'd keep in touch. He stood under the porch light until I drove out of sight around one of Hiawatha's curves.

I chose a route home by way of Eglinton and North Toronto's back streets. If someone I knew spotted me on the DVP, word might get out I was a closet suburbanite. It was ten-thirty, and I hadn't eaten since Cam Charles's spread. Falafel felt about right. I stopped at the Kensington Kitchen on Harbord and ordered a plate to go. Falafel, hummus, tabbouleh, and pita. The pita was whole-wheat.

I ate the food and drank two glasses of Soave in front of the CITY-TV news. The sports guy's sweater had more colours than a test pattern. He said the Blue Jays lost in the ninth and the Maple Leafs had a couple of promising defencemen. I switched off the set. When the Boston Celtics cranked up, I'd get interested in team games.

I dialled Annie's number. Her answering machine told me she'd return my call. The answering machine told everybody she'd return their calls. Impersonal. Wasn't I special? Annie must have been at the big bash that came after the Festival of Festivals' opening movie. Had Daniel Day-Lewis hit town yet? I didn't ask Annie's answering machine.

I took a book called *Jazzletters: Singers and the Song* to bed. It was written by a guy named Gene Lees, and I was up to the chapter on Johnny Mercer. When I fell asleep, the melody to "Skylark" was circling at the centre of my mind.

10

DAVE GODDARD was an item in "For the Record" in Friday morning's *Globe*. The first item was about a stockbroker and a half-million dollars; both were missing from a Bay Street investment firm. The second was about a man of no fixed address who got set on fire on the tennis courts behind the Moss Park Armoury. Dave was the third. "For the Record" runs every day in the back pages of the *Globe*'s news section. It's for readers on the run, six or seven one-paragraph stories, usually about crime, usually spiced up from routine police reports. The man of no fixed address probably didn't think the fire was routine. He was alive and in St. Michael's Hospital. So was Dave Goddard.

The *Globe* paragraph said he'd been assaulted early Wednesday morning in a lane near Queen and Spadina. An injury to the head, the paragraph said, and no arrests had been made. Dave was described as "an internationally known jazz musician". Someone on the copy desk at the *Globe* must have added the description. Or else the police guy who handed out the press announcement was more hip than the Toronto cops I usually cross-examined in court.

I got to St. Mike's before ten and didn't have to go farther than the waiting room on the first floor to find Dave. He was sitting in the middle of a row of five chairs, and behind him there was a counter and a glassed-in area where women in civvies were talking on phones and tapping numbers into computers. Dave had an official-looking form attached to a clipboard in one hand. He had a ballpoint pen in the other hand, and a bandage on his head. It wasn't easy to miss the bandage. It began just above Dave's eyebrows and reached into his scalp. A couple of inches of Dave's hair seemed to have been shaved to make way for the bandage. Dave was applying himself to the form on the clipboard.

I sat in the chair beside him. Dave's left eye panned over to me. The expression on his face was somewhere between blank and morose.

"What's happening, man?" Dave said to me.

"That ought to be my question, Dave. What happened to you?"

"The dude you were supposed to be tailing aced me."

I said, "He aced me too."

A woman leaned over the counter behind us and spoke to Dave. She had a Middle Eastern face and deep, dark eyes.

"How's it coming there, Mr. Goddard?" she said.

"Right with you, man," Dave said without turning his head.

The woman beamed her eyes on me and shrugged.

I looked at the form in Dave's lap. He was stuck at the entry for home address.

"Try 48 Hiawatha Crescent," I said.

"I can dig it," Dave said. "Ralph's place."

The tip launched Dave on a roll of right answers. He filled in his own occupation and Ralph's telephone number. His Ontario Hospital Insurance number stumped him.

I said, "Tell the woman with the eyes you'll phone it in."

Dave conferred with the woman, who asked him for a cash payment of five dollars and twenty-six cents. It covered a television set Dave rented. The woman said OHIP would pick up the cost of room, meals, bandage, and head shave. The woman's eyes were large and moist and almost black. I could drown in eyes like hers.

The Volks was parked in a lot on Dundas Street. Dave's clothes looked rumpled but not as ingrained with dust and grit as my Cy Mann navy blue. Dave and I walked up Bond Street. His hands were conspicuously empty of the gleaming new saxophone case. I asked Dave what had gone on between him and his assailant outside the entrance to the Cameron.

Dave said, "Enough of this shit."

"Dave," I said, "I think it'll help if we discuss your contact with the guy."

"That's what the dude said."

"'Enough of this shit?'"

"That's it, man."

"Next thing he made off with your saxophone?"

"Maybe what the dude said was more like, 'I got no time for this shit.'"

"Which shit would that be, Dave?"

"All I know, man," Dave said, "the dude wasn't in a mood for hanging out."

"He wanted your saxophone?"

"Grabbed my axe and took off up the street."

"No more conversation?"

"I went around the corner at the Cameron," Dave said, "and here's the dude with this big mother of a two-by-four raised up in the air."

"What next?"

"Twelve stitches and a concussion."

Dave and I crossed Shuter and walked past the St. Michael's Choir School.

"We got a gap in time and movement between the alley and the hospital," I said. "What I'd like, Dave, you fill it."

"Cat was loading a bunch of crates in his truck back of the Cameron," Dave said. "He dumped a crate on me. Surprised hell out of the cat. It's middle of the night, and me and the two-by-four's laid out in his truck."

"This truck, it have wheels like on a tractor?"

"I wasn't doing a size survey, man."

We cut off Bond Street and across the parking lot. I needed my daily hit of facts. Lawyers live off facts. Raymond Fenk bashed Dave with the two-by-four. He slung Dave in the back of the truck with the monster tires, and when I showed up, he wielded the two-by-four on me. I could figure out that much. Facts have a consecutive beauty. The consecutive part was my difficulty with Dave. He was a lateral thinker. I was a vertical thinker. Clash of two modes. The owner of the truck found Dave and drove him to the hospital. Or called the cops, who did the hospital run. If I wanted the ration of facts that covered events of the previous thirty-six hours, I'd have to wait Dave out. Brother Ralph was more my kind of thinker, painstaking but vertical.

"I wish you'd phoned me from the hospital, Dave," I said. "Me or Abner Chase or Ralph."

"I phoned Flip."

"Good thinking, Dave," I said. "Who's Flip?"

"He's pushing buttons to get me the loan of an axe till mine comes back," Dave said. "Flip Bochner."

We reached the Volks. Dave groaned a little when he stooped to sit in the passenger seat.

"You in shape to play?" I asked.

It was still and quiet inside the car. The bandage on Dave's head looked more ominous than it had in the hospital waiting room.

"Man," Dave said. He was facing straight ahead. "How about you drive me to Long & McQuade's? Be okay?"

Long & McQuade's is a music store on Bloor somewhere beyond Bathurst. The parking-lot attendant said I owed him three dollars. I paid and turned left out of the lot and drove west on Dundas.

"The doctor said it's cool to blow long's I take it easy," Dave said. "I told him, man, I usually do."

Dave almost smiled.

I said, "The guy who did the number on your head is named Raymond Fenk."

Dave was silent.

I said, "He's in the Hollywood movie business."

Nothing from Dave's side of the car.

I said, "You were working a club in his neck of the woods two or three weeks ago."

Dave came to life.

"Catch this, man," he said. "The club you're talking about's in a shopping mall. Dude that owns it, he tells me, you get to the shoe store, right next to it's the club. I'm thinking to myself, later for this, man. But I go inside, the place's groovy."

Dundas narrows where it bisects old Chinatown. The cars had jammed up, and the drivers were looking desperate. It'd be worse farther west where the newer, expanded Chinatown is as dense as Hong Kong. Dundas was a lousy choice of route unless I was scouting for dim sum.

"Whole gang of cats sat in with my band," Dave said. He was heating up on the subject of the Alley Cat Bistro in Culver City, California. "These cats got the studio gigs, you dig. Play for the TV shows, the movies. But nights, for a change, get a taste of jazz, they came out to blow at the club."

I was three cars and a dump truck back of the red light at University Avenue.

"Jack Sheldon did a couple sets with my band."

The light turned green, and the dump truck stalled. Nobody moved.

"Snooky Young fell by twice."

I let Dave run through his catalogue of happy California memories. The traffic was on my mind. Some rich guy with marginal taste donated a sculpture for the boulevard that splits University on the south side of Dundas. It's scrawny and metal, and at the top, maybe twenty-five feet high, there are parts like emaciated arms lifting straight up. People who question the sculpture's merit have a nickname for it. Gumby Goes to Heaven.

"Med Flory also," Dave said.

I turned right at University. Everybody was driving like Mario Andretti. I joined the race.

"Somebody brought around, probably Jack Sheldon brought around an alto player by the name of Joe Romano. Real hot player."

I asked, "What about Raymond Fenk, Dave?"

"Tell me his horn."

"Not a musician, Dave. Raymond Fenk was the guy I said handled the two-by-four."

"Don't know of the dude from anywhere."

I pushed gently at Dave. I prodded and probed, and made the effort at thinking laterally. I discovered for my pains that, according to Dave, his stay in Los Angeles had been monastic. He frequented the Alley Cat and a Holiday Inn, and rode cabs in between. No concerts on the side, no movie contacts, no freelancing.

"How about an all-day excursion to Disneyland?" I asked.

"I knew a cat once worked there. Steady bread but the cat freaked. You believe it, man. 'Some Day My Prince Will Come' fifteen goes a day?"

I found a space on a side street south of Bloor, and we walked back up to Long & McQuade's. Dave went to the counter. I browsed. There were rows of plastic guitars in the contours and colours of rocket ships from old Flash Gordon comics. I stopped in front of an IVL 7000 Pitchrider Guitar MIDI Interface with Pickup and Footswitch. Dave bought some saxophone reeds. Lucky for Dave. The Pitchrider Interface cost two thousand dollars.

Back in the car, Dave asked a question.

"How'd you find out this name—Fenk, you said's the dude?—is the name of the guy boffed me?"

"Luck," I said. "A little footwork, and help from a lady friend. Those three."

"I never saw the dude till I looked over my shoulder five days ago."

"Now he's got your saxophone and case, and you want them back."

"My axe anyway, man."

"The case looks new and shiny," I said. "Must be worth something."

"New isn't shit. I liked my old one."

"It wore out?"

"Some motherfucker swiped it."

"Too bad."

"From the club beside the shoe store."

I hadn't started the car engine. We were parked under a well-established city maple, and on the sidewalk beside us two girls about nine years old had a piece of chalk and were marking out squares for hopscotch.

"And where'd you get the new case?" I asked Dave.

"Same place."

"The original case was stolen the week you were playing at the Alley Cat?"

"I bought that case the day I bought my horn," Dave said. "Like forty years back, man."

"Concentrate on the present, Dave."

"One night the case's gone. You get used to a case, man. I must've carried it on a hundred thousand jobs. I felt like crying."

"What do you mean you got the new case at the Alley Cat?"

"You want to hear the truth, man?" Dave faced toward me. "I did cry. Back at the hotel, I bawled my eyes out for a couple of minutes. It was nice later when the dude gave me the new case. But . . ."

Dave turned back to the scene in front of the car. One of the little girls was bouncing through the hopscotch squares. She was using an acorn as a marker.

"Which dude are we at now?" I asked. "Who was it gave you the replacement case?"

"Never met with him, man," Dave said. "The guy that owns the Alley Cat comes up to me and says, guess what, a dude said he heard you got your case lifted and he left this new number for you. Fans like to lay things on musicians. A drink. A joint. Come to their place for dinner. I figure it was that way with the dude with the new case."

"Did the Alley Cat owner say what he looked like? The case's donor?"

"Just a fan. I never asked."

I could recognize a clue when it jumped up and tapped me on the shoulder.

"Dave," I said, "Raymond Fenk didn't want your saxophone. He wanted the case."

"Jesus, man, he could've asked."

"There must be something about the case."

"He didn't have to put me in the hospital," Dave said. "I would've given it to him before he came down with the two-by-four."

I pulled away from the curb and the hopscotch game, and drove on streets that would take us to the Cameron House. Dave was saying something about reeds. He was fussy about them. They had to be extra hard. Flip Bochner would provide the substitute saxophone, but Dave said he had to choose the reeds. That explained the trip to Long & McQuade's.

"At the hospital, Dave," I said, "what'd you tell the police?"

"What happened is what I told them," he said. "A dude was following me and finally caught up."

"You mention my name?"

"No. I told them I wanted my axe back."

"They seem interested?"

"One cop asked questions, and the other wrote stuff down, and both of them split. No, I don't think they were interested, man."

"I wonder what it is with the case?" I said. "Someone steals the old case and replaces it in Los Angeles, and someone else in Toronto from Los Angeles, Raymond Fenk, steals the new case."

"Forget the case, man," Dave said. "It's the axe."

"I think I know how to retrieve both."

"How?"

"Same way you lost them," I said. "Steal them again."

11

O**N THE TELEPHONE**, James Turkin's polite sister told me James had a room on Howland Avenue and was given to passing his late afternoons at a café called Dooney's. Howland and Dooney's were in the Annex. I thanked the sister and drove to the café. It was five o'clock.

Outside Dooney's, large block letters advertised cappuccino and gelati. Not a shamrock or shillelagh in sight. Inside, the room was long and narrow and bright. One wall was all window, and the tables were filled with talkers who looked serious about it. James Turkin was sitting alone at a table for two near the back. He had a coffee cup in front of him and an open magazine, and he was watching me walk the length of the room toward him.

"I don't need a lawyer," he said when I got close.

"The reason I came calling, James, I'm not selling my services. I'm retaining yours."

I sat in the other chair.

James said, "I don't do houses."

"We're still in business," I said.

"Or apartments."

"What's this?" I asked. "You experience a change of calling?"

"Factories I do, office buildings. As far as houses go, I got . . . scruples."

As a sideline, James worked at upgrading his vocabulary. The rest of the time, he was the best burglar I knew. One day the break-and-enter squad would come down on him, and I'd defend James in court. He had pale features and light-brown hair that he wore in a 1950s pompadour. He was nineteen. His nerves were as steady as the Dalai Lama's.

"Also," James said, "I took a course in another . . . endeavour."

"A course sounds like you found something on the straight and narrow."

"Picks," James said.

"Come again."

"Pickpocketing," James said. Nothing moved except his lips. "A one-week course."

"I can see it now," I said. "George Brown College offers night classes in Pocket Picking, followed by Extortion 101."

"This was two old Colombian guys came up from New York, and all it cost was four hundred including equipment."

"What equipment?"

"Mannequins," James said. "They had bells tied on them. The idea is you tried to lift the wallet off the mannequin, inside pocket, hip pocket, different places, and if the bell rang, you failed. One guy quit the first day. It was like all he had to do was breathe next to the mannequin and bells started like in a church. Anyway, soon as you got it so you could pick ten pockets and no bells happened, the Colombian guys took you down Eaton Centre. Work on humans."

"You think you got your four hundred dollars' worth?"

"I was the only student in the class the Colombians let do the newspaper routine for real."

"Am I going to want to hear this?" I asked.

"You're on the subway." James sounded as close to eager as he gets. "You hold the *Sun* in one hand, and the other, you reach into the guy beside you's pocket. Has to be quick. I got a teacher's wallet."

"Bad luck," I said. "The teacher must've been slim pickings."

"I mailed it back to the guy."

The waiter came by, and I ordered an espresso.

"You heard of this writer?" James was leafing through his magazine. It was *Harper's*. "Lewis Lapham?"

"He writes some very funny pieces. Acerbic."

"What I mean, is he any good?"

"Yeah, he's good. Got a nice style, and he keeps you turning the pages to find out what he's saying. I'd call that good."

"I thought so. I underlined twenty, I don't know, thirty words in this one story."

"Here's one for you, James. William Safire in the *New York Times*, especially Sunday. You'll go crazy underlining."

James didn't write down Safire's name. He'd remember. James was a kind of *idiot savant* in training. His fields were words and locks and now apparently other people's pockets. I'd acted for him on a charge of assault with intent when he was young and foolish and unfocussed. The judge put him on probation for two years. The probation had another ten months to run, and it hadn't dissuaded James from his new life of non-violent crime. He thought he was indestructible. Maybe he was, but I kept his file in my active drawer.

"What's the word mean?" James asked. "About Lewis Lapham?"

"A touch of the bitter. That's how you define acerbic. Astringent, okay? There you got another adjective. Put the two on the same list, acerbic and astringent. Use them when you want to say something has a taste of sour. Harsh."

My espresso arrived.

"End of today's lesson in etymology, James," I said. "I want to talk to you about a job in the category of piece of cake."

"I already said I don't go into houses any more or apartments, places where people live."

"How about where they reside temporarily?"

"Like what, an office where the guy sometimes sleeps over? That happened to me in this factory out in Etobicoke. I go in, three in the morning, and a man, must've been an executive, was sound asleep in the dark. Office as big as this restaurant, leather couch he was laying on, girl with him asleep also. No clothes on either one of the guy or the girl. I was ... mortified."

"Mortified is nice, James," I said. "Let me test your philosophy of residences vis-à-vis commercial properties. What does a hotel come under?"

"I've never done a hotel."

"People come and go. Hotels, at least not this one, aren't permanent dwellings."

"You shouldn't be asking me this stuff. You're a lawyer."

"You're right, James, the Law Society wouldn't approve. But, take my word, this is a worthy cause."

James hesitated. He was rummaging for a word.

He said, "That's your ... justification."

He'd settled for second-best. I wouldn't tell him about rationalization.

"Work it out, James," I said. "The bad guy took something from the good guy, and we're going to take it back from the bad guy."

"Is this a new hotel or old?"

"Thirty, forty years it's been up, from the architecture and everything else."

"You know what's a tough building? The library in North York, couple years old, and it's got the latest. I went in Tuesday night for practice. Guy told me about the electronic things in the ceiling, high tech, they track you everywhere you move."

"What'd you bring out? Dictionary?"

"Only practice. You don't believe me, I already had seven hundred dollars from the naked guy's wallet in Etobicoke."

"Electronic surveillance I don't think is a problem at the Silverdore."

"A hotel would look good on my résumé."

"I like it, résumé. Your profession's gotten into white-collar procedures?"

"Not written down. Just, some guy asks what places I've done, I can say hotel."

"This is rush, James, if you're telling me yes. I don't mean next week or two days from now. It has to be right away."

"Tonight I got something on."

"Make it tomorrow in the daylight. The guy, Fenk's his name, we aren't going in there and tiptoe around his room while he's in bed. Some time before noon tomorrow ought to be right. That suit you? Fenk'll be out and moving by then. Away from the room."

"You the lookout or you mean you're going in with me all the way?"

"Never send a man on a mission you wouldn't go on yourself, James, or something along those lines."

"What's coming out?"

"One portable object dearly beloved by its true and long-time owner."

"How much is my end?"

"Payment of two hundred dollars on completion of the operation."

James's face remained as immobile as usual. But I gathered the price met his standards, unless it was the idea of an addition to his résumé that attracted him. He agreed to meet me on Charles Street near the Silverdore at eleven on Saturday morning.

I said, "You're not likely to get detoured, are you, by whatever's on tonight, to the slammer maybe?"

"It's a beginners' class for dips. I'm the teacher."

I got the bill from the waiter for my espresso and James's coffee, and paid at the cashier's desk.

"You want to practise on me?" I said to James on the street. "I'll tell you if any bells go off. The wallet's in my rear pocket."

"No, it isn't."

I touched my pocket and felt nothing except a small wave of panic in my stomach.

"Here you go," James said.

He was holding my wallet out to me.

"When you were going out the door," James said, "I lifted it then."

"That was scary, James. Not even a tinkle."

12

IF IT WAS SIX-FIFTEEN in my apartment, it was three-fifteen at the Alley Cat Bistro. I got its number from California directory assistance and spoke to a man with an Hispanic accent who said the boss wouldn't be in for an hour. He called me *señor*.

The focal point of my living room, I tell myself when I'm thinking decor, is a sofa covered in greyish-brown fabric that has enough of a satiny sheen to make a luxury statement. Jackie O. would willingly sit on my sofa. It faces the front window and is set about ten feet into the room. In the mornings, the early sun hits the sofa. Sometimes, if duty doesn't summon me to office or court, I carry my breakfast coffee into the sofa and sun, and think of the Côte d'Azur. The fantasy doesn't work in the evenings. I poured a Wyborowa on the rocks and sat on the sofa in the semi-gloom.

What the hell was so precious about Dave Goddard's saxophone case? Not the old one. It was out of the picture. The new case. Raymond Fenk couldn't have been after the tenor saxophone. He didn't strike me as a guy who wanted to rehearse the John Coltrane songbook. He struck me as someone shifty who knew the saxophone case had value. Someone shifty and violent. Impatient too. And maybe kind of stupid. Couldn't he have displayed a more subtle touch in relieving Dave of the case? An act of grab and assault, Fenk's act, was a trifle obvious.

Arrogant even. That was a possibility. Combine arrogance and impatience and you might have Raymond Fenk.

I went into the kitchen and phoned Annie's answering machine to remind it of my dinner date with Annie. The machine was indifferent. I freshened my drink, two ice cubes and the same number of ounces of vodka, and got comfy on the sofa.

The saxophone case couldn't have value all by itself. The value was whatever was in the case. The saxophone was in the case. Scratch the saxophone. If something else was in there, Dave Goddard would have noticed it. Well, maybe scratch that supposition. Dave, for all his other fine qualities, mostly his honest-to-God musical artistry, might not be the planet's most observant occupant.

What if something was concealed in the case? Something Dave wouldn't notice no matter how observant he was. Whatever was concealed, if anything, would have to be light. Otherwise the extra weight would tip off Dave. On the other hand, the case was new and unfamiliar to Dave, and he wouldn't recognize anything out of sync about the case's balance.

I reached back of the sofa and turned on the lamp at its least bright level. The lamp sat on a dark wood table that Annie and I discovered on a foray into the antique-shop country up near Shelburne. Beside the lamp I kept a stack of magazines—*Vanity Fair*, *Jazz Monthly*, *Saturday Night*. James Turkin might have fun underlining the Mixed Media guy's column in *Vanity Fair*, James Wolcott. He was always good for a "palpable" and a "semiotics".

Things that could be tucked out of sight in a saxophone case. Not gold bricks. Money, though it'd have to be in bills of very large denomination to make the trouble and effort of concealment worth while. Jewellery, though we'd be thinking small and prized diamonds, rubies, and so forth for the same reasons of effort and trouble.

Or, oh shit, drugs.

"Crang, we know you're up there."

It was Ian from downstairs.

"You want to come down for a drinkee?"

I got off the sofa and walked to the top of the stairs. Ian was standing at the foot, a short, compact man, bald, a moustache, wearing white shorts and a Diana Ross T-shirt.

"Ian, how many times have I told you, drinkee's a dead giveaway."

"Who cares? It's Friday. I never watch my language on weekends."

Ian was the swishier member of Ian and Alex. He sold real estate, Alex was a civil servant. Ian was joking. He didn't care if he sounded like a queen. People buying houses preferred gay agents. Better taste in realty. Ian told me that, and I believed him.

"Thanks anyway," I said. "I'm out for dinner, and until then I got to ratiocinate up here."

"Get *you*. Ratiocinate."

"The mental equivalent of weightlifting."

"If you change your mind, Alex has done something super. It's got brandy in it and honey and lime and champers. Pitchers of it, I promise."

"Save me some for breakfast."

"Oh well, give our love to Anniepoo."

"Ian, I'll send someone around to wash out your tongue."

"*Please* do."

It was four-fifteen at the Alley Cat, and the manager was on the premises. He sounded friendly. Why do Americans get into all their wars? Most Americans I run into are too friendly for warmongers. The friendly American at the Alley Cat had practically total recall of the Dave Goddard saxophone episode. A guy came in with the new case early in the evening before Dave arrived for the first set, and said it was a gift of appreciation. He heard Dave lost his old case. Didn't want to meet Dave. Just a present from an admirer to show Dave not everyone in Culver City was a ratfink thief. I asked the manager what the man bearing gifts looked like. Big, strapping guy, the manager said on the phone. That was Fenk to a T. Claimed he was a fan, but the manager didn't remember seeing him around the Alley Cat. Still on stream for

Fenk. The guy smiled a lot. Well, Fenk could fake it. The guy was black. Oops. Not Fenk. I thanked the manager, who said to come by next time I was out their way.

I gave my glass a small snap of Wyborowa, a dressing drink, and sipped at it in the bedroom while I considered my wardrobe. The black guy who left the case for Dave could have connections with Fenk. He ran the delivery errand, and Fenk completed the arrangement by picking up the case in Toronto. Yanking the case out of Dave's hands and slamming him with a two-by-four wasn't precisely synonymous with "picking up", but it rounded out the enterprise that began at the Alley Cat. Say the black guy snitched Dave's old case, substituted the new, which had something hidden in it, and Fenk took delivery when the case reached Toronto with Dave.

Should I congratulate myself on this marvel of deduction? Definitely premature. The whole house of cards hinged on the presence of something concealed in the case, and until James and I checked out Fenk's room at the Silverdore, I wouldn't know about the case or concealment. If Fenk still had the case. If the concealed goods existed. If they existed and Fenk hadn't disposed of them. If you were the only girl in the world and I were the only boy. I got out the clothes for my date with Annie and put them on.

13

THE WAY I WAS DRESSED, someone would have asked for my autograph at the Belair Café. I had on a white linen jacket, a dark-red silk tie against a light-grey broadcloth shirt, and grey flannels fresh from the dry cleaner's hot press. Instead, I took Annie to Emilio's.

Our waitress brought us menus, and I ordered a bottle of Vouvray. The waitress looked like Cher's younger sister. Same pile of black hair, same lean curves, same expression that said attitude.

I said to Annie, "You don't suppose that girl's got a tattoo in a very private place?"

"Don't bother asking her."

"Not till we're better acquainted," I said. "Around dessert time."

Emilio's made me feel cosmopolitan and funky. It looked like it belonged in SoHo, the one in Manhattan. Which, in Emilio's case, didn't mean it had done a copycat act. The guy who owned it was a New Yorker who used to live in SoHo. I retained that bulletin of news from one of my intensive readings of *Toronto Life*'s restaurant reviews. Annie and I were at a table under a Canadian Opera Company poster for a 1986 production of *Un Ballo in Maschera*. Beside it was a black-and-white photograph of Emilio's staff softball team, and in my sightline I could contemplate a metal sculpture of a white pineapple. Annie had on a black silk shirt and black cotton pants. Both were loose and billowy.

Nat Cole was singing "Lush Life" on Emilio's tape, and when he finished, a Latin group began a rendition of a Beatles song whose title I couldn't remember.

"Hear that?" I said to Annie. "I've eliminated it from my thought processes."

"If 'Norwegian Wood' was clogging your thought processes, you were in serious trouble."

"Not just the song," I said. "The whole of Beatle lore. John, Paul, George, and Ringo are right out of my head."

"That's a laugh. I've never noticed *Sergeant Pepper* in your record collection anyway."

"I'm not talking music, kid," I said, "I'm talking information over-load."

Cher's Younger Sister arrived with the Vouvray. It was sweeter than I liked in my wine, but the fruitiness and acidity were close to the mark. I think I read that in *Toronto Life*'s wine column.

I said to Annie, "What I'm trying to deal with here, it's the bane of life in the 1980s."

"That's easy. The bane of the 1980s is shoulder pads."

"I'm serious."

"So am I. You realize how many jackets and blouses I haven't bought because they looked like they were made for some guy on the Pittsburgh Steelers?"

"You going to listen to my theory or shall we just order?"

"Both," Annie said. Her face wore about as much makeup as Annie permits—a touch of blusher on the cheeks, even less lipstick, and a hint of black eye-liner. For some people, perfection requires little elaboration.

We ordered. Annie wanted cannelloni that came with ricotta, spinach, and tomato. I asked for chicken Taipei, and we said we'd split a starter of mussels that were steamed in ginger and honey.

"Actually it's more than a theory," I said. "It's a route to sanity."

Annie started to say something and stopped.

"Yeah?" I said.

"Nothing. I'm all ears."

"It's about the bombardment of facts," I said. The Vouvray wasn't too sweet after all. "We get so many of the little suckers beaming in from radio, TV, printed page, wherever, our poor brains can't absorb and compartmentalize and recall as required. Makes for muddy thinking. But I got the solution. Eliminate. Get rid of whole topics."

"But, honestly, the Beatles?"

"Newspaper story pops up about a Beatles reunion, about the latest tally on Yoko Ono's fortune, George plagiarizing a song from Motown. Any of those, I can give them a pass."

"How 'bout another example?" Annie said. "Something with more muscle?"

"Red China."

"Nobody calls it Red China any more. Plain China will do."

"My point entirely," I said. "I've been so successful at blocking the subject I missed the change in name."

"Get out of here."

"China ruled out, that makes a couple of billion potential stories I don't have to account for."

The waitress brought the mussels. Little pockets of steam hovered over each open shell, and I could sniff the ginger in the air.

"Evangelists," I said. "On or off television."

I began to divide the mussels on the plate. One for Annie, one for me, another for Annie, another for me. Annie reached over and put her hand on top of mine.

"It's okay, sweetie," she said. "I trust you not to take more than your share."

I ate the first mussel and tried to come up with an adjective that went beyond delicious.

"Evangelists you were saying?" Annie said.

"Exclude them, and think of the *Newsweek* cover stories I don't have to read."

Annie said, "Now and then I really can't tell when you're putting me on."

A moment of quiet of the pensive sort came from Annie.

She said, "Another topic occurs to me you might jettison."

I can tell when Annie isn't putting me on.

"Criminals," she said.

My glass was empty. I poured more Vouvray into it and topped up Annie's glass. We'd finished the mussels.

I said, "That might involve a career change of large proportions."

"Well, maybe just some criminals."

"Which ones?"

"Ones who are guilty."

"According to the latest statistics from the courtrooms of the nation," I said, "that would be most of them."

The main courses came. Annie's cannelloni looked as other cannelloni does but smelled better than most. My chicken Taipei had the same two ingredients that elevated the mussels to gourmet class—ginger and honey. There was also some peanut and soy in there. A little corner of Thai paradise.

"That man you're defending who did the terribly clever things with the apartment building," Annie said. "He's got the money, he and his partner, and what they did was illegal, and I don't understand why you have to defend their illegal acts."

"First," I said, "a quote."

"Lawyers are always quoting somebody or other."

"From a playwright."

"Playwright doesn't necessarily make it gospel."

"Robert Bolt wrote this in his play about Thomas More," I said. "*A Man For All Seasons.*"

"Right, I saw the movie," Annie said. "Paul Scofield played More. Got an Oscar."

I said, "More was the Lord Chancellor, and in one scene he's having a conversation with this very idealistic guy, More's son-in-law, I think. More says to the son-in-law something like, 'I know what's legal, not what's right, and I'll stick to what's legal.' So the son-in-law thinks he's got More in a corner, and he says, 'Then you set man's law above God's.'

More comes right back. 'Not far below,' he says, 'but let me draw your attention to a fact. I'm not God.'"

Annie worked some cannelloni on her fork. I drank from my glass of Vouvray. Nothing like a few lines from the theatre to dry a man's throat.

"Where's this Robert Bolt stuff taking us?" Annie said. "I already know you're not God."

"You don't have to say it so emphatically."

Annie patted my arm. It was a pat that meant state the point.

I said, "A guy in my job can't think about idealism, playing God, or anything in that vein. That's what Bolt was talking about. A criminal lawyer deals with facts and law and the system."

"This is beginning to sound familiar from past lectures," Annie said. "The adversarial system. Presumption of innocence. Da-dah. Da-dah. Da-dah. What am I leaving out?"

"No fair sneering. It's a nifty system. Only one thing wrong with it."

"Yeah," Annie said. "You're in it. Which I think is why we're having this little heart-to-heart."

I took a bite of my chicken, drank some more wine, and pressed on.

"The thing wrong," I said, "is the system is tilted badly against the people accused of the crimes."

"Your noble clients."

"Noble doesn't come into it."

"Right there we agree."

I said, "Stick with me a minute. All the machinery gears up to put the accused guy on trial. There's the cops and the crown attorney, medical experts, forensic scientists, court officials, God knows who else, dozens of people all lined up on the same side. That's one tilt. Okay? But something else works against the accused guy, more fundamental even."

I stopped talking. Annie chewed away on her cannelloni. When Cam Charles paused for dramatic effect, people sucked in their breath and made sounds of awe and exclamation. I couldn't get a rise out of the woman in my life. I was also developing a dose of Cam Charles envy.

"The something else more fundamental," I said, "is a bias."

Annie nodded. It looked to me like the nod of someone who's turned out the inside lights.

I said, "The defendant is protected by what you mentioned earlier, the presumption of innocence. The court has to presume he didn't do what he's charged with until the crown proves it."

"Beyond a reasonable doubt," Annie said.

"Neat. You've been listening."

"Like I said, I've heard some of this before."

"But even with the presumption of innocence, there's this bias built into the system." I was talking slowly, like a lecturer addressing a class of jerks. I stepped up the pace. "It's a bias to get a guilty verdict. That's why everybody's sleuthing and investigating and questioning and keeping files and policing and prosecuting. To convict the guy."

Annie waited until her mouth was free of cannelloni.

"I'm in favour of that," she said. "Especially where the guy's ripped off a company for two million or so with a dishonest scheme. Arkansas?"

"Oklahoma," I said. "But you're leaving something out. There has to be a voice speaking against the bias I just told you about."

"A mouthpiece. Is that where the odious term came from?"

"It isn't odious," I said. "Listen, someone has to argue for the accused guy, one single voice that tries to make sure all that massive machinery on the other side doesn't screw up. That's where the defence lawyer comes in. He speaks against the bias. It's his duty."

"Duty to whom?" Annie said. "A bunch of guys you admitted your-self were more than likely guilty?"

"Not just to the clients," I said. "To society."

That rang pompous.

"A duty to everybody who might some time get pulled into court," I said.

That rang lame.

"A duty to the system," I said.

"You make it sound like the garbageman," Annie said.

"It's a dirty job, but somebody's got to do it?"

Annie took a little wine.

She said, "I suppose the part that really bugs me about you acting for these terrible people, you *like* it."

Annie had her hand up as a signal I shouldn't interrupt.

"Even if you are right about the bias and the lonely voice of the defence lawyer and all that romantic stuff," she said, "it seems, ah, unseemly you should get such a kick out of being on the side of crime."

"First," I said, "I don't defend crime. I defend people, and all of them happen to be innocent at the time they retain me."

"What's second?"

"You're right," I said. "It gives me a boot, the whole courtroom process, me and my client against the machinery."

"Hopeless."

"That's your rebuttal?"

"I'm regrouping my forces for a return engagement."

Annie had polished off the dish of cannelloni. My own plate was strewn with chicken debris. On the other hand, I'd made the larger dent in the Vouvray.

Annie said, "One thing in favour of your current client the musician, from what you say, he doesn't seem to be a threat to society or its money."

"On the contrary, Dave's the victim of the piece."

"That's novel for you," Annie said. "What're you going to do for him?"

"Make a call or two."

"Who on? The porn mogul, right?"

"Yeah, my sparring partner, Raymond Fenk. Just a small matter of a pickup from him is all."

Did dissembling come that easy to everyone? Or was I in the upper brackets of dissemblers, up there with Richard Nixon, Uriah Heep, all-time greats like them? If I revealed all to Annie about the planned covert operation at the Silverdore, our dinner date might turn flat. Better to get the job done, restore Dave Goddard's tenor saxophone to its rightful blower, make everybody happy, with the possible exception of Fenk, and when all was wrapped and packaged, tell Annie the story. That wasn't dissembling. That was postponing.

"I wouldn't mess with that Fenk," Annie said. "Mean face on him and built like a house."

"The dealings are going to be what you might call arm's length."

The waitress picked up our plates, and Annie asked for dessert.

"Bananas au rhum," she said, reading from the menu.

"With two forks," I said.

Emilio's had a Friday-night SRO crowd. The standees lined the wooden bar at the front. But the room was open and airy, and nobody's conversation spilled over onto Annie's and mine. It felt cozy in the crowd.

I asked Annie, "How's it shaping up for Cam's festival?"

"Nicely," Annie said. "He's bringing in at least a dozen movies you wouldn't see booked into the commercial theatres in a million years. *A Quarter to Three* isn't in that category. Harp Manley's film. It'll be in release all over the place later this fall. But, you have to hand it to Charles, it's a sweet little coup he's pulled, snagging the movie for its world premiere. All the press on Manley and the movie won't hurt Charles's festival one bit."

"At a cost in credibility," I said.

"Because *A Quarter to Three* doesn't fit the festival theme?"

"Political content, minorities, oppressed people, and all."

Annie said, "Well, Charles made a lot of noise at the press conference about Manley representing a breakthrough in American film for black actors."

"That'll come as news to Sidney Poitier," I said. "And Richard Pryor, Eddie Murphy, Dexter Gordon. Harp Manley's about the fifth breakthrough."

"The way Charles talked, it came across as very plausible," Annie said. "Criminal lawyers are good at that."

The bananas were slathered in brown sugar and nutmeg and cinnamon and a squirt of rum. The waitress forgot the second fork. I used a coffee spoon.

"The only trouble with Charles's festival is the timing," Annie said. "For me personally, I mean. It's already taking hell's own footwork to cover two festivals going on at once, and the Alternate hasn't even started showing movies yet."

"That's Cam's way of making a statement," I said. "Confrontation. Nose to nose. Up against the wall. Festival against festival."

"Take tomorrow," Annie said. "Between Charles and Helga Stephenson, I got a choice of four press conferences, not to mention I can't miss two movies the Festival of Festivals is running."

"And a party?"

"No more parties. Last night's was de rigueur, the opening bash and everything, but as far as getting material, forget it. Too many faces, too much crush."

"Dan make the party?"

"Dan?" Annie scrunched up her face. "I'm trying to think Dan. Dan Rather? Danny DeVito? Daniel Ortega? 'O Danny Boy'? Am I getting warm? Which Dan at the party?"

"Day-Lewis."

"Daniel Day-Lewis," Annie repeated, her face unscrunched. "Brother, you really got a bee in your bonnet about the man. No, he wasn't at the party. He isn't on my calendar until Tuesday or even in town till then for all I know. Besides, he isn't my only interview. I got two more solo and a bunch of others in general scrummy media conferences."

"Dumb word."

"Which one?"

"Media."

"Plural of medium," Annie said.

"You know what someone clever once said of medium?"

Annie said, "Your definition of clever doesn't always match up with Webster's."

"Television is a medium," I said. "So called because it is neither rare nor well done."

Annie laughed.

"For a quip," she said, "that one's worth stockpiling."

Annie did most of the damage to the bananas au rhum. We had coffee, lingered another half-hour, and left. The Volks was parked at a meter on Jarvis Street. Walking to the car, Annie had her arm around my waist, and my arm was draped over her shoulders. I made a U-turn on Jarvis and drove to Annie's place. It's a flat on the third floor of a fine old house in Cabbagetown with an equally fine reno job. In the bedroom, Annie had two more black garments under the black blouse and trousers.

"Want me to tear those off with my teeth?" I said.

Annie went into the bathroom, and when she came out five minutes later, she'd removed her makeup and her black bra and panties. I was already in bed.

Just before daylight, Annie and I came awake at the same time. We didn't make love again. We snuggled. Like spoons. I lay on my left side facing toward the window. Annie lay on her left side facing in the same direction. Her right arm was around my waist, and her body touched mine in nice places.

"I remember who said it," I said.

"Ummm."

"About medium."

"Um."

"Ernie Kovacs."

Annie was asleep.

14

BY THE TIME Raymond Fenk walked out of the Silverdore Hotel at two o'clock on Saturday afternoon, James Turkin and I had been lounging inside and outside the Volks for almost three hours.

A little after eleven, I'd gone into the hotel and asked for Fenk's room on the house phone. Someone male, presumably Fenk, answered. That you, Bill? I said. Wrong room, the male voice said. He sounded bad-tempered. Had to be Fenk.

The Volks was on the north side of Charles east of the Silverdore. The hotel was on the south side. James filled in the wait with tales from the pickpocket world. He said, apart from South Americans, Soviet émigrés ranked near the top of the craft in the United States. Émigrés was James's word. They had a touring company, James said. Hit the big conventions in the midwestern cities. Cute, I said.

At twelve-thirty, I sent James over to Yonge Street for coffee and doughnuts. I wanted my doughnut plain. James reported back none of them came plain. The one he chose for me oozed something in raspberry paste.

At one-fifteen, James asked did I know whether Fenk carried a hotel key with him or left it at the front desk? The one occasion I knew about, I told James, a key was in Fenk's pocket when he went into the hotel. James seemed to like my answer.

At two o'clock, Fenk emerged. He had on a deep-blue jacket with lighter blue piping around the lapels. The guy collected jackets like Lord Thomson of Fleet collected newspapers. Fenk walked west toward Yonge. He was carrying a briefcase. It was slim and black and had more locks than most bank vaults.

"I got another way," James said.

He got out of the car and crossed Charles. What other way? I hired him to pick the lock on Fenk's hotel room. That was the way.

James strolled Charles in Fenk's wake. I left the Volks and stuck to the north side of the street, watching the action. Fenk walked. James strolled. Some action. Just short of Yonge, Fenk wheeled into a small self-serve restaurant. The restaurant had six or seven tables on a front patio. Fenk went through the door. James stayed outside reading a menu mounted beside the entrance. Fenk came back carrying a glass of something in the hand that wasn't clutching the briefcase. He sat down at an empty table. James stuck with the menu. This was exciting stuff.

James disappeared into the restaurant. Fenk gulped at his drink and stared into space. Or maybe his eyes were trained on the building across the street. It was a Gold's Gym, and young women were entering and leaving in tight and shiny garments that made them look like exotic dancers in mufti.

James reappeared from the restaurant. He too held a drink. He stopped in the middle of the patio. He glanced right, away from Fenk, and left, toward the table where Fenk was sitting and eyeballing the entrance to Gold's Gym. James looked lost and indecisive. The hick from out of town. He took a step and stumbled. The stumble moved him into Fenk's space. Whatever was in James's glass—Seven-Up? soda water? something pale and fizzy—splashed onto the Fenk table. Fenk jumped up. James landed on his shoulder. Fenk sat down. James caught himself against Fenk and the table.

Fenk was concentrating on his briefcase. He gripped it with his left hand and used his right to yank his glass out of the spillage from James's drink. James fussed. He pulled a handkerchief from his side pants pocket and swiped at Fenk's table. Fenk stared thunder clouds at James.

James kept on playing the hick. Wiping the table, smiling the sheep-ish smile, babbling words I couldn't hear from across the street. The performance, all ninety seconds of it, ended when Fenk waved James away, and James beat his retreat in a posture that suggested homage to a Japanese emperor.

I got back to the Volks before James.

"Out of his pocket," I said to James as he was opening the door on the passenger side. "You bumped against Fenk, all that business about spilling the drink, mopping the table, you picked him for the hotel key."

"What the technique's called, it's a mustard-checker."

"I missed the mustard."

"Well, the thing I did was a . . . variant."

"Variation'll do."

"The Colombian guys, the teachers, they taught us you go up to one of those hot-dog stands on the street. Customer in a suit's stand-ing there. Got the frank in his hand. You squirt him with the mustard bottle, and it's all, Jesus, I'm sorry, mister, wiping the yellow stuff off. Same time you're dipping for his wallet."

James reached into the breast pocket of his shirt and lifted out Fenk's room key. It was attached to a round strip of plastic that had 814 cut into it.

"What're we waiting for?" I said.

James pointed through the windshield.

"Him down there."

Fenk hadn't finished his drink or his ogle.

"Might've only come out for a soda pop," James said. "We get in the room, and next thing he's back, gets another key from downstairs, walks in."

After ten minutes, Fenk left the patio. He didn't turn back to the hotel. He went the other way, out of our view into the pedestrian traf-fic on Yonge.

The Silverdore lobby had wallpaper that imitated marble, and plastic trim that suggested wood. A chandelier, on the gaudy side, hung from the low ceiling. It seemed to be made of real glass. The elevators were to the right. James and I rode one to the eighth floor, and James rapped smartly on the door to 814.

"Just in case he's got a roommate," James said. "Girlfriend, you know, assistant."

"Could only be Della Street."

James knocked again. The hall was empty.

"That one of your jokes?" James said. "The Della Street?"

"Very small."

"Sometimes you could explain them. I'm not totally stupid, you might not know it."

"You're not even a little stupid, James. Just a little young."

James put the key into the lock to 814.

I said, "But, sure, I'll alert you when a joke's gone by. Do some verbal underlining."

James opened the door, and we stepped inside. Fenk had a suite, and James and I were in the sitting room. It reminded me of Ralph Goddard's family room. It lacked Ralph's Motolounger, but for dubious decor it compensated with a painting of a dusky bare-breasted beauty. The painting was on velvet. There wasn't much sign of Fenk in the room. Some papers on the desk, the September *Penthouse* on the sofa. But there was a significant sign of Dave Goddard. His spanking new saxophone case rested on the sofa beside *Penthouse*.

"Bingo," I said.

I snapped open the case.

"Hold the bingo."

The case was empty. Or almost empty. It contained the strap that Dave wore to hold his saxophone when he played. It didn't contain the saxophone. The case's lining was ripped open at the top of one side, and the rip, carefully done as if with scissors, extended from end to end of the case.

James, standing beside me, said, "Something had've been in there. Inside the cloth. Only reason for it to be torn like that."

"I was thinking along those lines, something hidden in the case, just yesterday afternoon."

"You know where it probably is, whatever was in there? In the briefcase the guy was carrying who's staying here. Fenk's briefcase."

"Maybe. But where's the saxophone? It's the reason for this little break-and-enter. A tenor saxophone."

There were three doors leading off the sitting room, one to the hall and the other two, it stood to reason, to the bedroom and a closet.

"You know what a tenor saxophone looks like?" I asked James.

"Does it matter?" James said. "I find one musical instrument, it's the instrument we're looking for, I would think."

"Excellent logic, James."

James opened the closet door. The closet was empty of everything except wooden hangers, the kind you can't take with you.

"Do the bedroom," I said.

I crossed over to the desk. The first paper I picked up was a contract that said on page one it was between Wholesome Productions Inc. and Alternate Film Festival Limited. On the back page, Fenk had signed for Wholesome in a hand that was easily readable. Wholesome? The sinister smut peddler had a sense of irony. Cam Charles hadn't signed for Alternate. The signature belong to someone whose first name was Trevor. I couldn't make out the second name. But a guess wasn't hard. Couldn't be more than one Trevor connected to the Alternate Film Festival. Trevor Dalgleish.

The contract was thick with clauses that lawyers stick in to button down events that might screw up a deal. Bankruptcy of one of the parties, earthquake, end of the world, failure to pay the lawyers' fees. The only clause that counted was the one where the party of the first part granted to the party of the second part the right to screen the aforesaid *Hell's Barrio* one time only in the course of the aforesaid Alternate Festival. Criminal law was simpler, no parties or aforesaids, just the crown and the bad guys.

The rest of the papers on the desk were press releases and a program for the festival. Someone, Fenk I guessed, had circled *Hell's Barrio* on the program. It was being shown Monday night at eight. I leafed through the press releases. Three of them were devoted to *A Quarter to Three*, Harp Manley's movie. *The Hell's Barrio* release, one page long, had handwriting in the right margin. The writing was in black ink and in the same firm hand that signed the contract for Wholesome Productions, and it spelled out three names. The first two names were Vietnamese. I'd read *Fire in the Lake*, I'd seen *Good Morning, Vietnam*, and I knew Vietnamese names when I saw them. Another argument in favour of the well-informed life. The third name, the one after the Vietnamese, I recognized. Trevor Dalgleish's.

Trevor's had a line under it and a telephone number beside it. Same black ink, same firm hand. The phone number began with 921. That put it midtown, probably around Avenue Road. There was a white pen on the desk with Silverdore Hotel stamped on it and a scratch pad with the same designation. I used the pen to write Trevor's name on the pad and started on the phone number. I wrote 921, and that was as far as I got when someone out in the hall put a key in the lock to room 814 and turned the knob.

It was ten feet from the desk to the bedroom. What was the world record for the ten-foot dash? I broke it getting from desk to bedroom. James had left the bedroom door open. I closed it behind me.

"Someone out there," I said. My voice surprised me. It was low, which was okay, and shaky, which wasn't.

The room had two double beds. Fenk's suitcase sat on the bed closest to the door, and James was sifting through it. I didn't bother telling him the suitcase wouldn't accommodate a tenor saxophone. James stopped his sifting and slid under the bed. It was a move of remarkable grace and alacrity.

I chose the closet. It had two louvre doors, and both were shut. I eased one open. It made no noise. On the closet rack, Fenk had hung the beige jacket and the plaid. There were no others. Lord Thomson of Fleet had more newspapers than Fenk had jackets. There were a couple of shirts alongside the jackets and a pair of loafers on the floor. I hunkered under the jackets and shirts, and closed the louvre door. It was as noiseless shutting as it had been opening.

Inside the closet, all was black. Outside, all was silent. The black didn't change much over the next few moments, but the silence was broken by voices coming from the sitting room. Two of them, or possibly three. I couldn't make out words, but I could judge tone. None of the voices sounded happy. At a guess, I would have said it was a two-way or a three-way argument.

Ten minutes went by. The dispute continued, and my legs, in the hunkered position, throbbed. I dropped my bottom to the floor. My left buttock crushed one of the brown loafers. I moved the loafers and reached my legs half the length of the closet. Both feet struck something metallic and made a ping sound. I sucked in my breath and counted to sixty. Nobody launched an attack on my hiding place. I let out my breath. The ping couldn't have been loud enough to reach beyond the confines of the closet.

I leaned forward from the waist, in the kind of stretch one makes to loosen up before a set of tennis, and I touched the object my feet had hit. It felt smooth and slick and had curves and interruptions in the curves that could have been valves. Had I found Dave Goddard's tenor saxophone? Seemed close to a sure thing.

Ten more minutes passed, give or take an eternity. It was no fun in the closet. The voices kept on, definitely angry. Then, in a snap, they were gone. Had I missed something? I listened so hard my ears hurt. A minute or two later, I got my reward. I heard a door close. It wasn't loud enough to be the bedroom door but faint enough to be the door out of the suite and into the hall.

I sat and strained some more and heard nothing. The voices had fled, all of them except the voice that whispered from the other side of the louvre door.

"Okay to come out of there," James whispered.

I pushed back the door.

"Thanks, James." I was whispering too. "Close call."

"Had closer."

I shoved up from the floor and got myself tangled in Fenk's plaid jacket.

I said, "Fenk must have come back."

"Him and somebody else. There were two guys altogether. Maybe three."

Both of us were still whispering. James crossed the bedroom to the door. He opened it slowly, looked around the edge, and went into the sitting room. I slid back the other louvre door. It was Dave Goddard's tenor saxophone on the closet floor unless someone else owned a forty-year-old Selmer with no polish and elastic bands holding some of the valves in place.

James came back into the bedroom.

"Guy's in the next room," he said, not whispering.

"Why aren't you whispering?" I whispered.

"Guy won't hear us."

"Unconscious?"

I was still whispering.

"Probably was two, three minutes ago," James said. "No way he is now."

"Quit it with the laconic stuff, James." I'd given up on the whispering. "What's the mystery?"

I walked past James into the sitting room, and once again came face to face with Raymond Fenk. My face developed a quiver around the mouth. His stared up at the ceiling from the floor.

"Dead," James said.

Fenk had a cord wrapped into his neck so tightly that most of it disappeared into the flesh. His face was a high red, and his eyes were open and bulging. If he hadn't been garrotted, he'd suffered something as close to that technical description of strangulation as I cared to witness from up close. On the other hand, I couldn't take my eyes off him, and I'd lost the quiver around the mouth.

"You feel for a pulse or anything medical like that?" I asked James.

"The guy's out of here. You kidding?"

James was right. Fenk's vital signs had fled while I was hunkered down in the closet.

"Now what?" James said. "For us, I mean."

"We skedaddle."

I went back into the bedroom and reclaimed Dave Goddard's saxophone from the closet floor.

"Hey, all right," James said when he saw what was in my hands.

I fitted the saxophone into the case and snapped it shut just the way I'd seen Dave do it at Chase's three nights earlier.

James had the door open a crack.

"Don't get your speed up," he said. "People out there that got their names on their lapels, buttons, ribbons, stuff like that on."

At the desk, I looked for the *Hell's Barrio* press release. It was gone, and with it went the three names and the phone number that someone, undoubtedly the late Fenk, had written in the margin. The page from the scratch pad where I'd scribbled Trevor Dalgleish's name and the first three digits of the phone number remained in place. I tore it off the pad and crumpled it in my jeans pocket.

"People got something against their rooms or what?" James said from the door. "They're having a party in the hall."

Fenk's face was the colour of a Santa Claus suit. His mouth was slack, and his eyes popped in a way that made the irises seem smaller and the white parts larger. He didn't look as bad-tempered in death as in life. He looked scared. The cord must have hurt like hell.

"Oh my *God.*"

"What's the matter?" James asked, holding position at the door.

"Nothing that's part of your job," I answered James.

I opened the saxophone case. No strap. I looked back at Fenk. The strap was buried in his neck, the strap that held Dave Goddard's saxophone when he played it.

"People in the hall," James said, "they're . . . dispensing."

"Dispersing."

"Going to their rooms."

One saxophone strap looked like another. The police medical people would say Fenk died of strangulation brought on by the tightening of a saxophone strap around his neck. But there was nothing to connect the strap to Dave Goddard. How did that stand up as reasoning?

Probably had a flaw or two. But removing the strap from the folds of Fenk's flesh was a task for a man far less squeamish than I.

"Cleared up out there," James said.

I lifted the saxophone case in my right hand, and James and I fled the scene of our break-and-enter and Fenk's murder.

15

J AMES POINTED OUT out that Fenk's briefcase with all the locks on it had been nowhere in evidence in the hotel sitting room.

"I'd've liked to time myself on it," James said. "Three, four locks it had. Probably one had a key, others different combinations. Take me, I'd add up the work, six minutes to spring."

"You got the real competitive spirit, James. If the briefcase surfaces, I'll give you preference over a chisel."

"No extra charge. The two hundred'll cover it."

"Competitive, but a sportsman."

We were in Dooney's. I'd drunk two bottles of Perrier. The adventure at the Silverdore left me thirsty. It also left me enervated. I ordered a double espresso. James had coffee—milk, no sugar. He sipped it as if he'd just returned from a trip to Grandma's. The kid was immutable. I made a mental note to lend him the word.

"Two possibilities," I said. "Either Fenk didn't bring the briefcase back to the room or else the guy who killed Fenk took it when he left."

"You think one guy?"

"That's the other puzzle. One killer or two, I didn't pin down how many people were in the sitting room."

"Okay, one of the voices, I couldn't tell what he was saying, or anybody else, what they were saying, but he had a deeper voice."

"A deep voice would be Fenk."

"What I think too. When I lifted the key from him at the restaurant, he was talking some, giving me shit. His voice was like the father's on TV. *The Munsters*, that father."

"Young fella like you, James, you remember Fred Gwynne?"

"Reruns."

"Keep going, James. Let's hear you on the other voice. Or voices."

"Higher or lighter," James said. "Not like a girl's, but higher or lighter. And the way the words ran together, that was different."

"Trevor Dalgleish."

"Who's he?"

"His name was on a piece of paper on Fenk's desk in the sitting room. Trevor's got a light voice, tenor maybe, and his accent leans to mid-Atlantic."

"Middle of the Atlantic? No country out there I heard of."

"People who grow up in Rosedale, tony neighbourhoods like that, some of them speak in a mid-Atlantic accent. They want you to think, these people, Canadian, American, whatever, they're plugged into upper-class England. Kind of an affectation. You storing this away, James? That's roughly what a mid-Atlantic accent comes down to."

I checked for the waiter. Dooney's was doing a brisk Saturday-afternoon trade in the usual serious talkers, and I was getting desperate for my double espresso.

James said, "Doesn't mean this Dalgleish had to be the guy out there with Fenk."

"True, but just for theory's sake, let's use what's handy."

James's face had lost its customary sulk. The kid was getting a kick out of his phonetician's role.

"Mid-Atlantic, I don't know," he said. "But what it was like, me listening to whoever was with Fenk, it was like I'm on the subway, and people're talking beside me. Talking English, okay? But I feel like I'm right out of it."

"Very perceptive, James. Opens up another possibility."

"Yeah?"

"Tell you why. There were two other names on the paper I told you about on Fenk's desk, two besides Trevor Dalgleish's, and they belonged to guys from the Far East."

"Israel, in around there?"

"That's Near East. Far East is China, Thailand, Vietnam, teeming millions."

"Those people, yeah, high voices."

"Compared to Fenk's," I said. "Except I'm beginning to think Paul Robeson had a high voice compared to Fenk's."

My double espresso arrived. Lukewarm, but I didn't care. I needed an adrenalin boost, and I swallowed a quarter of the cup at one go. James stirred a spoon in his coffee. He looked like he'd run out of linguistic analogies.

I said, "Want me to sum up?"

"It's just . . . speculation."

"Hell, let's think wild, James. Reach for it. Plunge into the realms of might be." Was I getting hyper? Must have been the double espresso. Or a reaction to the afternoon's crime spree. "What we might have in the sitting room," I said, "is either one Trevor Dalgleish or two Vietnamese."

"And that was who wrapped the thing around the dead guy's neck."

"It's surmising, but what the heck."

"*And*," James said. The kid had gone into a dogged mode. "*And* it would also be who might've walked out with the dead guy's briefcase that had in it that stuff that used to be inside the lining of your guy's saxophone case."

"Well, as long as were surmising, we might as well take it all the way."

James developed the expression of a man having second thoughts. He said, "There's one place, you follow me, we don't take it."

"I know," I said, "to the cops."

"No way."

"Too fanciful for the police, James, all our theorizing about voice tones and speech patterns."

"That's not the reason I'm thinking about."

I lifted my cup of lukewarm espresso and drank another quarter of it. That took ten long seconds. James didn't look like he was enjoying the ten seconds.

"Besides," I said, "if we approached the police, we might have to answer for several crimes of our own."

"Now you're talking," James said. He exhaled a long breath. First time I'd seen the kid show a small flash of nerves.

"One thing," James said, "the guy's gonna be happy to get his instrument back."

"Well, let's see, you picked a pocket, we did a burglary, Fenk got strangled, I sat in a dark closet for a century or two, but, yeah, Dave Goddard should be one happy tenor-saxophone player."

"Personally, what happened today, I liked it."

I finished the espresso, reminded James I was available for the defence if his career in crime foundered, and drove home.

The first chore was to store the saxophone and its case in the hall closet. I'd return them to Dave later in the evening, after I'd caught a nap. Exhausting work, the break-and-enter game. Dave could get by with the Flip Bochner saxophone for one more night of music. Was there a need for me to brief Dave on Fenk's murder? Maybe the fact, but not the cause. If the cops couldn't trace the saxophone strap to Dave—how could they?—why should I burden him with the news? By recovering Dave's sax, I'd made up for the botched tail job. Or almost. What about Fenk's murder? Did I have a duty there? The questions were getting tougher by the second.

I lay on the bed with my clothes on and read again at the Gene Lees book, *Jazzletters*. Something to take the mind off crime and my part in it.

Lees had a theory in a chapter called "Pavilions in the Rain" about the demise of the great bands. Claude Thornhill. Jimmy Lunceford. Boyd Raeburn. Lees thought the bands were hurried to their decline when the American transportation system shifted and changed. Cars came along in bigger numbers, pushed by money men who had interests in road construction and rubber firms. Lees said the money people lobbied successfully for the dismantling of the trolley systems and the electric railroads that carried people, among other destinations, to the pavilions and dance halls in the countryside where the big bands played on weekends. Goodbye trolleys, goodbye pavilions, goodbye bands. Sounded convincing, but I was always a sucker for a guy who could pitch a well-reasoned theory.

I fell asleep, clothes on, Lees book on my chest, and woke up three hours later. If I had a dream, I didn't remember it.

16

DAVE GODDARD cut a bizarre figure on Abner Chase's band-stand. The white bandage on his forehead glowed eerily in the overhead spot, and the way he handled the borrowed saxophone, he looked how I feel when I drive a Hertz car. He looked awkward.

But none of it, not the bandage or the strange horn, got in the way of Dave's playing. Harp Manley gave Dave a featured solo on "What Is There To Say", and he made gorgeous music. His sound was more tart than usual, lemony, and his improvisation, subdued and reaching into French impressionist territory, packed little mysteries in the melody line. It was a few minutes of unrepeatable beauty, and the audience in the club, even the Saturday-night people on their night to howl, knew it. Patrons kept the silence, waiters stayed at their stations, nobody hit the cash register. And at the end, after the last phrase of Dave's music, there were five seconds of hush before the cheers came.

The quintet played a semi-fast "Rhythm-a-ning" to wind up the set. It was the final set of the night and of the week, and I slid away from the bar and pushed through the crowd to head off Dave. I wanted to tell him about the magic of his solo, but I knew Dave wasn't a guy for a complimentary word. I'd settle for letting him know I had a surprise at home he'd like.

Dave was at the musician's table, standing, holding the Flip Bochner saxophone and listening, impatiently I judged, to a trio of fans who were heaping on him the kind of praise I had in mind.

"Happening, man?" Dave said to me, mostly a mumble, talking against the eager fans.

"You want to come by my place, Dave? It'll be worth the detour, I promise."

"I don't know, man. My head's beating like a bitch."

"Ten minutes, Dave."

He left the club with me, not precisely kicking and screaming but not as if he were on the way to a banquet in his honour either. Dave was tired and down, and conversation on the walk up Beverley was desultory.

"You get to Raymond—what's his name, Fenk?" Dave asked.

"Me, among others, I got to him."

"What about my axe, man?"

"Hold your horses, Dave."

I led the way up the stairs to my apartment. It was quiet downstairs. Ian and Alex's custom was to go a little crazy on Friday nights and settle in with a couple of rented movies and early to bed Saturdays. I switched on the lamp in the living room and got Dave's saxophone case from the closet.

Dave reached out, not quite believing, for the case. The fatigue dropped away from his face. He put the case on the sofa and lifted out the saxophone. He cradled it. His baby'd come home.

"Can you dig it, man? It's been like the last couple nights, only half me was on the job."

Dave raised the mouthpiece to his lips and blew a dozen quick, light notes.

"Man, you saved my life."

"Well, there's a little story that goes with the recovery, Dave."

Dave turned back to the case on the sofa and ran his hand around its interior.

"I don't want to come on I'm not grateful, man," he said, "but something's missing."

"That, the rip in the lining, is probably part of the story."

"Rip doesn't matter, man. My strap's nowhere's here."

"Dave, let me get to the story."

"Man, remember I told you the axe and the old case, the one before this one, I bought them the same time, sort of a package deal? The strap came too."

"Of the three, saxophone, case, strap," I said, impatience in my voice, "the strap's the easiest to replace. Must be. One strap's like another."

"Not exactly."

"Dave, the sooner I tell you my story, the sooner—" I stopped. "What do you mean, not exactly?"

"I lost the old case already, so okay, I cooled out about that. But the strap, well, man, if it's possible, you know where it's at? The cat at the store I bought everything from, like forty years ago, he really cared, that cat. He cut my name into the strap, the metal part, in the clip. It's still there like he did it yesterday."

I straightened the magazines on the table in front of me. *Vanity Fair* was on the top of the pile. It had Tom Hanks on the cover.

"Dave, you want to sit down."

"Not really, man. The whack on the head, I feel wonky on account of it still. I'm gonna split."

"This isn't an invitation, Dave. More like an order. Sit down, I'm serious."

I went into the kitchen and made a drink, a big Wyborowa and one small ice cube.

In the living room, Dave was still on his feet, beside the sofa, holding his saxophone.

"Whatever way you want, standing up, sitting down," I said to Dave, and I told him the whole story. I thought I was particularly vivid in the passages that described the manner in which the saxophone strap with Dave's name on it cut into Fenk's neck.

"Down there at the police station, Dave, they got computers, all that state-of-the-art crap. The cops who called on you at the hospital, maybe they looked like they didn't give a damn, they still punched the facts into the computer. Man named Dave Goddard, David no doubt, reports he was assaulted and had his saxophone stolen." I walked around the living room, to the window and back, talking, working on the drink. "This afternoon, tonight, tomorrow, whenever the chambermaid or somebody finds Raymond Fenk's body, pretty ugly by then I imagine, another cop is going to punch into the computer. This cop, homicide division, he'll punch in a long report, take him an hour, and at the end, he'll punch cause of death. A saxophone strap with a name on the clip. Dave Goddard. The computer'll go nuts. It's got the same name twice, it's got saxophone, it's practically solved the case."

"Man, I'm fucked," Dave said.

He sat on the sofa. I sat in a wing chair that was positioned kitty-corner to the sofa. Annie took charge of my furniture and its arrangement a year earlier. The wing chair was in a pattern of pale-green and brown stripes.

"You got a driver's licence, Dave?"

"Where you at, man? Driver's licence got nothing to do here. This's murder I'm in shit about."

"You got one?"

"I been driving since I was, like, sixteen."

"You can borrow my car. A place to stay, you got that? Quiet, out in the country, a place like that?"

"Ralph's cottage. But, man, I didn't kill anybody. I had the strap, I said already, forty years. You think I'd leave it around the dude's neck?"

"Where's Ralph's cottage?"

"Muskoka. Well, not exactly Muskoka. It isn't on the water or anything. Kind of back in the woods. I hate it, man."

"Borrow my car, okay? Drive up there, to Ralph's Muskoka cottage, but don't tell Ralph. Can you get into it otherwise, without Ralph knowing?"

"There's a key, Ralph leaves it in this shed. But, man, you don't know, owls, crickets, it's noisy. All those birds, the kind of animals they are, they're out of tune."

"Take my car. Never mind the musical judgments about the owls. Just drive up there. There's a phone?"

Dave nodded.

"Car's out back, the white Beetle," I said. "Pick up your stuff at the Cameron and call me from Ralph's place so I know you got there. It'll take you, go up the 400, cut over at 11, how long, three hours?"

"Less. Except, man, what am I dodging up there for? I had nothing on with the dead guy I know of."

"It's your strap killed him."

"I don't dig this scene."

"Dave, I'm advising you now partly like a lawyer and partly like a guy in a George Raft movie. Get out of town. I got an idea, two or three of them, and it'd be better in all ways if I have a free hand to follow up on them. You around, get arrested, I'd be using up time out at the jail, doing a bail application, talking to the homicide people, that kind of dance. For both our sakes, I know it's unorthodox, drive up to Ralph's tonight."

"I don't get it, what's going down."

"Neither do I, and I was the guy in the closet."

I took Dave back downstairs and around to the alley where the Beetle was parked. First crack, he missed the timing between the clutch and the accelerator, and stalled the engine. Second crack, he steered smoothly out of the alley. I forgot to tell him to stick to the inside lane on the highway. Dave'd learn.

My second Wyborowa wasn't as large as the first. I sat in the kitchen with it and the phone book. Trevor Dalgleish had two entries, home and office. The office was on John Street. Cam Charles & Associates, of whom Trevor Dalgleish was one, worked out of a renovated house downtown near the Amsterdam Café. It had three storeys with a lot of glass and ferns and native Canadian art. Dalgleish's home was on

Admiral Road, and the phone number began with 921. Admiral was a short, windy street in an enclave of large one-family houses between Avenue Road and St. George Street. For a young lawyer, a criminal lawyer, Trevor had a swell address.

It was almost two o'clock. I could telephone Dalgleish and ask him about Raymond Fenk or I could wait till first light. First light seemed more civilized. Calling Dalgleish was my number one idea. I told Dave I had two or three ideas. I exaggerated. The case was hurling me into a moral abyss. Prevaricating, postponing, exaggerating. I went in search of the Gene Lees book and the chapter on Edith Piaf.

17

CAM CHARLES'S phone call came at orange-juicing time. Fourteen minutes past nine.

I said, "You rad lawyers get a fast jump on Sunday office hours."

"I'm at home, Crang."

"Me too. That keeps us even so far."

"Obviously I know where you are." Cam caught himself. "Why am I always getting into foolish exchanges with you?"

"Must be chemistry."

"I'd like us to meet this morning."

"See, I told you it was chemistry."

"If you can grasp this, Crang, I want the meeting to be confidential."

"What you mean, you don't want me around your office."

"Correct."

"Or home. I might lower the tone."

"There's a potential problem, and I hate to say this, you may be the man I need to find out how close to real it is."

I asked, "This wouldn't, any chance, have something to do with the late Raymond Fenk?"

Cam hesitated.

He said finally, "It may have to do with a lot of unpleasant things, but not that one."

"I have to say, Cam, I admire your way with the auxiliary verbs."

"What?"

"All those mays."

"Crang, can we just for God's sake make an appointment."

"Some place off the beaten track."

"For reasons I haven't got time to go into right now, I don't want anyone from my office seeing us together, anyone from the criminal bar for that matter, and people from my firm happen to be in the house at this moment."

Cam lived in a big house in Forest Hill. Trevor Dalgleish lived in a house on Admiral Road that had to be just as big. Where did I go wrong?

"I got the perfect spot," I said.

"Where?"

"The AGO."

Silence from Cam's end.

"You know," I said, "paintings on the wall, Henry Moores on the floor."

"I *know* the art gallery, Crang. I'm thinking about it for a meeting place. Weighing it."

"All the criminal lawyers I ever heard of'll be in bed or out visiting clients at West End Detention."

"You're probably right."

"One thing, there might be a lawyer's wife on cash at the gift shop."

"I'm not acquainted with lawyers whose wives do that sort of volunteer work."

"Understand what you mean, Cam. Bourgeois."

"I'll meet you at ten."

"Sorry. Place doesn't open till eleven."

"All *right*. Eleven then."

Cam hung up, and I got another orange out of the refrigerator. Had Cam slammed down his receiver? Slamming the phone is a wasted gesture. All the guy on the other end hears, the slammee, is a click. Interesting metaphysical question. Slam at one end, click at the other. If

Bishop Berkeley had lived in the age of the telephone, he would have dissected it. I pressed a fourth orange and had myself a full glass.

I hadn't phoned Trevor Dalgleish. I hadn't done anything constructive. I hadn't thought up any more angles to pursue in the quest of Fenk's killer. I hadn't slept much. Dave Goddard woke me at four-thirty with his call from Ralph's Muskoka cottage. I asked Dave a question I'd overlooked earlier. Where was he on Saturday afternoon when Fenk was expiring in the Silverdore sitting room? In bed at the Cameron, Dave said, all afternoon, all alone. Terrific alibi, I said, and tossed and turned until the sun came up.

Cam Charles's phone call and the orange juice gave me a kick-start on the day. I sliced two raisin buns into halves and put them in the oven to toast. The day was overcast, and in the living room, no sun-beams warmed the sofa. I made more orange juice and buttered the raisin buns. "A potential problem," Cam said on the phone. Little did he know. Or did he? My mouth was full of raisin bun. I stopped in mid-chew, and in my head I heard the tumblers click into place.

"Something," I'd asked Cam, "to do with the late Raymond Fenk?" Uh-oh.

I got the Wyborowa out of the freezer and poured two fingers into the orange juice. How did I *know* Fenk was dead? How did *I* know? Is that why Cam hesitated before he said his problem didn't concern Fenk's murder? The vodka in the orange juice wasn't making me feel much better about my gaffe. What was the drink called? Orange blossom? No, screwdriver. One right answer for the morning.

At ten, I flashed the radio around the dial to on-the-hour newscasts. None mentioned a murdered person in a midtown hotel. I walked down to Queen Street and bought a *Sunday Star*. Raymond Fenk didn't make the front page or any of the pages after it. He was dead, and nobody seemed to know except Cam Charles, me, and, undoubtedly, the police. It must have been the cops who told Cam. That'd be natural, given Fenk's presence in town for Cam's film festival. The cops hadn't phoned my place. No one had informed me of Fenk's death, not cops, radio, or press. This is a fine mess you've got us into, Stanley. I cleaned the breakfast dishes and sauntered up Beverley Street to the AGO.

Cam was facing the entrance to the gallery, and his reflection came back at him in the bright glass of the doors. He had on a brown and grey tweed jacket and chocolate-brown slacks, with a crimson foulard at his throat. Sunday-slumming attire for your prominent criminal barrister. He didn't see me walking up the stone steps behind him.

"You want to look at the show while we talk, Cam?" I said to the back of the tweed jacket. "It's Harold Town, kind of stuff that'll bump us out of the mundane."

Cam turned from his image in the glass.

"There you are, Crang," he said. "At last."

Imperious bastard. It was two minutes past eleven.

"If you don't mind," he said, "I'd prefer to do this sitting down."

"They got benches in there," I said. "In front of the paintings."

There was a small congregation of people at the ticket counter. I bought admissions for two. That was seven bucks I'd have to charge to my client. Who was my client? Dave Goddard? I'd swallow the seven.

The Harold Town retrospective was on the second floor in the Sam and Ayala Zacks Wing. Sam and Ayala were a wealthy couple who had more taste than the guy who put Gumby Goes to Heaven on University Avenue. Cam said nothing on the way up the stairs. In the first room, where the Towns were hung, there was so much colour on the walls they gave me the sensation they were in motion. I stopped at the door. Straight ahead, dead centre, was a collage that looked like an abstract slice of ancient Babylon. There was another painting, mostly reds, of a toy horse, and one of a strange enormous seal—the kind that kings and potentates used to slap on their written pronouncements—against a midnight curtain. Cam made a beeline for a bench that had a black leather covering and no back. I sat beside him.

"What's shaking, Cam?"

"Two points, and that's one more than I had before I phoned you this morning. The first, really the second but never mind, is this—you're in a bind, Crang, you know that?"

"Well, I'm pretty good at identifying binds, Cam. This current one, I've got no doubt, you're wondering how come I knew Raymond Fenk was recently departed, not as in on his way back to Los Angeles but as in dead."

Cam looked wonderfully pleased with himself. I didn't take it as a comment on my present predicament. Cam always looked wonderfully pleased with himself. Maybe it was his barbering. Up close, on the black leather bench, studying Cam's head, I had never seen a man shaved, trimmed, shampooed, and cologned to such perfection. Beside him, I felt shabby. That was worse than feeling in a bind.

Cam said, "You know what's your trouble, Crang? Always has been? Don't answer. You don't want to know, but I'm going to tell you. You're impetuous, irreverent, and too much of a smartass."

Cam kept on looking pleased with himself.

I said, "We got to the part yet about what my trouble is?"

"My call two hours ago, the purpose was to ask you, to *retain* you actually, if you'd carry out a little job, something in the, shall we say, quasi-legal line. I still want you to do the little job, but now I'm not asking you. I'm telling you."

"Because of the, shall we also say, previously mentioned bind?"

"I don't care how you know about Fenk's murder. I'm not even going to inquire about your embarrassing display with the man at the Park Plaza press conference. I don't think any of that is relevant to my problem. But the fact is you know about Fenk and his murder and you shouldn't, and I'm going to use that information for my own purposes."

"For pressuring me into taking on the little quasi-legal job."

"Correct."

"Maybe I would've said yes anyway."

"Maybe you would have."

"Just so we clear the decks, Cam, satisfy my own curiosity, how'd you find out about Fenk's murder?"

"Stuffy Kernohan's first call was to me. As soon as he saw Fenk was connected with my film festival, after the body was found, by whom I don't know, Stuffy rang me at home, and we agreed he'd low-play the announcement to the press. I don't need that kind of publicity on the day the festival opens. Later in the week perhaps, but not right on top of the opening. Stuffy understood. He owed me one."

Stuffy Kernohan? Should I know him? The Silverdore's manager? A police guy? With a name like Stuffy Kernohan, he could be the Chicago Black Hawks goalie.

"If you're finished with your questions, Crang," Cam said, "let's get to business. I'm on a tight schedule."

"Who's Stuffy Kernohan?"

"Oh, *Crang*." Cam was good at scorn. "Stuffy's been on the homicide squad since before we came out of law school."

"I don't do murder cases, Cam, remember?"

Criminal lawyers get slotted. I had a mini-specialty in fraud charges. The rest of my files were a hodgepodge of hold-ups, break-and-enters, other crimes against property. Alleged murderers seemed to go elsewhere. Just as well if it meant sucking around guys like Stuffy Kernohan who sucked around guys like Cam Charles.

"Everything I tell you from now on is in strictest confidence," Cam said. He was into his earnest routine. "This concerns an associate of mine. Trevor Dalgleish."

"Funny, his name's been crossing my mind lately."

"I talk, Crang, you listen."

You had to hand it to Cam—I did—he knew how to run a briefing. Crisp sentences, no wasted motion, and he was right into Trevor Dalgleish's bio. Thirty-one years old. Member of a FOOF. Fine old Ontario family. Undergraduate degree in economics. Scored high in the LSATs. Came out of the University of Toronto Law School clutching a prize in criminal law. Articled with Eddie Greenspan. Switched to Cam's firm when he got his call. Worked fifteen hours a day. Smooth in court, something I'd seen for myself a few times. Trevor, Cam said, was a rising star, and versatile. He sat in on the discussions when the Alternate Festival was hatched. And took over responsibility for a block of films—booking, contacts, drawing the documents, getting names on dotted lines. Leading up to the festival, Cam said, Trevor was working twenty hours a day.

"So what's the problem?" I asked. "Paragon like that, some other law firm's liable to steal him away."

"All his life," Cam said, now sounding concerned, wise, avuncular, and a pain in the neck, "as long as I've known him, which is very nearly all his life, Trevor's been a man who takes short cuts."

Cam had an illustration. It seemed that as a young buck at St. Andrew's College, the very prep school that Cam had attended earlier, Trevor ran a lucrative scam that involved bribing a printer's apprentice to slip him exam papers in advance. Trevor peddled the papers to his fellow preppies. A suspicious teacher nailed a group of students who got uncharacteristic As on the exams. The fuss was short-term but scandalous.

"Look at the bright side, Cam," I said. "Trevor probably learned a lesson. Cheaters never prosper."

"That's just it. Trevor wasn't caught."

"The mastermind, and he got away with it?"

"And may still be getting away with something."

"Like what?"

"Like that's what I'm retaining you to find out."

"Closer to blackmailing me to find out."

"Don't take it personally, Crang."

On the wall opposite the bench where we were sitting, there was a Town oil, about seven feet high by five wide. Green was the major colour, hundreds of tight little green balls with tiny black centres. A long, jagged white line cut through the entire middle of the painting, top to bottom. What was the picture supposed to be? Maybe a close-up of a monster zipper?

"Give me some help, Cam, teensy little hints," I said. "Why's Trevor got you nervous?"

"Number one, my read on Trevor is he spends more money on himself than his billings at the firm warrant."

"Is it that big? Trevor's house on Admiral Road?"

"It's also the scene of very lavish dinner parties."

"Never been invited."

"Doubt you ever will," Cam said. "Besides the house, Trevor has his place in the country up in King."

"Let me guess—he rides horses out there."

"What else does everybody in King do? Trevor's very expert at it. Jumps his horse at the Royal Winter Fair, that kind of thing. All of which costs a great deal of money for a man just past thirty."

"Sure, Cam," I said. "But a minute ago you told me Trevor comes from good stock. Ever think it's family money that finances his conspicuous consumption?"

"An excellent family name, I said that, grandfather associated with E. P. Taylor, all the rest. Trevor's got the name, but the family money evaporated with Trevor's father."

"Isn't that just the way, always a wastrel in there to blow the ancestral fortune."

"Number two, Trevor's too intimate with clients."

"Ho boy, that could be risky around your place, Cam, guys with the dreadlocks, smoke the ganja."

Cam went through the motions of looking disgusted, but his heart wasn't in it. He was more interested in surging ahead with the briefing.

"You and I know it happens, Crang, criminal lawyers overly involved in the lives of the people they're defending."

"Rubbing shoulders with the bandits, yeah. Start out drinking in the same bars, end up sharing a cell."

"Precisely."

"One problem, Cam, the way you described young Trevor, workaholic, nice way about him in front of a judge, I've seen that, he doesn't give off the feel of lawyers I know've gone down the tubes."

"I hope I'm wrong. Probably am. But I want to find out if Trevor has troubles."

"If, you mean, if *you* have troubles."

"With Trevor."

I gave the Harold Town more study, the greens and the white line zigging down the centre. If you turned the picture on its side, it'd look like an ECG printout. Guess again, Crang. If Town wanted it on its side, he'd have painted it on its side.

"Why me, Cam?" I asked.

"You've acquired a bit of a reputation, you must be aware, for this kind of thing."

"What? Nosing around?"

"If you want to put it that way. The qualities I criticized you for a minute ago, don't be offended, they have their uses in situations like this. Irreverent, push in where don't necessarily belong."

"Really glad I came to our little meet, Cam. Swell boost for the ego."

"I can't ask about Trevor myself, obviously, or delegate one of the other people in the firm to make inquiries into our own associate."

"Lousy for office morale."

"And I'm not inclined to hire some sloppy private investigator."

"So it's sloppy me."

It was more fun to think about the Town oil than about Cam's proposition. I had another idea about the painting. It was a glimpse close up of a giant fissure in a rock. Bet it had Rocky Mountains somewhere in the title. Cam wasn't talking proposition. He was talking arm-twisting. My arm.

I said, "I need material to get me going, Cam."

"It's yours."

"Clients' names. Trevor can't be playing footsy with everyone who comes through the door. Make a list of the people you think are too much into Trevor. Or vice versa."

Cam reached into his inside jacket pocket and brought out a pen and a small pad. The pad had a dark leather cover, and the pen was slim and gold. What had Annie said? Cam goes first cabin.

"Something else," I said. "I want the names of the movies Trevor lined up for your film festival."

Cam stopped jotting.

"No, Crang," he said, dragging it out, exasperated. "The festival's unrelated. No bearing whatsoever."

"Think of yourself, I know this is hard, Cam, as the client here. I'm the guy you do what I ask."

Cam got his gold pen busy again.

"Raymond Fenk," I said. "The deceased."

Cam tightened up around the mouth, but he didn't speak. Cam had discipline.

"Get onto your pal at homicide, the old Stuffer," I said. "Tell him to phone the Los Angeles police, telex, fax machine, whichever's fastest. Find out if Fenk has a record. Had a record."

Cam was a swift notetaker.

"That's it," I said.

Cam put away his implements.

"Expect a package of information by three this afternoon," he said, and walked away from me and the Harold Town retrospective without a nod for either of us.

I'd run out of guesses about the green canvas. Fissure in the Rocky Mountains was what I was going with. I went over to the small card on the wall beside the picture. "1965," it said. "Oil on Canvas. The Great Divide." Well, what the hell, fissure and Great Divide were close. I took twenty minutes to look at the rest of the show, and on the way out, I bought a catalogue for ten bucks. I'd swallow the ten.

18

THERE WAS A BOWL of five-day-old homemade chili in the refrigerator. The home it was made in was mine. I peeled back the Saran Wrap that covered the bowl, and sniffed. My nostrils didn't shrivel, and no blue mould lurked at the bowl's edges. I scooped the chili into a pan, and put the pan on the stove at a low heat.

On television in the living room, CBS was showing U.S. Open Tennis. Ivan Lendl was playing. When wasn't Ivan Lendl playing? I had a vodka and soda and the Harold Town catalogue. *The Great Divide* was reproduced in its whites and greens near the front of the catalogue, and on the opposite page there was an explanation of the picture. It said Town took his first plane flight in 1965. He was in his forties, and the experience of looking at the world from the new perspective of straight down blew him away. He went home and painted *The Great Divide*. It was his interpretation of a telescoped view out of the window as the plane came over the runway at the end of a night flight. Nice guess, Crang, fissure in the rock. Not even close.

I turned the catalogue's pages, and on television the tennis match went on. By and large, tennis makes genteel noises. The light thonk of the ball coming off the racquet, the polite handclapping between points, the referee's moderate tones. The occasional roar of planes heading into LaGuardia Airport near the U.S. Open stadium was a pain in the eardrum, and the now-and-then hollers from yahoos in the stands. But mostly the background tennis sounds seemed about right for a browse through the Town catalogue. After a while, I ate the chili.

At ten past three, the doorbell rang. The young man on the front step looked like he'd just been let out of Sunday school. He was wearing a light single-breasted black suit, white button-down shirt, and a tie that was so discreet I couldn't tell whether it was black or deep purple. He said he was present on an errand for Mr. Charles, and handed me a large brown envelope.

"You haven't been inconvenienced, sir?" The kid had taken lessons in earnest from Cam. "I was supposed to have this to you at three."

"Just listening to tennis. No inconvenience."

"Of course, Mr. Crang. Thank you, sir."

The kid didn't kiss my hand. No one's faultless.

I opened the brown envelope at the kitchen table. There were two single sheets and a bunch of other papers clipped together. The top sheet dealt with Raymond Fenk. Ha, he had a record. Not much, but a record. Two convictions in California for possession of an illegal drug. On both, he'd been charged with trafficking but pleaded guilty to reduced counts of simple possession. Must have had a defence lawyer who was a winner at plea bargaining. Fenk paid a fine on the first charge and did ninety days on the second. The drug in question was described on the sheet of paper in formal laboratory language. But, scraping away the Latin and the chemistry, we were talking cocaine.

The second sheet was headed "Trevor Dalgleish Clients". These had to be the people Cam thought Trevor might be romancing. Ten names altogether. The first six were separated by double spaces and had complete addresses and phone numbers after them. None of the names rang bells. The other four names were grouped and had one address for the lot and no phone number. Nho Truong. Dan Nguyen. Nghiep Tran. My Do Thai. I was in business. The names were Vietnamese. Were any of them matches for the two names I saw on Saturday afternoon? Written above Trevor's name on the press release for *Hell's Barrio*? In Fenk's hotel room? My memory was okay, but not photographic.

The address for the four men put me on more solid ground. It was an Oxford Street number. Oxford ran off Spadina Avenue south of College. It was in the Kensington Market area. Portuguese fish stores. West Indians peddling live chickens and rabbits and ducks. Fruit and vegetable stalls on the streets. Annie and I did monthly excursions to the market for provisions. I don't think we'd run into Nho Truong and the guys. Hadn't bought a live duck either.

The papers clipped together were publicity blurbs, cast listings, and other informative bumpf on six movies. *Hell's Barrio* came first. Raymond Fenk's name was front and centre as producer. I didn't recognize the names of the rest of the *Hell's Barrio* people: the actors, director, cinematographer, the best boy. On the other five movies, my recognition quotient was a total zip. The people who made the movies had names that meant nothing to me. Neither did the movies' titles. All I knew was, the same guy was in charge of lining up the six for the Alternate Festival. Trevor Dalgleish.

Was there a common thread in the six? *Hell's Barrio*, I already gathered, was about Hispanics having it tough in L.A. The second movie was about AIDS. I couldn't tell from the literature whether it was feature or documentary. Next was a film "as relevant as today's headlines and just as explosive", the publicity said, about black street gangs in a city that wasn't identified. Hispanics, AIDS, and gangs? So far, not much of a common thread. People who weren't getting a kick out of life? Maybe film analysis wasn't my long suit.

My vodka and soda was empty. This seemed to be a job—figuring out what the six movies shared—for the in-house film critic. If I asked Annie to take a shot at it, I'd have to go all the way. Tell her everything that had gone on: the tail job for Dave Goddard, Fenk's murder, the rest. Well, I was due to let her in on the events to date. Overdue. Then she could look over the six movies for points in common. She could also tell me what the hell a best boy was.

19

ANNIE DIDN'T THINK I'd used my most mature judgment.

"This is a case," she said, "damn near terminal, of you losing your marbles."

"It seemed a good idea at the time, the part about swiping the saxophone back. It still does if it weren't for the dead person."

"You have to call the police. Come on, this is murder."

It'd taken me a half-hour to tell the story of the stolen saxophone, my expedition with James, Fenk on the sitting-room floor. Start to finish, it was good for no more than ten minutes, but Annie interrupted with many variations on "say that again" and "you did what?" The food and wine got in the way too. Annie made us a platter of tuna-salad sandwiches with olives and tomato slices and gherkins, and she opened a bottle of white Dao. It was an early supper or a light dinner, whatever meal came at six-thirty before we went off to the premiere of Harp Manley's movie. I ate my half of the platter and more. Annie's appetite was on hold.

"So?" she said. "You want my opinion? There's the phone over on the table."

"One point emerges, I think. I'm in kind of deep."

"Take the sun ten years to reach you, that deep."

I expected Annie to be upset. She wasn't. She was mad, which was better than upset. Mad is closer to rational analysis. I needed a little of that, as long as it didn't include a call to the cops.

"The police," Annie said, "solve murders. They get paid for it. You, what you get paid for, the way you explained it to me one or two hundred times, you come along later, *after* the murder. You say to the judge, oh, no, it wasn't *my* client who did the murder. Or it wasn't *murder*. Or some such."

"Yeah, well, events seem to have got out of the normal sequence."

"No kidding."

"Another factor, kind of crucial, the cops' idea of solving Fenk's murder, they'll charge Dave Goddard."

"And you."

"It went through my mind."

"And that JD sidekick of yours."

"James Turkin is delinquent, no question there, but juvenile, no. If you ever meet him, Annie, you wouldn't think of the word."

"If I ever meet him, I'll kick his ass."

Annie's temper had just about run the course. We were sitting at the butcher-block table in the window of her apartment. The chairs were bentwood knockoffs, and Annie had been perching on the edge of hers. She poured wine into both glasses and eased back in her chair.

"I'm scared for you," she said.

"Feeling nervous myself."

"I don't suppose that means you're going to do anything sensible."

"There're beginning to be facts, you think about it, that dovetail."

"For instance? The voices you and your pet criminal heard in the hotel sitting room? I don't care about accents or timbre, that could've been practically anybody."

"Theoretically, yeah. But we know Fenk had some kind of contact with Trevor and two Vietnamese guys. There names were on his desk, and whoever offed him took the paper with the names when he or they left."

"'Offed' gives me the creeps."

"I used it to show you I was macho and unafraid."

"Didn't work."

"Whoever *murdered* Fenk left the room with the paper with the names on it."

"Better. And the person or persons probably left with the briefcase too."

"Now you're getting into it," I said. "And another conjunction of facts: Trevor must be acquainted with Fenk from booking his movie into Cam Charles's festival, and Trevor for sure knows some Vietnamese guys who are his clients."

"Hm."

"Does that, the hm, mean I should go on?"

"Hmmm."

"I produce for your perusal the contents of one brown envelope."

It was the envelope that Cam's delivery kid dropped off at my place. I'd left the two separate sheets at home, the one with Fenk's record and the other with the four Vietnamese names. The movie info was still in the envelope.

"These," I said to Annie, "are the six movies Trevor's got the responsibility for. Signing up the people, contracts, nitty-gritty details. What I wonder, Fenk's one movie and five others I never heard of, do they link together somehow?"

Annie pushed the platter to my side of the table and organized the movie material in six piles. The platter had three-quarters of a tuna sandwich on it. I ate the three-quarters.

"I only recognize the titles," Annie said, lifting the papers, reading, putting them down. "And that's just from seeing them earlier in the program Cam's ladies handed out at the Park Plaza."

Annie got up from the table and went to the corner of the living room she calls her office. It has a white wicker desk and chair, a bookcase full of movie tomes, a typewriter, and the cursed answering machine, and on the wall there's a poster from *The Man with Two Brains*. I gave Annie the poster. *The Man with Two Brains* is my favourite Steve Martin movie. Annie came back with a program that had a glossy cover in silver and blue.

"Give me five minutes," she said. She looked at the title of one of the movies and began flipping through the program. It was the program for the Alternate Film Festival. "Another thing I was wondering," I said. "All the movies, you see in the credits 'best boy', usually right next to 'grip' and 'gaffer'. You got any idea what a best boy does?"

"Five minutes," Annie said, "of silence."

I occupied myself with the Dao and the view out the window of Annie's corner of Cabbagetown. The sky was still overcast. Might rain. A leaf fell from a tree in front of the house across the street. I wasn't a whiz at marking time.

"Well, I don't know." Annie gave the program an impatient shove. "If these've got something the same about them, it beats me. Different themes, different producers, sounds like different techniques."

"You tried, kid. It was just a thought."

"California, but so what?"

"So what, what? Where's California come in?"

"That's where the six movies were made, but so were probably six hundred other movies this year."

If there'd been wine left in my glass, I would have poured it down my throat in one large, dramatic flourish. The glass was empty, and so was the bottle. I settled for giving Annie my best meaningful look. The gesture was wasted. Annie spoke first.

"I see what you're going to say, yeah," she said. "Fenk's a Los Angeles person."

"So doesn't it mean something that Trevor's booked only movies from California? Trevor who's been maybe up to fishy business with Fenk of the same state? Must be a tie-in."

"California."

"Why didn't you let me say it first, about the connection between the six movies and Trevor and Fenk?"

"Come on, you were going through all that nonsense about checking the wine and staring into my eyes like you were Sherlock Holmes. What was I supposed to do, sit here and look stupid?"

"Dr. Watson would have."

Annie smiled. It was her first from the time I arrived and began the story that revealed all. Or almost all. I didn't get graphic in describing the look of Fenk on the sitting-room floor.

Annie said, "I wouldn't be mistaken, would I, if I guessed you want me to ask around, see who knows the dirt on the other five movies besides *Hell's Barrio*?"

"There must be people at the festival up from California for those. Producers, directors, writers, stars, best boys."

"Actors in the movies in the Alternate Festival, except for Harp Manley, I think they're too lowly to be called stars."

"If they're here is all that counts. Maybe they're hooked into Fenk or Trevor or both, some of the California types, and maybe there's a pattern of links somewhere."

Annie said, "Well, I've got the right cover for a person asking pertinent questions. Impertinent questions too."

"Everybody'll say, oh golly, it's just that adorable Annie B. Cooke doing interviews. Her occupation."

"Part of my occupation."

"Chatting up the stars, present stars, future stars, mega stars. Daniel Day-Lewis."

"Again? You're bringing up the man again?" Annie said. She made a little gesture of semi-annoyance with her arms. Then, switching manner, she said, coquettish, "Well, just because he's one of the world's divine males . . ."

Why had I mentioned Daniel Day-Lewis? I didn't know his name was on my tongue till I let it roll off. What was this? Incipient green-eyed monster syndrome? Who was the dolt in the Preston Sturges movie? The one where the symphony conductor imagines his wife's having an affair with another guy? *Unfaithfully Yours.* Linda Darnell was the wife. Funny movie. Ah, Rex Harrison was the conductor. I was playing Rex Harrison. Not as suave, but as doltish.

Annie was looking at her watch upside down.

"We got half an hour," she said. "You know what? I'm starved."

She carried the platter back to the kitchen, and I followed.

"I'll find out what I can about the five movies." Annie had her back to me and was mixing canned tuna, Hellman's mayonnaise, and chopped green onion in a small bowl. "You do what it is you've made up your mind to do. But I still don't get it."

"Did I leave something out?"

"The part about the dead man and Trevor Dalgleish and the six movies, I'm in it up to there. I understand why you're poking around them. To see what they're up to, if anything. But who's your client? I know *who* he is. He's Dave somebody or other the jazz player. But who is he in the *story*?"

"An innocent bystander."

"I don't believe this, I honestly don't," Annie said. She kept on making her sandwich.

"Here's as far as I've got," I said. "Things start with Fenk's confederate at the jazz club Dave worked in Culver City."

"Confederate, I like that."

"He stole Dave's old saxophone case at the Alley Cat, and next night this guy, a large black guy I gather from the Alley Cat boss, made Dave an anonymous gift of a new case. One difference, the new case had contraband hidden in the lining."

"First, confederate. Now contraband."

"In the lining, I'll give odds, it was cocaine."

Annie turned around. In her hand she had a plate with one sandwich on it.

"Weirder and weirder," she said.

She opened the refrigerator door with her free hand, took out a quart bottle of mineral water, and swung her rump at the fridge door. It closed. Annie had a great rump. We went back to the table in the window.

"Cocaine is Fenk's background," I said. "Two guilty pleas for possession. And Fenk was the guy who went to all the trouble of relieving Dave Goddard of the case. He knew the cocaine was in there."

"I never heard so much hypothetical in my life."

"You don't like it?"

"I'm crazy about it. It's just hypothetical."

When Annie ate her sandwich, she held it with both hands. Women do that. You hardly ever see a man use two hands on a sandwich. I poured mineral water into the two empty wineglasses.

"Thanks," Annie said.

"Think of what I just said as in the early formative stages. What I'm doing, I'm gathering the elements I'm sure of. I'm sure Fenk has a cocaine record. I'm sure illicit stuff, about the size of a few kilos of cocaine when you think of it, was hidden in the saxophone case's lining. Why else was it ripped? And another thing I'm sure of, I'm sure Fenk knew the cocaine was in there, in the lining."

"Which Dave the musician didn't?"

"Goddard's the name, and no, in this, from word go, he's totally in the dark."

"He better be totally in Muskoka or you got trouble."

Annie finished her sandwich and wiped her hands on a paper napkin. She wiped so gently that the napkin showed hardly any creases. Another difference between the sexes. My paper napkin was a shredded ball.

"Not to upset the applecart," Annie said, "but why? Why would Fenk and the black confederate go to all the trouble? Hiding cocaine in the case and bashing Dave Goddard to get it back?"

"I might come up short there. But, what about, it was a nifty way, foolproof practically, of transporting cocaine from California to Toronto?"

"Could be," Annie said.

She looked at her watch again.

"Better call a cab, sweetie," she said.

I stood, and Annie put her hand on my arm.

She said, "There's one thing makes me feel kind of warm about this whole awful schemozzle."

"I can't imagine."

"You told me what was going on instead of clamming up."

"You're welcome."

"So what's the excuse you didn't come clean sooner?"

20

A **QUARTER TO THREE**, starring Harp Manley, was a heist movie. *Rififi, The Italian Job, Bellman and True*, that genre. Harp played a cop who went undercover into a gang that worked out a scheme to bust into the Philadelphia Museum of Art. No mean feat. The place looked like a cross between the Parthenon and the Acropolis. But it had an exhibition of jewels the gang planned to loot. The break-in was in the classic mould—shutting down the museum's alarm system, duping the guards, climbing through a skylight, other intricate acts. Harp's character was supposed to stick with the gang long enough to catch the gist of the caper and bring in the rest of the cops at the penultimate moment. But he got tempted. Maybe he'd go along with the gang and pocket his share of the loot. Harp and his wife had a teenage daughter with some fatal illness. He and the wife did much discussing of options. Duty to law and order versus money to ease the dying daughter's last months.

"Je-sus," I whispered to Annie. "You hear that? Harp's voice?"

"Crang, do me a favour, I'm enjoying this."

"It didn't hit me before."

"What're you mumbling about?"

"Another high-pitched voice, just like the one at the Silverdore, whoever killed Fenk."

"Next you're going to say it was Tom Selleck in there."

Toward the end, the movie turned sappy. Harp's character got the whole works. He wiped out the gang, snaffled some big money the gang had put together to finance the heist, and retired to New Mexico, where the air was going to work miracles for the daughter with the dread disease.

"Would you call that pat?" Annie said. "The denouement and climax?"

"Except Harp made me a believer."

"If he's as good on his horn, whatever it is, as he is on screen, you should play me his records."

I didn't tell Annie I'd sat her down for two or three Harp Manley albums over the years. Some jazz made an impression on Annie, some passed by her ears. She liked Bill Evans, she said, Paul Desmond, the Modern Jazz Quartet. She went for the romantics. Harp didn't fit the category.

The lights came up in the theatre, and a small group moved to a microphone that was in position down front. Cam Charles led the way. Harp came right behind him. Both had on tuxedos. Cam's shoes were patent leather.

"Wasn't that a triumph, ladies and gentlemen?" Cam shouted into the microphone. His right arm was slung over Harp's shoulders, and his left was raised in the air in a power salute. The crowd in the theatre applauded lustily, and there was a sprinkling of bravos.

Cam made a speech, and Harp said a few words, and a grey-haired gent droned on about the pride he and his company took in sponsoring the opening night of the Alternate Festival. I didn't pay much attention. Neither did Annie. We only had eyes for the theatre. The Eglinton is on the shrinking list of Toronto's grand old movie palaces. Not that old either, maybe sixty years. It came from the age of Art Deco. Opulence and vulgarity, curves and geometry, all that stuff in nutty balance. I felt at home in the place when I was a kid at Saturday matinees, and I felt at home at the Harp Manley premiere. There was a high ceiling, rows of long, thin lamps up there, and an alabaster nude on either side of the screen. It was fussy and elaborate and kind of effeminate, but it beat hell out of the cramped boxes the movie chains were passing off as theatres these days.

"You know what?" Annie said. "I'd come here even for a rotten movie."

Down front at the mike, Cam invited everyone to stay for a reception in the Eglinton's lobby. "An opportunity to mingle with the stars," he put it. Not everyone took Cam up on the invitation. That was a blessing; the lobby was as lovely as the rest of the building but not exactly ballroom-sized. Cam's chic PR ladies were once again on deck, moving through the crowd with words of welcome and trays of red and white wine. I took two glasses of white, handed one to Annie, and we rubbernecked. Harp had a fawning crowd around him. So did the guy who played the chief heavy in the movie, the mastermind behind the bank robbery. Was it Charles Durning or Brian Dennehy?

"It's neither actor you think it is," Annie said, following my stare.

"You into mind-reading now?"

"Everybody mixes them up. The actor over there is Ned Beatty."

"Maybe there's really only one of them. He uses three names and works a lot."

Annie waved at a tall, slim, short-haired guy who waved back.

"Jay Scott?" I said. Jay Scott was the *Globe*'s movie critic.

"Another smart move from Cam Charles," Annie said.

"Yeah?"

"He didn't give the reviewers an advance screening of *Quarter to Three*, which means Jay and everybody else, if they want to see it, and they definitely do since it's for certain going to be a hot movie later this fall, they had to come to this gala opening."

"Gives the event more prestige."

"And the festival more press coverage."

Annie and I simultaneously spotted somebody. They were different somebodies. I didn't notice Annie's target, but mine was Trevor Dalgleish. He was moving away from the bar that had been set up where popcorn was normally peddled, and he had one glass of red wine in his hand.

"Sweetie," Annie said, "you excuse me for a minute?"

"That was going to be my line."

I weaved through the mob in Trevor's direction. So far no one had intercepted him. He wore a tux and a confident smile. I caught up to him before he could join a group of three other people in formal gear.

"Congratulations, Trev," I said. "Festival's off to a boffo start."

"Hello, Crang." Trevor didn't sound overwhelmed by my company. "The little lady got you in tow again?"

His accent wasn't as mid-Atlantic as I'd thought, but the flavour was there, the inflections built in from his Old Toronto upbringing and the St. Andrew's education. And the voice was on the right pitch, in the tenor range.

I said, "Too bad not everybody could be here."

"Oh, I don't know." Trevor swept his free hand in a general gesture meant to encompass the lobby. "Look around. An A-list gathering if I'm any judge."

"I had Raymond Fenk in mind, Trev."

Trevor dropped a heavy hand on my shoulder and steered me toward the side of the lobby opposite the bar. It was an accomplished bit of ballet, the way Trevor executed it. I ended up with my back to the wall, and Trevor had his to the crowd. I felt hemmed in and vaguely threatened.

"Ray Fenk's death, a tragedy really, isn't common knowledge, Crang." Trevor's voice went grave, and his face developed a light flush. "How's it happen you know? Cam indicated to me the news wasn't going beyond our office and the homicide people, not until the police develop a lead they have."

"What's the lead?"

"Pardon me, Crang, that isn't the question."

"The way I know about Fenk's murder, Trev, a client of mine may be implicated."

"How odd," Trevor said. He looked to me like a guy who was both curious and uneasy. "May I ask who your client is?"

"If I can ask what the lead is."

"That's confidential."

"You mean it's staying in the family of three: Cam, your good self, and Stuffy Kernohan."

"D'you know Kernohan?"

"Heck, Trev, when it comes to the homicide squad, Stuffy's a Hall-of-Famer."

Around the right side of Trevor, I could see Annie in profile. She had on a short jacket and short skirt. Both were black and tightly tailored. Her blouse was white, and it came with a neckline that showed a little breast bone. She was talking with great animation to a guy I didn't recognize.

"My client you're wondering about," I said to Trevor, "he's a musician. Plays the tenor saxophone. That's of the reed family. Has a curved bell, valves for the fingers to play, a long, thin cord. The cord's a leather thing that drapes around the neck."

It wasn't subtle, banging away at Trevor that way. It may not have been awfully bright. But time wasn't an ingredient I was in ample supply of. If Trevor had first-hand information about Fenk's murder, if he had a hand in the killing, maybe I could wedge something out of him with a few blunt remarks. When it came to blunt, I was a master.

"This is all very fascinating, Crang," Trevor said, his face deepening from blush to medium pink, his hands flexing to fists. "But I seem to recall you had your own encounter with Ray Fenk."

"The dust-up at the Park Plaza," I said. "That seems to be on the list of everybody's favourite memories."

"It was Ray's first trip to Toronto. He knew no one here, just myself and one or two others at the festival. It does seem strange, new in town like that, just arrived, he'd apparently been irritated so soon by you."

"Little trick of the personality I have, Trev."

The guy on the receiving end of Annie's animation was slim and medium height. His hair was dark and clipped close to the head, and he had an angular face. Not a terrific smiler, from where I was standing, but you could say attractive.

"You'll already know this, Trev," I said, "but your Mr. Fenk wouldn't win any good-citizenship awards. Porno movies, they were his specialty, and he had a couple of cocaine convictions back home."

Trevor shifted his feet, got a knowing smile on his pink face, and made little circling motions with the hand that held the wineglass. The way I interpreted the gestures, Trevor was about to say something patronizing.

"Both of us," he said, "—don't let me sound gauche, Crang—are men of the world."

"I know what comes next."

"You do?"

"And cocaine is a fact of life."

"In contemporary society," Trevor said.

"I shouldn't have left that out."

Trevor shifted again. His first shift had blocked my view of Annie and her companion. Now they were back in sight. Annie's animation continued.

"Well, my God, Crang," Trevor said, "some of the best people I know—I hate it when I hear myself speaking in thundering clichés—they serve cocaine in their homes like an appetizer. What's the harm, within certain sensible bounds? Ray Fenk's troubles, as far as cocaine went, were no more than unfortunate. Really, I've had clients, you must have too, who've done worse and suffered less."

"The Vietnamese guys, for example, speaking of clients?"

Trevor looked like a guy who might be having trouble with anger—the colour of his face, the nervous clenching of his hands.

"What *is* this conversation, Crang?" he said. "You're all over the map."

"Just comparing notes, Trev."

Annie's companion turned full-face. I gave him a once-over. Hot *damn*, the guy was Daniel Day-Lewis.

Trevor glanced over his shoulder in the direction I was doing the once-over.

"I'm keeping you from someone," he said to me.

"Not yet," I said. "What're they like, clientwise, the Vietnamese?"

"Very obliging. Why? You've had bad experiences yourself?"

"Haven't represented any Vietnamese so far."

"Then what the hell are you on about? If it's any of your concern, which I very much doubt, I'm just on retainer for my Vietnamese. Nothing's come up yet."

"What might come up? What field they in?"

"Businessmen. They're in business."

"High risk, I betcha."

"You just went past the bounds, Crang." Trevor pushed back his sleeve and read his watch. "I have other duties here tonight."

I said, "Look forward to more of it, the conversation."

"Perhaps when you're less opaque."

Trevor moved away. Across the lobby, Daniel Day-Lewis was nowhere in view. Annie was talking to a woman who looked like she'd borrowed her clothes from Diane Keaton's wardrobe. I moseyed through the crowd, had another glass of wine, and chatted with people I knew from other movie bashes. After an hour of it, Annie and I flagged a cab on the street in front of the theatre.

In the back seat, Annie laced her hand through mine.

She said, "Don't even mention his name."

"Daniel Day-Lewis."

"How'd you get such a hang-up about the man?"

"Well, you did give the impression back there, you must know, you were sort of bowled over by the guy, hanging on his every word, and one of the world's most *divine* men you said earlier."

"Crang, honey, listening to Daniel Day-Lewis, that's called work."

The cab was headed down Avenue Road, and when we got to Upper Canada College, the driver cut over to Oriole Parkway and kept going south.

"Some of what he told me," Annie said, "I can sneak into *Metro Morning*, and the rest I'll use for the *Chronicle* pieces."

"So you cancelled the Tuesday interview? Got all you need from Mr. Daniel Day-Lewis?"

"Are you joking? Tonight was luck. Tuesday's serious."

Annie leaned over and kissed my cheek.

"Crang, whatever's in your mind, Day-Lewis is not my type, it turns out. A nice man, sexy on the screen, but in real life, nothing emanated for me. Happy now?"

"Not your type?"

"No tingles."

"Well, listen, good-looker, who is your type?"

Annie put her head back and was quiet for three or four seconds.

"My type?" she said. "Ted Koppel."

21

ANNIE WAS SITTING at my kitchen table. She had a ballpoint pen with red ink, and she was writing in a nimble hand on pages in a ringed notebook. It was just coming up to 7 a.m.

"Know what I'm getting you this Christmas?" she said. "A typewriter."

"Really romantic." I was standing in the doorway in my maroon dressing gown. "What should I get you? A snow shovel?"

"If you had a typewriter," Annie said, "nights when I sleep over, I could type the notes for the radio program. This way, longhand, I get in front of the mike and can hardly read my own writing."

Annie was due on air for her *Metro Morning* movie review at around ten to eight. She was dressed and had a cup of coffee beside the ringed notebook. There was more in the Mr. Coffee machine. I poured a cup.

"Which one you going to talk about?" I asked. "The Harp Manley?"

Annie made a grunting noise that I took to be affirmative.

"Want some background stuff?" I asked. "About Manley as a jazz musician?"

Another grunt that I interpreted as negative.

I sat at the table and let my coffee cool. Three or four minutes went by, and when Annie's writing seemed to be slowing down, I spoke again.

"Study the guy closely," I said, "and Ted Koppel bears a striking resemblance to Howdy Doody."

"Eye of the beholder," Annie said without raising her head from the notebook.

"With an overlay of Alfred E. Newman."

"The man exudes intelligence." Annie looked up. "I can't help myself, Crang. Ted speaks from the TV screen and I get all unglued."

"Must be the hour."

"He does come on late, which is a shame."

"Not Koppel's hour. This hour, right now, seven in the morning. It's too early for rational talk about sex appeal."

"For talk maybe." Annie let go a slinky smile. "But I've known you to show fantastically sexy moves at ridiculously early hours."

I looked at the wall clock. Ten past seven.

"Not now, idiot," Annie said. "A girl needs a little foreplay."

"How 'bout a quickie?"

Annie went over to the phone and dialled for a taxi.

"Just end the suspense about one thing," I said.

"It isn't true," Annie said. "I'm not seeing Ted Koppel on the sly."

"Another subject altogether," I said. "What in hell's a best boy?"

"Persistent cuss you are." Annie was organizing the notebook, pen, and other utensils in her shoulder bag. "A best boy. He's the person on the movie set that runs the errands, fills the coffee cups, opens the limo doors, sharpens the pencils."

"A gofer? That's all?"

"Don't blame me. I just supply the answers around here."

"I was hoping for something more exotic."

"Shoot the messenger, why don't you?"

I went around the table and kissed Annie's forehead.

"Did I sound like an ingrate?" I said. "Truth is, it's a heck of a load off my shoulders. All those years, sitting in movies, reading the credits, not knowing what best boy meant, feeling stupid."

The taxi came just after seven-thirty. Annie was cutting it fine. *Metro*

Morning broadcast from studios over on Parliament Street, about ten minutes from my place.

I had a shower and shave and switched on the radio to the CBC. The sweet little number who reads the news and weather was in the middle of the marine forecast. Then the unflappable guy who does the traffic spoke of a three-mile backup on the Don Valley Parkway. He didn't say DVP. Then the host made a joke about Annie's clothes. Said she was dressed for a gala night on the town. Annie said some gala nights on the town just never ended. The host made a noise like a chuckle. And Annie talked for five minutes about *A Quarter to Three*. She brought up stuff that was new to me. I sat through the same movie she did, but she saw more than I saw. Amazing.

I turned off the radio and practised pronunciation in front of the mirror in the bathroom. Nhu Truong. Dan Nguyen. Nghiep Tran. My Do Thai. The four Vietnamese people Trevor Dalgleish might or might not be palsy with. I didn't have much trouble getting my tongue around the names. The two spots where "N" and "g" ran up against one another were tricky. But I wasn't trying to come on like a recent arrival from Ho Chi Minh City. Just a snoop looking for four guys who had an address on Oxford Street.

There were a few delays before I got out of the house and on with the quest. First came breakfast. Followed by incoming phone calls. Dave Goddard rang from Muskoka to complain about the birds.

He also said he wanted to throw himself on the mercy of the police. I persuaded him to give me until Wednesday. It took much talk. Cam Charles phoned as soon as Dave hung up. Cam requested an update.

"Update?" I said. "Cam, I haven't been on the job twenty-four hours."

"Trevor spoke to me this morning," Cam said. "He's of the opinion you should be reported to Stuffy Kernohan."

"I'm supposed to be checking *him* out, and he wants to turn *me* in?"

"You apparently said something last night that piqued Trevor's interest."

"Part of my ongoing design, Cam."

"Well, it had better not go on too long. If something's not right about Trevor's conduct in the firm, I want to know it fast."

"Wednesday latest, Cam. Two days."

I don't know why I arrived at Wednesday as a deadline for solving everybody's problems: Dave's, Cam's, mine. If nothing happened in the next two days, I could stall for more time. I wouldn't have trouble buying an extra day or two from one of the trio. Me. The other two, Dave and Cam, might be a smidge recalcitrant.

By eleven, I was mooching through the streets behind College and Spadina. The neighbourhood had textbook Toronto history. It was the area that a lot of immigrants to the city chose as a first perching-spot. In the late nineteenth century, Jews arrived from Russia and Middle European countries. They settled in the College-Spadina environs. Portuguese and Hungarians followed to the same streets. Chinese moved in during the 1950s and 1960s. And after the Americans pulled out of Vietnam, the "boat people"—dumb term—made their appearance.

Nobody put down their roots for good in the neighbourhood. It was a way station until families got prosperous and travelled north to the suburbs. For them, suburbs equalled success. But signs of all nationalities remained behind. The Kensington Market was a monument to the foods of every Toronto culture except Wasp. Jewish businessmen ran the garment industry from their factories on Spadina Avenue. Portuguese bakeries and pool halls dotted the streets. Restaurants that were big on goulash and wiener schnitzel. Places that cooked Cantonese. Szechuan. Peking. Mongolian. Lately, Vietnamese was all the rage. Plenty of vermicelli dishes.

I turned off Spadina at Oxford and walked past a carwash and another half-block into the neighbourhood. The number I was looking for, the four guys' address, was on the north side. I stopped on the sidewalk.

"Son of a gun," I said, more or less to myself.

The address was a restaurant, another vermicelli outlet, and the sign on the door told me it was closed. "Open at noon," the sign read. That was thirty-five minutes away.

I ambled on down the street. A chestnut tree was dropping its nuts on the sidewalk. I picked one up. It felt cool and smooth and the end of something. It felt like the lyric Johnny Mercer wrote for the Ralph Burns tune. *When an early autumn walks the land / and chills the breeze / and touches with her hand / the summer trees / perhaps you'll understand / what memories I own.*

I kept on going to a mini-park and sat on a bench. I had nothing to read. Why hadn't I packed along the Gene Lees book? I sat and looked at my watch a couple of dozen times until it got to be noon.

The restaurant didn't seem to have a name, and I was its first customer. The furnishings and decor were rudimentary. It had a low plaster ceiling, and below it were heating pipes painted white and entwined with fake ivy leaves. The walls were covered in mirrors with patterns in them that distorted the reflected images. Plaques that advertised Canadian beers were another favourite in the place's aesthetic scheme. I sat at a table for two, wooden table and the same in the chairs. The chopsticks were plastic.

"You care for beverage?" the waitress asked me. "Beer maybe?"

She had a tiny voice. It matched the rest of her, small-boned and fragile. Her smile was lovely and tentative.

"Sure," I said, giving her my best grin, putting her at ease, getting her on my side, priming her for questions about my quarry. "A light beer would be wonderful. And thanks kindly."

I like beer about as much as I like baseball, but if the waitress thought I looked like a beer guy, okay for me. She brought a Carlsberg and a menu. The menu was eight typed pages, the Carlsberg smelled vaguely skunky. To me, all beer smells vaguely skunky. I ordered an imperial roll and a dish that featured chicken and vermicelli. The restaurant had about a dozen tables, and they were beginning to fill up. I seemed to be the only patron who wasn't Vietnamese. Maybe that's why the waitress's smile for me was lovely but tentative. Not used to Caucasians. That balanced things. I wasn't used to Vietnamese.

The waitress came back with the imperial roll.

"These fellas happen to be around?" I said to her. "Nho Truong, Nghiep Tran, Dan Nguyen, My Do Thai?"

I felt proud of the way the names tripped off my lips.

The waitress's smile turned less lovely and more tentative. She looked over her shoulder in the direction of the kitchen, and left my table without answering the question about the four guys. At least she put down the imperial roll before she did the fleeing act. It was warm and had a zingy taste.

A skinny guy in his forties leaned out the kitchen door. He was wearing a white singlet and a white chef's apron and had a cigarette in his mouth with an inch of ash dangling at the end. If he was the cook, I'd check my chicken and vermicelli for traces of nicotine. He studied me for fifteen seconds and ducked back into the kitchen. I seemed to have aroused somebody's attention.

The tiny waitress didn't take away my empty imperial roll plate and empty beer bottle. The chore was handled by a muscular guy in a short-sleeved white shirt that hung outside his pants. He brought me the chicken dish and a second Carlsberg. I got exclusive service. The waitress looked after everyone else in the place. Mr. Muscles took care of me.

I ate and drank and surveyed the room. None of the customers appeared to be taking special notice of me. None looked suspicious. Suspicious of what? Of bumping off Fenk? Of playing fast and loose with Trevor Dalgleish? That was what I was hanging around to find out. Put that way, it didn't seem like much of a plan.

Two guys, if I had to single out suspects, emerged as my leading candidates. They were sitting at a table next to the entrance. One had on a dark-blue warm-up outfit, zippered top and pants that ballooned at the knees. The other wore a Hawaiian shirt that draped below his waist in the same style as my waiter's shirt. Both guys looked younger, sharper, less working-class than the rest of the restaurant's clientele. The guy in the Hawaiian shirt had his black hair tied in a rat's-tail at the back. Really cool.

One o'clock came, and I'd had my fill of chicken, vermicelli, Carlsberg, and surveillance. But I wasn't leaving, not after the small signs that I'd stirred a little interest around the place. The waitress's nervousness, the chef's inspection, the muscular guy's ministrations. I ordered a pot of tea, and walked over to the counter and picked up a copy of *Now* from the stack beside the cash register. Something to pass the time. *Now*'s movie reviewer dumped on the Norman Jewison film that opened the Festival of Festivals, and its restaurant reviewer dumped on the food at the Belair. Seemed to be a pattern there. I tried the personals.

"Burt Reynolds look-alike," I read. "Successful, huggable, and available. Seeks relationship with tall, lean, model-type woman who is bright, happy, stable, and Candice Bergen look-alike."

Burt Reynolds look-alike? Who's that, someone with a toupee and a silly little moustache? And the guy who placed the ad didn't have a clear picture of the girl of his dreams. Lean and model-type was okay, but not in the Candice Bergen mould. Candice has great looks, but her figure's too substantial to qualify for model-type. Besides, her taste in men runs to Louis Malle. Wasn't anybody editing *Now*'s personals?

Two beers and a pot of tea. I needed to use the bathroom. It was through a door beyond the kitchen entrance. I was out of the restaurant for only three or four minutes, but when I came back, the place had undergone a transformation.

The two sharp guys were seated at their table. Their eyes were on me. My muscular waiter was giving me the same stare. He was leaning against the wall by the front door. The rest of the room was deserted. No patrons, no nervous waitress. Just me and the three guys. And one other Vietnamese gent. He was sitting at my table, and he wasn't reading *Now*.

"How'd you do that?" I said to the man at the table. "Make all the customers disappear? I've heard of sleight-of-hand, but this is fantastic."

The man had a wispy goatee and horn-rimmed glasses. He was wearing a shirt and tie and no jacket. He looked like an accountant who'd slipped out of the office on a coffee break.

"You do not have an appointment," he said. He spoke in an even, civilized kind of voice.

"Well, no," I said. "Just came on the off chance."

"This is about a transaction," the man said. "Sale or purchase."

"The transaction part's right."

"You want Big Bam," he said. The guy didn't deal in questions. Only statements.

"If I want Big Bam," I said, "my pronunciation's a little faulty. It was four other people I mentioned to the waitress."

The man in the shirt and tie listened while I recited the four names. I spoke them in the same order each time. Easier to keep them right that way, like memory work in public school.

"I wonder who gave you this address," the man said.

I thought about that for a second or two and decided to invoke an old maxim: when in doubt, improvise.

"Trevor sent me, as a matter of fact," I said. "Dalgleish."

The man turned in his chair and said something in a language that must have been Vietnamese to the other three men in the room. My muscular waiter and the guy in the Hawaiian shirt made identical motions. Both reached under their overhanging shirts and went for something on their belts. Guns? My stomach gave a lurch. The guys unclipped metal boxes from next to their hips. Not guns. My stomach righted itself. The two guys had walkie-talkies in their hands. They spoke into them in Vietnamese.

"Nice," I said to the man at the table. "All the technology."

The man said nothing, and I felt a compulsion to babble.

"Had those two fellas pegged," I said. "Your friends over there, in the Hawaiian shirt and the warm-ups. Distinctive types, you know the way it goes. Stand out every time."

"Big Bam's waiting for someone to make compensation," the man said in his civilized tones. "Three days now."

"Three days?" I said. "Not good at all."

"No."

The two guys were still broadcasting into the walkie-talkies. Make what compensation? And who was Big Bam? A pseudonym for one of the four men on Trevor Dalgleish's list? Probably not. Probably someone else altogether. One fact was sure—my new pals in the restaurant knew Trevor. The two walkie-talkie fanatics wound up their broadcasts.

"Ten-four," the guy in the Hawaiian shirt said.

"Ten-four," the muscular waiter said.

"Some language is universal," I said to the man at my table.

He wasn't paying attention to me. He was busy talking to the other three. The language wasn't universal. It was Vietnamese, and it sounded like a set of orders. I sipped the last of the cold tea in my cup and sat by for further developments.

The man at the table got out of his seat and smiled. I did the same with a lot of emphasis on the smiling part.

"Big Bam is going to be at the park," the man said.

"Great," I said.

"He wants us to take you there with us."

"Even better."

The other three guys assembled to my right. The man in the shirt and tie nodded, and the three guys were on me as fast as a Road Runner cartoon. The one with the muscles held my wrists tight at my sides. The other two patted me down. Hawaiian Shirt took the upper half, Warm-up Suit took the waist down. It was over in a few seconds, and the three guys stepped away from me. They left everything behind, my money, wallet, keys, and a tingling in my wrists.

"The brass knuckles and the blackjack, they're at home," I said to the man in the shirt and tie. "I could've told you. Saved the bother."

"Good business is built on precaution," he said.

The four of them started for the door.

"Just a sec," I said. "Two beers, imperial roll, chicken dish, tea. I haven't paid the waitress."

"Big Bam's treat," the man in the shirt and tie said.
I told him I was mad about treats.

22

TWO CARS WERE PARKED in front of the restaurant, half on the sidewalk and half in Oxford Street, and of the two, I would have chosen to ride in the Datsun coupe. It had a sporty look I liked. But I didn't get to choose. The man in the shirt and tie, definitely the leader of the pack of four even if he was the least prepossessing, pointed me into the other car. It was a white Cadillac Seville. The Datsun was dark brown. Both were new models and had all the optionals. These guys shared something with Cam Charles. First cabin all the way.

Hawaiian Shirt and Warm-up Suit drove away in the Datsun. Mr. Muscles got behind the wheel of the Seville. Shirt and Tie and I sat in back, and we followed the Datsun.

"One thing I'm kind of a stickler about," I said to Shirt and Tie, "is names. For instance, I'm Crang."

"Mr. Crang?"

"That'll do."

"Very good. I'm Truong."

"Nho Truong?"

"Exactly. Your pronunciation is excellent."

"Been practising," I said. "And who's that up front?"

"Our driver is Tran."

"Nghiep Tran?"

"Ah," Truong said. "Not so accurate this time, your pronunciation."

"I guess it's back to the mirror."

"Pardon?"

"Just a little Occidental habit," I said. "How about the fellas in the Datsun? Dan Nguyen and My Do Thai?"

"You know us all, Mr. Crang." Truong shook his head. "But you make one error in the pronunciation."

"Where the 'N' and the 'g' come together?"

"Exactly."

Truong spoke the two names, Nghiep and Nguyen, four times each, rapidly. I repeated the names after him. He shook his head again.

"Back to the mirror?" Truong said.

"I promise."

Truong smiled sympathetically. He and I were getting on famously. I decided to go for the whole enchilada.

"That leaves one more," I said. "Big Bam."

"He earned the name," Truong said.

"I didn't think it was Vietnamese."

"No mirror for it," Truong said. He was making a joke. I laughed.

"How'd he earn it?" I asked. "Big Bam?"

"Perhaps when the matter is rectified," Truong said, "he will tell you himself."

"The matter he's been waiting three days for someone to make compensation on?"

"Not just someone," Truong said. "Trevor Dalgleish. And now you."

"Count on it."

The Seville turned on to College Street, then west to Bathurst and north. I could see the Datsun up ahead on the same route. Whatever Trevor Dalgleish had going with these guys, principally with Big Bam, he must have screwed up. That was interesting. Even more interesting, the time frame for the apparent screw-up, going back three days, took in Fenk's arrival in town and his murder at the Silverdore. The Seville hung a left at Harbord. How long could I keep Big Bam and his guys thinking I was connected to Trevor? That'd be delicate. It had to be long enough for me to weasel out a few more facts, but not long enough for them to figure me for a fake. The car wound north of Bloor and on to Christie Street. I knew what park Big Bam must be waiting at: Christie Pits.

The Seville parked on the street that overlooked the Pits from the north side. The Datsun was at the curb about a block further west on the same street. Three or four other cars were parked in between the two. One car stood out, a red Porsche convertible. No one was in it.

Truong got out of the back of the Seville, walked around to the front, and climbed in the passenger seat beside Tran. Truong opened the large glove compartment and slid something out. I leaned over the seat. Truong had a money tray in his lap. Each compartment was at least partly filled. Twenties, fifties, hundreds. The hundreds compartment was close to overflowing.

I sat back and looked out the side window into the park. It took up ten or twelve acres, and it dropped about thirty feet below street level, which is where the name came from. The Pits. Christie Pits. There was a swimming pool on the far western edge of the park, a wading pool, a fenced-in baseball diamond, and three or four softball diamonds. At the south end, old men played bocce, and spread around the acres there were benches, drinking fountains, other amenities. So what brought Big Bam, whoever he was, and his activities, whatever they were, to this haven of rest and recreation?

Tran, the muscular guy at the Seville's wheel, got on his walkie-talkie. As best I could make out, he seemed to be in touch with two or three good buddies. The guy who had the walkie-talkie under his Hawaiian shirt had to be one, broadcasting from the Datsun. Who were the others? Tran gave me a clue. As he talked, he kept glancing into the park. I followed his glances. A guy sitting on a bench beyond the baseball diamond's right outfield looked like he was talking into his sleeve. He must be another of the communicators. And a man in a green windbreaker squatting on the slope that ran up the Christie Street side of the hill had his head hunched over a small object, probably a walkie-talkie.

Tran lowered his own walkie-talkie.

"Set," he said to Truong.

Truong looked at his watch and nodded. I looked at my watch. Two o'clock on the button. Truong and Tran were focussing on the part of the park immediately below us. I did likewise. They knew what they were watching for. I'd have to learn.

It was a slow day in the Pits. Two o'clock on a Monday afternoon. The kids were in school, and it was too early for the office softball teams to hit the diamonds. A couple of mothers were guiding toddlers through the wading pool, and two or three dog-walkers, paper bags in hand, were airing their mutts. That was it, apart from the man sitting on the bench at the bottom of the hill on our side of the park, the north side.

The man had his back to us, and he was reading a newspaper. Looked like the *Globe*. He had on a light-grey suit, no hat, and his hair was black. I guessed—his hair, build, all-round persona—that he was Vietnamese.

Another guy was scrambling down the hill behind the bench that the Vietnamese with the *Globe* was sitting on. The scrambler, on the portly side, was wearing a suit, tie, and summer fedora, and didn't give the impression he was used to coping with steep hills on foot. He stumbled to the bottom and sat on the bench beside the Vietnamese. They chatted, and in the course of the conversation, not long, the guy in the fedora looked back, first at the Seville, then, craning around, at the Datsun down the block. He was making a lot of motions that seemed to say, yeah, sure, he understood, he agreed. The Vietnamese wrote something on the top sheet of a pad of paper, ripped off the sheet, and handed it to the other guy. The two shook hands, and the man in the fedora started back up the slope. His progress was slow, and he was aimed at the Seville.

"That Big Bam down there on the bench?" I asked Truong.

"Of course."

"How about the sluggish chap?"

Truong twisted in the front seat and gave me his version of an impatient look.

"Oh," I said. "Customer?"

"Of course."

The customer arrived at the Seville, at Truong's side. Truong pressed the button that lowered his window, and the customer beamed at him. His face was pink, and his upper lip was lined in small beads of sweat. Apart from that, in his nice linen suit and rep tie and new fedora, he seemed the model of respectability. He was holding out his sheet of paper to Truong.

"Hell of a climb, heh, heh, the hill, heh, heh," he said. He was breathing hard.

"Twenty-eight hundred," Truong said to him. Truong was reading the figure on the sheet of paper.

The portly man had money in his hand, six five-hundred-dollar bills. Truong accepted the bills. He took two one-hundreds out of the appropriate compartment in the money tray and handed them to the man. To the customer. Truong wrote something in the corner of the sheet of paper. It seemed to be his initials. He gave it to the man and raised the car window. The portly guy headed down the street in the direction of the Datsun. He wasn't wasting any tune.

"So far," I said to Truong, "it looks all take and no give."

"Wait," Truong said.

"Always been a failing of mine. Waiting."

I waited, and didn't get much wiser. The portly guy hurried up to the window on the Datsun's passenger side and handed his sheet of paper to the guy in the blue warm-up suit. Was he Dan Nguyen or My Do Thai? Whoever he was, he handed the portly guy a second piece of paper in exchange for the first, the one with the twenty-eight hundred and Truong's initials on it. The portly man pocketed the second piece of paper and disappeared out of sight beyond the Datsun.

Somebody else was on the bench with Big Bam, a younger guy in jeans and a terrific black sport jacket. Had to be a Giorgio Armani jacket. He followed the same drill as the portly man, except he wasn't breathing hard when he got to Truong's window. He was in for an even five thousand. He paid, took back his initialled paper, and trotted on to the Datsun. He looked smooth.

It kept up that way, people moving from Big Bam on the bench to Truong in the Seville to the guys in the Datsun. Money changing hands and sheets of paper getting traded. I lost track of the customers. There were two kids who were about seventeen and had on Upper Canada College blazers. There were numerous guys who looked like they sold life insurance. There was one matron in a flowered dress. One black guy about the size of Kareem Abdul-Jabbar and with the same amount of hair. One tough little guy who had a lip on him and complained about the price. Truong ignored him. Truong had other matters on his mind. Mostly money. The money tray overflowed. Truong counted five-hundred-dollar bills into stacks of twenty, bound them with large rubber bands, and pushed them into the back of the glove compartment. He did the same with the hundred-dollar bills. Bound them in stacks of fifty. There was a fortune in money in the glove compartment. I lost track of it too.

Close to four o'clock, a tall guy with the beginnings of a gut took his place on the bench beside Big Bam. They talked. The talk lasted longer than the conversations with other customers, and it was accompanied by much arm-waving from the tall guy. He left the bench, but he didn't have a piece of paper in his hand, and he didn't climb the hill to the Seville. He crossed the park and sat next to the guy with the walkie-talkie on the Christie Street slope.

Two more customers went through the usual drill: a chat with Big Bam, up the hill, pay at the Seville, collect paper at the Datsun. When they were done, Big Bam waved the tall guy with the incipient gut back to the bench. This time, he gave the tall guy a slip of paper. The tall guy started up the hill. Big Bam stuck out his right hand and pointed first at the guy on the Christie Street slope and then at the guy on the bench beyond right field. Those two, it stood to reason, had to be lookouts, watching for cops or other transgressors. When Big Bam signalled them, both got on their walkie-talkies. Voices came over the walkie-talkie in the Seville. Tran took the messages without answering back. It was all Vietnamese to me.

The tall guy arrived at Truong's window and handed in his piece of paper. It was, on the basis of the amounts that had been established by the other customers, for comparative peanuts. Six hundred and twenty-five dollars. The tall guy was in his early thirties, and besides the swelling stomach, he had a face scarred by ancient acne. The six-twenty-five he passed to Truong came in a fat wad of crinkled fives, tens, and twenties. Tran gave the bills a look of disgust. Truong, the old pro, treated the money as business as usual. He initialled the paper and gave it back with a polite nod.

Big Bam and the two lookouts had come up the hill and settled inside the Porsche. They sat there. Nothing else. No revving of engine or other indicators of imminent activity. But something was up. I could feel a tightening of the mood inside the Seville.

The tall guy, outside the window, looked at his piece of paper and turned away from Truong's window in the direction of the Datsun. But he didn't step away from the Seville. He didn't need to. The two guys from the Datsun seemed to be coming to him. Dan Nguyen and My Do Thai, whichever was which, were on the run toward us, past the Porsche, up to the Seville and the tall guy. The two of them, Hawaiian Shirt and Warm-up Suit, were carrying baseball bats, and I had a terrible feeling they didn't plan to use them for the same purpose Darryl Strawberry wields his bat.

The tall guy looked like he was nailed to the street. He didn't budge, and the expression on his face said he was petrified. He held out his right hand, beseechingly, to the two men with the bats. The hand held the slip of paper. The two batters didn't care about the paper. The tall guy took a quick, scared, hopeful look at Truong behind the raised window. No use. Truong was concentrating on the money tray.

"But I got the fucking paper!" the tall guy screeched at the men with the bats, and he started to wave his arms, the way he waved them when he talked to Big Bam on the bench.

I didn't think any of it—the arm-waving, the screeching, the displaying of the paper—was doing the tall guy any good. He probably didn't think so either.

The man in the blue warm-up suit swung his baseball bat at the tall guy's knees. He connected. The tall guy's feet flew about a yard in the air, and he hung up there a second or two before he dropped. I opened the door on the right side of the Seville and pushed it out. The tall guy hit the road hard, shoulder and hip first. He didn't bounce. The man in the Hawaiian shirt was on him for more licks. He gave the tall guy's gut three swift whacks with the bat. I got out of the car. The tall guy was a couple of feet from me. Vomit spurted from his mouth. Warm-up Suit was still on the job. He rapped the tall guy's ankles. Once, twice, swift and vicious, a third time and a fourth. The tall guy grabbed his stomach with one hand and reached for his ankles with the other. He rolled on to his back and over on the other side, and when he rolled, the slip of white paper came loose on the pavement.

The two guys from the Datsun had wrapped up batting practice. They were hotfooting it back to their car. Truong seemed to be absorbed in his study of the money tray. No one saw the loose piece of paper except me.

"You!" Tran yelled from behind the Seville's wheel. "Get the fuck back in!"

He was yelling at me. But from where he was sitting, Tran had no line of sight on the paper. I squatted, palmed the paper, straightened up, and slid into the Seville's back seat. One easy, fluid, sophisticated motion. So how come my armpits were dripping sweat?

The Datsun up ahead gunned away from the curb. Big Bam and the two lookouts followed in the Porsche. And we were right behind in the Seville.

I slipped the piece of paper into the breast pocket of my shirt and looked through the back window at the tall guy in the street. He was wrapped in the fetal position, curled up, both hands holding tight to his body, vomit running down his front. His shoes had come off, and his pants were pulled halfway up one shin. A bone seemed to be sticking out of the leg at an angle bones don't normally choose.

"A dissatisfied customer?" I said to the back of Truong's head. My voice had a croak in it.

Truong turned in his seat to face me.

"Worse," he said. "A duplicitous customer."

23

FROM THE ROUTE Tran took back downtown, I thought we were aimed for the restaurant where I had lunch. I thought wrong. We got into the same general neighbourhood, but a few blocks further west, closer to Toronto Western Hospital. I considered suggesting to Truong we might have dropped off the tall guy at the Western. I kept my mouth shut.

Tran drove along a side street lined with narrow, two-storey houses painted in fabulous shades. Magentas, emeralds, blood reds. In Toronto, English Canadians sandblast their brick. The other nationalities make like Robert Rauschenberg with theirs. Tran turned left off the street and through the opening in a ten-foot-high chain-link fence. The guy in the Hawaiian shirt was standing at the opening. He closed a gate into it after we passed by. Tran steered around to the back of a building and pulled up in a line with the Datsun and the Porsche. The gang was all here.

The building towered over the houses to the east by two and a half storeys. It had a run-of-the-mill industrial look, yellow-brown brick, flat roof, large rectangular windows. There was something different about the windows. They were painted over and projected nothing but black. Did evil lurk within?

Everybody was out of the cars except Truong. The five underlings—Tran, Hawaiian Shirt, Warm-up Suit, and the two lookouts—strung themselves in a loose line between the Seville and a steel door into the back of the building. They checked rooftops, peeked around corners, seemed to be watching for anything that might move. Give them two-piece dark suits and wires plugged into their ears and they'd look like your average platoon of secret-service agents guarding the prime minister. Truong, in the Seville with the cash, had the prime-ministerial role.

Big Bam was at the steel door, fitting a key into a lock. Two keys, in fact, in two locks. He hadn't directed his attention my way. First things came first, and getting the money inside the building qualified as a definite first. I was glad to settle for second place. Gave me time to work out my strategy. What strategy? Examine the slip of paper? Not if it might cost me time in the batting cage with the two Saigon sluggers. I'd save the paper for later in the privacy of my own living room.

Big Bam opened the door, and simultaneously Truong was out of the Seville and stepping in expeditious fashion down the line of guards. He carried the tray in both hands, gingerly, like a precious possession. Which it was, probably in the vicinity of a hundred grand for the day's curious commerce.

Truong went through the steel door followed by Big Bam. Tran motioned me to take a place in the procession. The light was murky inside and got murkier when Tran slammed shut the door and threw the pair of locks. We went single file, nobody talking, up one flight of stairs, turned left, and climbed a shorter flight. At the front of the file, someone opened a door, and bright light flooded down the stairs. I was second-last in the group, trailed by Tran, and when I stepped through the door, into the brightness, and looked around, I came close to tumbling backwards into Tran the trailer.

"Well, damn," I said.

"Fantastic, you know?" Tran said from behind me.

"And here I thought I'd seen all the city's architectural wonders."

The space in front of me might have been smaller than the inside of Maple Leaf Gardens, but not much. The whole of the interior of the building had been ripped out from side to side and from first floor to the ceiling, three and a half storeys up. No inside walls, no floors, no skylight, no windows that let in light. There was plenty of light from other sources, and all of them were in operation. Bars of pink neon at least thirty feet long ran vertically up all four walls. Tiny red bulbs, like the kind for Christmas decorations, were strung over every available surface. And the surfaces were manifold. A bar, much longer than Abner Chase's salad bar, occupied one end of the room. It didn't peddle arugula. It was in the spirits business. Bottles of all things alcoholic sat on shelves behind the monster bar, and the shelves were festooned with the ubiquitous tiny red bulbs. Several dozen small tables and four times as many chairs were grouped around a large dance floor. It was painted midnight blue. Enormous speakers for a sound system hung about twelve feet up in the room's four corners. And giant grainy blow-ups of famous folks, three times life-size, were mounted at regular intervals around the walls. Marilyn Monroe. Elvis Presley. James Dean. I recognized the famous folks who were deceased. I drew a blank on most of the others. Must be rock stars. If I learned who they were, I'd put them on the list of subjects I was eliminating from my thought processes.

"What's this place called?" I asked Tran.

"Booze can."

"I know that. But what's its name? When a guy comes here in a cab, where's he tell the driver to take him?"

"Big Bam's place."

"Should've guessed."

"Only word of mouth, you know?" Tran said. "Not many cab drivers can find this place, only the ones who are our friends."

"Oh sure," I said. "Wrong sort might get in."

"No trash, you know?"

It didn't seem prudent to continue the conversation. Tran and I might get into a debate over trash. He was sure to win.

I knew about booze cans, but this was my first venture into one. That gave me the edge over Toronto's cops; they knew about booze cans too, but apparently hadn't been inside one long enough to make a bust. Booze cans like Big Bam's place, so I'd learned from the grapevine, opened for business around ten-thirty at night and sold liquor, drugs, and high-stepping times until the sun came up. Those activities broke many laws, but, as I gathered from the same grapevine, the police hadn't penetrated the booze cans' security and caught owners and customers in the lawbreaking. What was this informative grapevine of mine? The series of articles that the *Globe*'s investigative reporter wrote on booze cans a month or so earlier. Wonder if the investigative reporter knew about Big Bam's place with the steel door and the guys with the baseball bats? That was real security.

"You and me got to wait," Tran said to me.

"Doesn't come as a surprise, the way my day's been going."

Big Bam, Truong, and their protectors were across the floor, about the width of a football field from Tran and me. A door led out of the huge room at the point where the bar ended. Big Bam and company disappeared through it.

"You want a drink?" Tran asked me.

"Now you're talking."

Tran didn't inquire after my preference in beverages, and I wasn't certain we were palsy enough for me to speak up. A guy with muscles like Tran, maybe nobody got palsy enough with him to speak up.

Tran went behind the bar, and I sat down at one of the tables next to the dance floor.

Tran came back with two cans of Sprite.

"Not exactly the kind of drink I had in mind," I said.

"Big Bam makes the rule," Tran said. "No booze on the job."

"Speaking of the job," I said, "what was going on up at the Pits? All that collecting cash and trading paper?"

"You don't know?"

"Wouldn't ask otherwise."

"You don't know," Tran said, "I don't tell you."

"Another Big Bam rule?"

"You got it."

Tran finished his Sprite and crushed the can in his right hand. It was probably as thrilling as life was going to get in Tran's company. I asked him about the other guys. He told me Hawaiian Shirt was Dan Nguyen, and Warm-up Suit was My Do Thai. I said it was nice to have the fellas straight. He told me the names of the two lookouts. I didn't commit them to memory.

Tran walked back to the bar and picked up a newspaper from the counter.

"That thing come in two sections?" I asked.

Tran separated a pair of double sheets from the paper and shoved them across the table to me. It was printed in Vietnamese. Or maybe Sanskrit. I leafed through my share of the paper. There was a photograph of someone who looked strikingly like Lyndon Johnson.

"What's this about?" I asked Tran.

He studied the photograph and the accompanying story.

"President of the United States," Tran said.

"Not for a while now."

It came up to six o'clock. Tran had two more Sprites and gave his newspaper a real going-over. I passed through three phases. Impatience, fear, inertia. What if Big Bam in the other room was in touch with Trevor Dalgleish, and Trevor blew the whistle on me? That thought accounted for the fear. So did the memory of the tall guy in spasms on the road by the park. I didn't think I'd suffer his fate, not immediately, and I didn't think Big Bam would be in early communication with Trevor Dalgleish. Truong's remarks in the restaurant and in the Seville, the stuff about waiting three days to resolve something or other, gave me the impression Trevor was being elusive with his Vietnamese clients. Clients? That was another question. I was developing more than a glimmer of suspicion that Trevor and the Big Bam bunch had something other than a traditional solicitor-client relationship.

Around six-thirty, things perked up. Dan Nguyen and My Do Thai came back out of the door they'd gone through hours earlier. They said nothing and left by way of the back entrance we'd all entered by.

Ten minutes later, the two lookouts made a similar passage, except their exit was by way of another steel door in the far wall opposite the bar. This door was double-sized and had a peephole in its centre. Five minutes after that, I did a definite ID on one of the people in the blow-ups on the walls. It was Sonia Braga, world's third- or fourth-sexiest woman. She looked different in the blow-up, but still sexy. Next time Annie raised Ted Koppel, I'd counter with Sonia Braga. After that, events in the booze can calmed right down again.

"Would you come in, Mr. Crang?" Truong said. He was standing at the open doorway to the inner room. His voice caught me with my head down. Maybe inertia had given way to forty winks.

"Nice to see you again," I said to Truong.

I followed him into the office. It was smallish and had a cluttered feel. It also had the only window I'd noticed in the place that wasn't painted over. The office window was covered by a black blind.

Big Bam was on his feet behind a desk, smiling broadly, his arms held out to the sides, expansive, a gesture of apology.

"What can I say?" he said. "Waiting like you been doing's a drag. But what can I say? Basically, it's got to be business before pleasure, you catch my drift."

"No bother," I said. "Gave me a chance to do a little marvelling out there."

"Bottom line," Big Bam said, "my place's real strong, do I lie?"

I allowed that he didn't. Big Bam was about five-ten, slim and dark, and he had the sort of old-time handsome features that were the rage in 1940s movies. The shape and arrangement of his nose, cheeks, mouth, chin were like Turhan Bey's. Sexy, if you don't object to bland. Big Bam's grey suit jacket hung on the back of the chair he'd been sitting in. The suit was raw silk. His shirt, a fainter grey, was pure silk, and he had two thick gold chains round his neck. His watch was a Rolex.

"Let you in on what's going down here," Big Bam said, sitting in his chair. "Truong and I're into some serious number-crunching."

"That so?" I said.

I sat in the chair across the desk from Big Bam. Truong had another desk at an angle to Big Bam's. The top of Truong's was a jumble of thick logbooks of the kind that accounting records are kept in, loose sheets of paper with long columns of numbers, and smaller pieces of paper, also jammed with numbers, ripped from notebooks. Truong had a pocket calculator in his hand. Big Bam kept his desk executive style. Clean except for a telephone and an appointment diary.

Big Bam said to me, "I laid it on Truong, best-case scenario, go for it. Say the price holds at one-twenty-five, what's my profit margin?"

Big Bam looked at Truong.

"Between thirty-four and thirty-six per cent," Truong answered without consulting anything, the pocket calculator or the stuff on his desk.

Big Bam said, "And this is at a point in time when purity's way up. Eighty per cent. The buyers are where it's happening. Basically their market, but what can I say?"

"Everybody's got problems," I said. That seemed innocuous enough.

"*Tell* me about it," Big Bam said. "But, hey, babe, deal another scenario. Say we get it on in the crack market. More volume, more dinero. What's my profit margin?"

"Forty-eight per cent," Truong said, no hesitation.

"But what're my priorities? I want crack on the agenda?" Big Bam was still pointing the conversation at me. I trusted he didn't expect an answer. He didn't. He kept on talking. "Basically not really. Crack's for the low-rent trade. Teenyboppers, riffraff. My call, it's a thumbs-down."

"Except in profit margin," I said, getting an oar in.

"Right on, bro," Big Bam said. "But crack, you got more mess, you got extra employees. Bottom line, I say hold down the overhead and stay with the straight coke. Go for it. Ride it out."

Maybe I was inching my way into Big Bam's line of gab. Not into his jargon. The guy talked like he might have proceeded without pause from native Vietnamese to ad agency English. Anybody'd take him for a career account exec at J. Walter Thompson. It was his subject I might be getting a handle on. He was talking cocaine. No difficulty reading that. And he was talking prices, weights, purity. The "one-twenty-five" must be dollars, and it had to be price per gram. Drug dealers always seemed to work on the metric scale. Big Bam was currently selling cocaine at one hundred and twenty-five dollars a gram. As for the purity part, cocaine that was eighty-per-cent pure must be powerful stuff. Maybe it was safe for me to stick in a question.

"Tell me, ah, Big Bam," I said, shifting in my chair, striving for the learned air of an old hand, "what purity we talking about back there when you got into the, um, business?"

"Bitchin' times they were." Big Bam's beatific expression reminded me of the way old folkies look when they reminisce about the years before Dylan went electric. "Customers used to think sixty per cent, hey, it's heaven, and they'd pay one-eighty, not blink once."

"Those were the days," I said.

"Right on," Big Bam said.

"You get into crack," I said, bluffing along grandly I thought, "you need, what, a laboratory to handle the work?"

"Basically, yeah," Big Bam said. "Don't have to be a nuclear scientist, catch my drift. Mix your baking soda in with your coke. Cook it up on a medium heat. Let it cool out. Get hard. You got your crystals. That's crack. Package it up and sell it for twenty-five buckaroos a pop. One kilo of coke, how many bags of crack that make?"

The question was directed at Truong.

"Between nine thousand, five hundred and ten thousand," Truong answered.

"Large money," Big Bam said to me. "But basically I don't get it on with the crack crowd."

"You're more carriage trade," I said.

Big Bam stood up and rubbed his hands together.

"I'll drink to that," he said. "What's your main taste, Crang?"

"Tran took care of me earlier," I said. "A little Sprite goes a long way."

Big Bam laughed. It was a tinkling sound, entirely without menace.

"Hey, it's happy hour," he said. "Let's get down."

"In that case," I said, "vodka on the rocks."

I thought Big Bam would dispatch Truong on the bartending duties, but he left the room to fetch the drinks himself. Truong stayed at his desk.

"Real captain of industry," I said to Truong. "Big Bam."

"Mr. Crang," Truong said, "may I have the piece of paper in your shirt pocket?"

My heart let go an extra thump.

I said, "I don't suppose I could say I was planning to return it?"

"I would have trouble believing you."

I took the slip of paper from my pocket without fumbling. It came out blank side up. I turned it over. There was an address written on it and, in the corner, a number. I handed the slip to Truong.

"You don't miss much," I said.

"Big Bam pays me not to."

"What'd the guy who had this paper do, the tall guy, to get the home-run hitters sicced on him up there at the Pits?"

"He altered the script."

That didn't tell me much. Told me nothing, as a matter of fact. Truong the inscrutable. I went for another question of more danger-ous relevance.

"Big Bam know about this?" I asked. "About me and the piece of paper?"

"There may be no need."

I assumed that qualified as a no. Truong opened the top drawer in his desk, dropped in the paper, and shut the drawer. At the same moment, Big Bam came through the door. He was carrying a tray with three glasses on it.

"A little Russian for you, my man," he said, handing me a drink in a heavy crystal glass.

Big Bam settled behind his desk. His drink looked like Scotch. Truong's looked like Sprite. Big Bam jumped up again. There was a compact-disc player on the shelf behind him. He chose a disc from a stack on the shelf and slid it into the machine. Soft rock thumped into the room.

"Hey, that'll work," Big Bam said, back in this chair.

He raised his glass in a silent toast. All of us sipped. Big Bam was right about the vodka. Russian. It was made from grain, the same as Wyborowa, but it had a stiffer taste.

"So," Big Bam said to me, "where we at, Crang?"

"Well," I said, going for a concerned look, "I gather there's a little misunderstanding about Trevor."

"Shorted me four K," Big Bam said. "From where I'm sitting, that's a big misunderstanding."

"Four K?"

"Hear me talking," Big Bam said. "I got a lot of time for Trevor. He's a righteous man. But, hey, our deal this time's for twenty-four K. I fronted him like I been fronting him the last year and a half. The deal on the twenty-four was twelve thousand a K."

Big Bam looked at Truong.

"Correct," Truong said.

"And delivery came in last Friday night as per arrangement with Trevor. But what's this? Delivery wasn't twenty-four K. Only twenty K."

Another check with Truong.

"Correct," Truong said.

"Stranger things start going down," Big Bam continued. "Truong phones Trevor about the shortfall. The four K. And, hoo boy, Trevor ain't taking no calls."

"Correct," Truong said without being asked.

"We dial Trevor's home, get on to his office," Big Bam said. "What do we get? Secretaries and answering machines. The man's avoiding me. I thought I knew Trevor, and now I can't tell where he's coming from."

Big Bam got up and changed discs on the compact player. I took a swallow of vodka and wondered how far over my head I'd put myself.

As far as I knew, K had two meanings in the vernacular: thousand and kilogram. Big Bam had to be talking kilogram, as in kilograms of cocaine. As in kilograms of cocaine that Big Bam had paid Trevor for in advance. Fronted him. As in twenty-four kilograms at twelve thousand dollars a kilogram. I didn't take time to do the multiplication. It was serious money. And Trevor was evidently short by the delivery of four kilograms. Or, another way of looking at it, four times twelve, more my speed in multiplication, Trevor had forty-eight thousand of Big Bam's dollars he wasn't entitled to. I needed to go into a big-league stall and think through the implications. For me, not for Trevor. I already seemed to have confirmation that Trevor was up to his eyeballs in the cocaine industry. Cam Charles wouldn't be delighted to receive the news.

"How can I put this?" I said to Big Bam. "Trevor's embarrassed. That accounts for what might strike you as his evasiveness. Understand, the trouble originated at the supply end. Trevor's supplier, I mean to say, and it left egg on Trevor's face."

I paused. Would that line of guff wash?

"Trevor's supplier, *tell* me about it," Big Bam said. "I sent my guys around the other day to put the grab on the rest of the cans. But nothing shaking there. Cans had no coke in them."

As he talked, Big Bam waved his hand in the direction of the corner of the office near Truong's desk. There was a squat combination safe in the corner, and beside it, in three careless stacks, there were the cans Big Bam must have been talking about. I wouldn't have called them cans. Containers maybe. They were three or four inches thick through the sides, which were large and flat, and they were in something like a hexagon shape around the outer edges. They had handles for lifting them, and they were a dull silver colour. They looked familiar, but I couldn't place why. The can on top of one stack had a yellow sticker with printing on it.

"You know what went down with the cans?" Big Bam said to me in a tone of voice that assumed of course I should know.

"Yeah, sure," I lied.

"Basically, I'm a patient man," Big Bam said. "For one day, I'm patient." He smiled. "After three days, I'm looking to get even."

"Which explains my presence here," I said, producing an expression I trusted was reassuring.

"Lay it on me."

"Trevor's difficulties at the supply end are on the verge of a successful conclusion," I said. Jesus, would Big Bam swallow this? Maybe he had no choice. He wanted his coke or his money. Or somebody's neck. "I came over, as a friend at court you might say, to extend Trevor's apologies and let you know the coke is on its way."

"When?"

It was Truong who asked the question.

"Tomorrow," I said. "Tomorrow night. Right here. This office."

When I improvise, I don't kid around. But the timing seemed smart. Big Bam probably wouldn't kick up a fuss over one more day. And the twenty-four hours would give me a chance to develop something more elaborate in the way of logistics.

Big Bam was spending a lot of time sipping at his drink and not saying anything. Too much time for my comfort.

"You pay attention to what went down at the park this afternoon?" Big Bam finally asked me.

"I found it all very, um, instructive."

"That's what it was supposed to be."

"Instructive?"

"Right on."

"I guess you're referring to the part where your fellas worked on their batting strokes?"

"You might keep that part in mind, my man."

"It's emblazoned."

"And paint the picture for Trevor."

"I catch your drift, Big Bam."

Big Bam broke out another smile and swung to his feet.

"Let's have the other half of these drinks," he said.

He collected the empty glasses and left the room. Truong and I sat in silence. That suited me. I had to deal with a small dose of aftershock. Big Bam wasn't exactly subtle when it came to threats. Straighten out the misfired cocaine deal, he was saying, or expect a few broken bones.

Strange guy, Big Bam, strange set of priorities. He wouldn't deal in crack even though it'd earn him more profit. The decision about the crack seemed to come out of some misguided notion of what was and wasn't classy. Crack wasn't. But Big Bam wouldn't hesitate to lay on the violence when it suited him. Hard man to figure. And not a man to trifle with, which was what I seemed to be doing. Trifling.

Big Bam returned with the refills, same all round. He picked out a new disc and stuck it on the compact player. It may have been new, but it didn't sound different to me. More thumping soft rock.

"So you're a lawyer," Big Bam said from back of his desk.

I didn't remember telling him that. Or any of his entourage.

"Got an office on Queen Street," Big Bam said. "Duplex on Beverley."

"Well," I said, "I'm in the phone book."

"Take mostly clients who're up on fraud charges," Big Bam said.

That wasn't in the phone book.

"You don't do the same kind of law they do over at Trevor's office," Big Bam said. "They're into minorities stuff."

Was Big Bam toying with me? I'd call it that. He kept on smiling as he talked. Still no menace in the smile, but it suggested a guy who enjoyed toying with people. With me anyway.

He said, "So I guess it's through movies you and Trevor got it on. You know, as friends."

I pretended to be occupied with my vodka.

"Movies," Big Bam said, "is one of your scenes. And jazz."

I said, "Bet you don't know what kind of car I drive."

"White Volks," Big Bam said.

"Convertible," Truong said.

I said, "This's very impressive, guys."

"You should see what we got in the file on Trevor," Big Bam said.

"You know about the exam-paper scam at St. Andrew's College?" I said.

Big Bam looked over at Truong.

"No," Truong said to me. "Perhaps you'd tell us."

Big Bam waved his hand.

"Stay cool, Crang," he said. "What's going down here, I like to know where people I do business with are coming from. We only had this afternoon to run you down. Truong made the calls. Basically he got enough background to let you in the door."

I said, "And, I hope, out the door later."

Big Bam liked that.

"I love this guy," he said, spreading his beaming smile on me. Truong had no smile. Didn't he love me? Or was he just sore because his research missed the story about Trevor and the exam papers?

"Well, listen, Bam," I said, "as long as we're in a biographical frame of mind, I was wondering about something. Your name."

Big Bam lifted a leg over the arm of his chair and swirled the ice cubes in his drink with a finger.

"Lay the brief version on you," he said. "The very brief version. A year ago March, there were two posses in this part of town selling coke."

"Posses?" I said.

"Gangs. Outfits. Organizations."

"I thought you guys called them triads."

"Posses," Big Bam said. "You want to hear the story or not?"

"Sorry."

"I ran one of the posses," Big Bam said. "Me. Ng Thai. The other posse used to set up in a restaurant over on St. Patrick. One night I went in the basement of the restaurant. Had twelve sticks of dynamite and a timer. Set the stuff for next day. At noon, the dynamite went."

Big Bam stopped talking and shrugged.

"And," I finished for him, "there was the sound of a big bam."

"Hardly anybody except my parents call me Ng Thai these days."

"Just curious, Bam," I said. "But, ah, what hours was this restaurant on St. Patrick open for business?"

"Oh, yeah, the whole posse went up with the place," Big Bam said. "Except Truong wasn't there that day. He'd already decided to come over to me."

Nobody in the room said anything for a moment. Big Bam was silent because he seemed to be relishing the ancient triumph.

Truong was just being his inscrutable self. And I was having enough trouble getting the numb feeling out of my brain, never mind my lips. This guy, Big Bam, was a champion killer. Murderer on a mass scale. Fenk, jeez, dusting off Fenk would have been swatting a fly for someone like him.

"One for the road?"

Big Bam was speaking to me. He had the smile on his face, not a trace of menace. How'd he manage that? All he'd done and no sign of it in his smile. In his whole face.

I held out my glass and nodded, yes, I'd have one for the road.

24

I**T WAS CLOSE TO NINE** and the sky was fading to black when I left Big Bam and his hospitality. I walked up to College Street and bought two Coffee Crisps and a tin of apple juice at a variety store. A sugar hit to keep me functioning. Maybe I didn't need the chocolate bars. The day with Big Bam had my energy pumping at a scary rate.

I ate one of the bars anyway and went north on Brunswick Avenue above College. I was looking for a number on Ulster Avenue. Found it. It was across from a small park on the southwest corner of Brunswick and Ulster. The house with the number I wanted was semi-detached and three storeys high. It had decorative woodwork around the top of the porch, filigree almost, and it had a tiny well-tended front yard planted in flowers that bloomed white even in the dark. I sat on a bench at the edge of the park and watched the house across the street.

It was the address written on the piece of paper I palmed after the tall guy dropped it at the Pits. When I handed the paper back to Truong in the booze can, I looked at it long enough to memorize what was written on it. Sometimes the old brain just never quits. What was written on the paper was the Ulster address and, in the corner, a number. Five. The porch on the house across the street was in darkness, but there was a light on in the room to the left of the front door. I figured

I had enough stamina to stick around for a couple of hours and maybe find out where Ulster Street and the number five worked into the story.

At nine-thirty, a man in a suit walked down the sidewalk and turned in to the Ulster house. The man was carrying a briefcase and looked law-abiding. He could pass for one of the insurance-salesman types who had dealings with Big Bam at the Pits. He rang the bell at the house. No porch light came on, but a small woman opened the door. She didn't open it far, a foot and a half. She accepted a piece of paper from the man, read it, and handed him a package. The woman closed the door. I thought she was Vietnamese, and very old. The man put the package in his briefcase and walked away. He had a pushy kind of stride. Definitely an insurance salesman. The entire transaction lasted twenty seconds.

I took a turn around the park to stretch my legs. The park had a kids' slide, a small wading pool, and a big rock with a plaque drilled into it. "Margaret Fairley Park", the plaque read. "A citizen who cared for her community." Well, Margaret, I thought, standing by the rock, wherever you are, give a care for the house on Ulster Street. It's in your community, and something screwy is going on over there. Something that makes it a cog in the Big Bam cocaine operation. Probably wasn't around in your day, Margaret, whatever day that was. Probably bath-tub gin and blind pigs were the scourge back then.

I took up position on the bench in time for another arrival on the porch. This visitor I recognized. No mistaking the jacket. It was black and sharp and Giorgio Armani, and the young person wearing it was the second customer Big Bam had serviced at the park that afternoon. The guy came away from the Ulster porch with a small package in his hand and a swagger in his walk.

I got off the bench and intercepted him.

"Evening there," I said. I was right in front of the guy. "Spare a minute?"

For a flash, the young guy looked shocked, guilty, and nervous all at the same time. But only for a flash. He had a lot of bravado to him.

"What's your story?" he said. "I'm in a hurry."

"Just checking up on a few points."

"You a cop?" the guy asked. He was about my height and had squinty eyes.

"Not a cop," I said. "I'm on the other side. Your side."

"Didn't think you were a cop," the guy said. "You don't look ballsy enough."

I skipped right on over the insult.

"Want to know if you've got any complaints," I said. "About the way you've been treated today."

"What're you talking about?"

"The transaction," I said. "Start to finish. With Big Bam."

The guy's eyes got squintier, but he started to answer.

"Well, like always," he said. "Told Big Bam what I was in for this week. He gave me the paper, and I paid the guy with the glasses. Listen, it was like every time I do a deal. I got my other paper, the script y'know, from the two guys in the Datsun, and for this deal it said to come here, which is the only thing different since I never been to this house before."

The guy stopped.

"I know you," he said. "You were sitting in back of the Seville."

"Great memory," I said.

"So how come you're standing around out here?"

"Think of me as Big Bam's quality-control manager. Just making sure our best customers get satisfaction."

The guy didn't have an answer for that, and I ploughed on.

I said, "Now you mention this is your first visit to this particular address. That'd be to pick up delivery of the cocaine?"

"Yeah, naturally, but what—"

I talked over the guy. "The paper from the men in the Datsun tells you the address where you go for the coke and the amount you've paid for?"

"Something's wrong here," the guy said. His eyes had squinted to slits.

"Helps if we run through the entire itinerary," I said. "Ensure none of our people slip up."

I'd lost the guy. He was looking over my shoulder and waving at someone back there.

"Petey," he shouted. "Get the fuck over here."

I looked behind me. A Trans Am was parked at the corner, and someone was climbing out of the driver's seat. If it was Petey, Petey was a long, lean drink of water, and he had a flashlight in his hand. The flashlight wasn't turned on.

"You've been a big help," I said to the guy in the Armani jacket. "So thanks and let's call it a night."

I turned, but the guy grabbed a handful of my shirt. His other hand was busy with the package of cocaine. Petey was closing in fast.

"The fuck you pulling?" the guy said to me. I tried to yank away, but the guy had my shirt too securely. We'd passed the point of negotiation.

"Whap this asshole, Petey."

The guy in the Armani jacket had real destruction in mind. I pivoted enough to get my right elbow in position and jammed it into the guy's stomach. He made an oomph sound and let go of my shirt. Petey had the flashlight raised over his head. That put it very high in the air and gave me time to dodge. I chose left, and the flashlight whistled past my right ear and clunked against my shoulder. It stung, but things could have been more painful.

Petey went back into his windup, and at the same time the other guy was recovering from the poke in the stomach. He straightened up, but I figured a couple of items put him at a disadvantage. The package of coke and his Armani jacket. Both represented big money, and he'd have it in mind to protect them.

I shot a fist at the package and knocked it out of the guy's grasp. He reached to catch it while it was still in the air. I juked to the right, and Petey's flashlight went by on the left. A clean miss. The other guy couldn't get his hands on the package fast enough. It hit the sidewalk with a small noise. *Pooph*. The package burst open, and white powder dusted the sidewalk. Five thousand dollars in white powder.

"Shit, oh shit, oh shit." The guy in the Armani jacket dropped to his knees and scraped his hands at the spilled cocaine. His shoulders heaved in something close to convulsions.

Petey wasn't doing anything new and dangerous with the flashlight. His attention was directed to the disaster on the sidewalk. I had the impression Petey wasn't the brains of the duo. I snatched the flashlight out of his hands and threw it spinning into Margaret Fairley's park.

"How's that for ballsy, fellas?" I said, and made a swift departure down Ulster.

At the corner, where the Trans Am sat, motor running, I looked back. Both guys were on the sidewalk brushing the cocaine on to the paper it had been wrapped in. They didn't have eyes for me. I slowed down and walked home.

25

I'**D GONE PAST THE HUNGER STAGE**. It was ten-fifteen. Or maybe a drink would reactivate my appetite. I poured a Wyborowa on the rocks.

A loose end. That's what the episode on Ulster was. It was peripheral to the major issues, which were Fenk's murder and where Big Bam's cocaine cartel blended into it. I took the drink into the living room and didn't turn on the lamp. Peripheral, yeah, but it was satisfying to know how Big Bam conducted his sales force. And now I knew. Resourceful me.

Big Bam wanted to minimize the physical contact he and his staff had with the cocaine. That explained the mechanics of his set-up. Cut down the chances of the cops nabbing him red-handed with the drugs in the course of the dealing. So he concocted a convoluted system of paper and payments and rendezvous.

The way I doped it out, the way it *had* to be, the customer had an initial meeting with the Bam himself. On the bench at Christie Pits, some prearranged place like that, maybe a different designated spot on each day of the week. Known only to the customer. Big Bam approved the amount and the price of the customer's coke purchase. Wrote it on a piece of paper. Customer took the paper to Truong, who collected the cash and initialled his okay. Customer traded the paper for another paper. That was handled by the lads in the Datsun. The slip of paper they issued gave the customer an address where the coke could be picked up. The paper also indicated the amount of coke the customer was entitled to. Very cagey.

The tall guy, for example, the tall guy who ought to be undergoing major surgery about now. The number on his paper was five. Five grams of coke he paid six hundred and twenty-five dollars for. The mathematics worked; at Big Bam's current rate of one-twenty-five per gram, the six-twenty-five bought exactly five grams. And the other thing on the tall guy's piece of paper was the address where he was supposed to pick up the five grams, namely the small and ancient lady's house on Ulster.

The same address must have been on the paper that the guy in the Armani jacket bought from Big Bam's outfit. The number on his paper would have been different, the number of grams. Much higher. I saw him count out five grand to Truong. How'd that calculate? One hundred and twenty-five divided into five thousand—click, click—came to an even forty. Forty grams of eighty-per-cent-pure cocaine. All of it spilled on the sidewalk by me. No wonder the guy went a little crazed.

What about the old woman at the Ulster house? Did she know what she was distributing? Maybe not precisely, but she must have surmised it was something more precious and dangerous than herbal tea.

Clever. Better, it was diabolical. Big Bam probably had a network of little old ladies in houses all over the city dishing out thousands of grams of cocaine every week. Probably paid them a small fee, and the whole scheme kept Bam himself safely distanced from the illegal transactions.

Except he'd have to take initial deliveries of the coke in bulk form before he and his guys divvied it up in gram units for retail. That'd be the only occasion when Big Bam and company got close to the coke, but it was a whole lot less risky than a few hundred weekly retail transactions.

And, speaking of bulk deliveries, who did Bam take them from? Probably from a bunch of different wholesalers. But I'd learned the name of one wholesaler.

Trevor Dalgleish.

Something stirred in my stomach. Hunger pangs. I put together more vodka and ice, and studied the inside of the refrigerator. Not promising. A tomato that was just barely on the edible side of mushy. A loaf of bran bread. And some other stuff that mostly had to do with breakfast. Should I send out for pizza? There was something about waiting for the pizza delivery man to ring the doorbell that generated tension in me. Dealing with the guy at the door always made me edgy too. How much to tip him? Another thing, cooked food wasn't meant to be transported in beat-up little trucks painted orange and pink. Cancel the pizza idea. I went back to the living room and lay in the dark some more.

Trevor peddled coke on a wholesale basis. Confirmed. Done and done. No doubt whatsoever. But as a killer? A killer of Raymond Fenk? I didn't make him for the role. Trevor was too lawyer-like, too Waspy. He lived in a house on Admiral Road and owned a tuxedo. Guys like that didn't go around strangling people. Of course, they didn't go around peddling coke either.

Big Bam made a better fit for killer. Any gent who could blow up a whole posse could bump off one Fenk. Or, if not Big Bam personally, then his faithful servants. I'd seen them at work with the baseball bats. A little matter of garrotting wouldn't raise a sweat for them. Or a qualm.

But there was a fly in the ointment with that line of reasoning. I had a direct link between Trevor and Fenk, but no direct link between Big Bam and Fenk. Or, put it another way, I had a link between Big Bam and Fenk, but the link was Trevor. He sold coke in large amounts to Bam, and one of the sources for Trevor's bulk stuff, at least recently, was Fenk, who smuggled in a quantity from California.

Which brought me around to Dave Goddard. My client. The guy whose predicament was the point of all this cogitating. It was Dave I was supposed to be getting off the hook, and how he got on the hook, to my way of deducing, was that Fenk must have used Dave's saxophone case to bring in part of the California coke shipment. Not all of it. Big Bam told me his current deal with Trevor was for twenty-four kilograms of coke. No way twenty-four K would have fitted in the lining of Dave's case. Three or four K, all right. Not twenty-four.

So how'd Fenk transport the rest? Something to do with the cans in the corner of Big Bam's office. Whatever the cans were, they eluded me. Maybe they didn't count anyway. What the heck, it was the coke hidden in Dave's saxophone case that tied together Fenk, Trevor, Big Bam, and the murder of the former by one or other of the latter. Concentrate on that point, Crang.

My stomach gurgled, not enough to yield to the pizza man but enough to go for a slightly soft tomato. I went into the kitchen and sliced up the tomato and built the slices into two sandwiches with the bran bread. Mayonnaise and black pepper for taste. I ate them in the living room, lights on, with a vodka and soda.

Big Bam and his gang for Fenk's killer. I liked the feel of it. Somehow they must have got through Trevor to Fenk as a cocaine source. Maybe they tried to strike a deal with Fenk. Cut out Trevor the middle man. Fenk balked. Or something else went wrong, and Fenk's life ended with a saxophone strap around his neck. Not bad as a piece of reasoning. It might explain why Trevor was steering clear of Big Bam. He knew Bam put the hit on Fenk and wanted to avoid the same fate.

Did that theory account for Trevor's other problem with Big Bam? The four kilograms of coke he still owed Bam? Not quite, but there must be a way of tying all the damned strands together. And still nail Bam for the killing. And put Dave Goddard in the clear.

Twenty-four hours.

That was how long I had to make sense out of things. Seemed a ridiculously short time. I had to get the cops on to Big Bam, on to Trevor too, and protect my own hide. Keep from taking the kind of licking Bam's swingers laid on the tall guy at the Pits.

Speaking of whom, why'd the Big Bam empire come down on the tall guy? Why him? "He altered the script," Truong said when I asked. That rang a little bell. Script? *That* was the word the guy in the Armani jacket used. It's what he called the piece of paper with the address and the number of grams on it. Must be a piece of lingo in the Bam circle of sellers and buyers. So if the tall guy altered the script, what'd he do? He changed it. Rewrote something on it. Not the address. That made no sense. The *amount*!

Well, yeah, of course. Say he paid for five grams of coke, he might have changed the amount on the slip of paper, on the *script*, to read six. Something along those lines. Maybe it was a one and he made it a ten. Nah, that was too blatant. Whichever number was involved, he upped it. And got caught. And got the stuffing knocked out of him.

Nice analysis, Crang. Heck, guy, take a bow. Better, take another drink.

I didn't feel like another drink. After the day I'd put in, my body said it was tired, but my mind said it was still in overdrive.

I wasn't close to sleep. But I went into the bedroom, took off my clothes, and got under the covers with the Lees book. I'd been saving up for the chapter on Dick Haymes. The best ballad-singer of them all. A romantic. An innocent. My kind of guy.

26

I **THOUGHT** it was a Vietnamese hit man.

I marked the place in the Dick Haymes chapter and switched off the lamp on the bedside table.

Somebody had opened the door down below into the apartment. Now the somebody was on the stairs. Quarter of the way up, I calculated. I crept out of the bed on the side away from the door and tiptoed across the floor. Did the footsteps on the stairs sound stealthy? Not really. They were soft but deliberate. Maybe Vietnamese hit men considered small details like stealth unnecessary.

I opened the closet door. The hell with that. I'd exhausted my in-closet hiding time. But there was a tennis racquet in there. I picked it up by the grip and tiptoed back to the bedroom door. I raised the racquet in the air. It wasn't in the conventional overhead-smash stance. It was in a position to sock the invader. The footsteps paused in the dark outside the bedroom door. I started to bring the racquet down with maximum force.

"Crang?"

The voice was whispering and female.

I stopped the racquet about three inches from Annie's dark and lovely head.

"What *are* you doing?" she said.

I reached past her and switched on the bedroom light.

"I thought it was somebody else," I said.

Annie's eyes were on the tennis racquet.

"You had a neat welcome for them, whoever it was," she said.

I walked over and sat on the edge of the bed.

"Putting it mildly," I said, "you surprised me."

"What else have I got your key for? Surprises, right?"

"This one was a lulu."

Annie sat on the bed beside me.

"Hey, is that what you wear at night when I'm not here?" she said.

I had on a Boston Celtics number 33 T-shirt. That's all I had on.

"Really sexy, your outfit," Annie said. "I love Magic Johnson."

"Larry Bird," I said. "Magic's number 32 and he's the other guys, the Lakers."

"Oh yeah, Los Angeles."

"Glad you think it's sexy."

Annie put her arm around my shoulder. I hadn't let go of the tennis racquet, and my hand was trembling. Annie didn't seem to notice.

"The reason I'm here," she said, "apart from all this male flesh, I've got fantastic news."

"Don't tell me, Ted Koppel's in town."

Annie took her arm off my shoulder.

"Crang, you're spoiling it."

"I'm a little jumpy is all it is. You want coffee or something, a drink?"

"If there's white wine open."

My jeans were on the chair. Annie goosed me when I stood up to get them. I laughed. It was a trifle forced. I put on the jeans, and we went into the kitchen. I poured Annie a glass from the bottle of Soave and made myself yet another vodka on the rocks.

"The other five movies?" I said. "Is this what it's about? You talked to people who're connected to them, Trevor's five besides the Fenk movie?"

"The point I'll get to in a minute is I *didn't* talk to anybody from them," Annie said. "But, anyway, on the scale of hot bulletins I bring from the front lines, the info about the five movies is in at least second place."

"I think you want me to ask what's in first place."

All sorts of whiffs were coming off Annie. Perfume. Cigarette smoke from whatever gathering she'd been at. Excitement. The perfume was Vivara by Pucci, impressed on my memory from past shopping expeditions.

"Fenk's movie?" Annie said. "*Hell's Barrio*? It was, get this, it was *stolen*."

"Ho boy, wasn't Fenk the light-fingered guy. Swiped everything that wasn't nailed down, Dave's saxophone case, a whole Hollywood movie. Who'd he steal it from?"

Annie was shaking her head.

"You're not following. Or I'm not saying it right. Fenk didn't take the movie from someone and say it was his. That's not the kind of theft I'm talking about. Somebody stole it from the *festival*. It was scheduled to run tonight. But there was a substitute instead, this really sincere thing from Sri Lanka. So afterwards I go asking about *Hell's Barrio*, and I'm persistent and charming as the dickens and the rest of it, and I find out the entire movie, the *physical* movie, has gone missing. Somebody walked off with the actual cans of film."

Annie was in one of the kitchen chairs, the heels of both shoes hooked on a rung under her. I was leaning against the counter. When Annie got to the end of her spiel, I bounced my bum gently on the edge of the counter. Otherwise, I gave no indication I was a man putting a big two and two together.

"They sort of chunky metal things, these film cans?" I said. "In a hexagon shape around the outer edges?"

"Yeah, silver-coloured usually," Annie said. "So it must be significant, you agree? The cans that had *Hell's Barrio* in them are gone. Disappeared. Vanished in a puff of smoke."

"They got big handles on them, these cans, for lifting?"

"Yeah, yeah."

"I think I know where the cans are."

"Aw, come off it, Crang. What're you? The man who's always one step ahead?"

"The cans I saw, I couldn't tell they had the film in them for *Hell's Barrio*. But the tipoff is they weren't in a place where film cans should be. There were seven or eight of them, my guess, and the one on top of the pile had a yellow sticker and a line of black type. A title probably. I should've done something about a closer look."

Annie had her hand on her chin, and she was wearing her concentrating look, the eyes a little wider, a small frown line between them.

"Seven or eight cans is too many for one movie," she said. "Except maybe *Gone with the Wind*, which *Hell's Barrio* isn't in length or probably in anything else. It'd take up only three cans of film, maximum. The rest you saw must be other movies."

"Cans of film," I said. "Got that. Keep going, honeybun. You're doing great."

Annie took her first sip of wine, enough to wet her lips.

"Okay," she said. "Late-breaking piece of news number two. The other five movies Trevor Dalgleish booked? There's nobody up from California for any of them. No actors, no producers, no persons whatsoever. But I asked a very nice young woman from the festival, one of those long-stemmed beauties you admired at the press lunch, and she told me, no problem—they all say no problem a lot, the tall girls—any inquiries on those films go to one man, same rep up from California for all five, da-dah, da-dah, da-dah. Guess who she said?"

"Raymond Fenk."

"Dammit, Crang, you get a kick out of ruining my revelations?"

"Fenk *was* here for *Hell's Barrio* and the other five California movies?"

"The long-stemmed one didn't seem to know he was dead."

"And you didn't enlighten her?"

"'Course not. But now we're cooking, you think so? Trevor Dalgleish is responsible for six movies at the festival, and the deceased, Raymond Fenk, is the California contact on the whole six."

"Great sleuthing," I said. "Where'd you get your touch? Read the complete Nancy Drew when you were a kid?"

"I'm not finished yet."

"Maybe I better re-fortify myself."

I got more ice cubes from the freezer. The Wyborowa was on the table. I put a small splash over the ice.

"All of this is happening up at the Eglinton," Annie said. "Those receptions in the lobby after the last film of the night are apparently a regular feature. Cam Charles's there playing the host. A few press people, the ones who aren't down at the Festival of Festivals. Patrons, guests, a couple of people from the Sri Lanka movie. Very sweet they were, but I couldn't get two useful sentences out of them for my San Francisco articles. So I'm poking around, getting the scoop on the stolen movie cans and everything, and I can't help noticing that Trevor Dalgleish has a new companion. New to me anyway."

"This is terrific, kiddo, the scene-setting," I said.

"But you're wondering where's the action?"

I didn't answer.

"All right," Annie said. "The guy hanging in at Trevor's side, he has four out-front, can't-miss features. Some of this I got from personal observation, the obvious parts. The others I just walked up to Trevor and the guy and put myself in their conversation."

"Bold as brass."

"They didn't exactly make me welcome."

Annie raised her left hand with the four fingers pointing up and the thumb tucked in.

"One," she said, "the guy, name of Darnell Gant, about your age, fortyish, he's black."

Annie brought down her forefinger.

"Two, Darnell is big, even bigger than I remember Fenk being."

The middle finger came down.

"He just flew in, some time in the last couple of days, from his home base, which is none other than Los Angeles."

Only the little finger remained up.

"That's number three, about Los Angeles. Number four, Darnell Gant, the large black man from Los Angeles, was grumpy."

No fingers.

"He was grumpy with Trevor?" I asked. "Or grumpy in general?"

Annie paused for reflection.

"Both," she said. "He was really mad about something, and he was laying it on Trevor because Trevor was maybe part of the cause. It was more than Trevor just happened to be handy."

"And you think," I said, "this new arrival, Mr. Gant, might be Fenk's confederate, the man described to me as large and black and he left the new saxophone case for Dave Goddard?"

"At the place near Los Angeles with bistro in the name."

"Alley Cat Bistro in Culver City."

"That's who I decided it must be when I was thinking about it in the cab over here."

"The other deduction," I said, "you think the reason the guy's angry is he's just heard his buddy Fenk is murdered."

"Isn't it wonderful when we're on the same wavelength?"

"Well, your theory's not bad at all."

"Come on, way better than not bad."

I went around to Annie's side of the table and lifted her up in a hug. She let herself go loose in my arms.

"I'm just starting to come down, you know?" she said after a minute. "So much's been happening. That awful man strangled. Your client's involved. You're in it even deeper. All the stuff I picked up tonight. I mean, holy cow."

Annie was talking into my chest. She leaned away and looked up at me.

She said, her voice less speedy than it had been from the time she arrived, "You think it's useful, about Darnell Gant from L.A. and the rest? In the cab, I kept going back and forth in my mind. First it was far-fetched, then it was crystal clear. Crystal clear was my final decision, but now . . . what the hell?"

"Sweetie," I said, "you were the one, I seem to recall, wanted me to ring the police. All of a sudden, you're out there digging up leads. I love it. It *is* helpful. More than helpful. But, you involved this way, I'm grateful and stunned."

"You started it, buster." Annie slid out of my arms. "Asking me to check out the people from the other five California movies. Don't forget that. The rest, well, it's kind of fascinating, and I know you're not going to let go till everything's straightened out anyway."

"So you declared yourself in for the long haul."

"Not quite. I still think you should get on to the police with all these developments, facts, suspicions, you name it."

Annie picked up her wine glass in one hand. I took the other hand and led her into the living room.

"Let's let it ride for now," I said. "We keep talking about theories, suspects, whether to call the cops, we'll never get any sleep tonight. This kind of thing—you notice—has a tendency to race the blood."

"I noticed."

Annie sat at the end of the sofa and curled her legs under her dress. It was wheat-coloured and clung smashingly to her body. I went over to the record player and looked through the albums in the section where I kept vocalists.

I said, "I have a man here, he'll take away the tension."

I put a record on the player, and Dick Haymes began to sing "Mam'selle."

I sat beside Annie on the sofa, and she said, "With a voice like that, the guy has to be incredibly gorgeous."

"He was."

Annie went to sleep on my shoulder after Haymes sang "What's Good About Goodbye?" I waited until the album finished. The last song was "When Lights Are Low." I carried Annie into the bedroom and undressed her on the bed. She made small noises but didn't wake up. I crawled in beside her. First I took off the Larry Bird T-shirt.

27

BEFORE ANNIE GOT UP, before the *sun* got up, I was on the phone in the kitchen.

No, the operator at the Silverdore Hotel told me, nobody named Darnell Gant registered there.

Too much to expect I'd get lucky first time out.

I opened the telephone book's Yellow Pages. Entries under "Hotels". Nineteen pages of them. Intimidating, but Darnell would probably book into a midtown establishment. Or downtown. Some place handy to Trevor Dalgleish's home or office. That cut down the possibilities.

I got a pen and made check marks opposite the likely hotels. Plaza II. Hampton Court. Carlton Inn. Further downtown, the Holiday Inn behind City Hall, the Royal York. When I finished, I had thirty-six check marks and started dialling.

I snagged Darnell on the nineteenth try.

"I'm putting you through to Mr. Gant's room, sir," the operator said.

"No, no." I was almost screaming into the receiver. "Don't ring him, operator. I just wanted to know if Mr. Gant was at the hotel."

"Yea-hus," the operator said and clicked off.

Darnell had put himself up at the King Edward.

"Making a big racket in here," Annie said from the doorway. "For a heck of an early hour."

It was just coming up to six-fifty.

"I'm hot, kid," I said. "Getting together a little scheme here that ought to wrap up my troubles. Our troubles. Dave Goddard's troubles."

Annie yawned. It was her turn to wear the Larry Bird T-shirt. I had on the maroon dressing gown.

Annie said, "Think you can climb off that high you're on long enough to make coffee?"

Before I answered, Annie wandered toward the living room. Her walk was of a person who wouldn't object to another ten hours of sleep. I put the kettle on the stove and measured four cups' worth of Folger's into the Mr. Coffee. Before the kettle boiled, Annie was back in the doorway.

She said, "I don't suppose, since this time yesterday, you bought a typewriter?"

"I'm hanging on for Christmas."

"'Fraid of that."

Annie went back to the living room.

Ten minutes later, when I took her a tray of orange juice, toasted bran bread, and coffee, she was sitting on the sofa, alert, and scribbling in the ever-present notebook.

"Not yet," she said. "Don't tell me about the scheme yet."

I turned for the kitchen.

"And, hey, thanks," Annie shouted after me. "This smells scrumptious."

I had a shower. Annie finished her piece for *Metro Morning*. I drank coffee in the kitchen. Annie had a shower. I looked out the living-room window into the park. Annie put on the wheat-coloured dress and called a cab.

"Thumbnail sketch," she said to me. "And slide over any parts where you might get your head bonged again."

"Simple," I said. "I'm getting all the suspects together in one room and let the guilty party reveal himself."

"Just like Hercule Poirot."

"Maybe not that cut-and-dried," I said. "But the clues are falling into place."

"I hope you're not banking on the guff about the voices in the other room at the hotel."

"Hum, now you mention it, these Vietnamese guys I was having a drink with yesterday, they talk in a range that might get them tryouts with the Vienna Boys' Choir."

Annie put her hands on her hips and gave me a ray of a look that might have withered lesser men.

"Just kidding," I said.

"What's this about all the possible guilty parties in one room?" Annie said. "That's not such a sterling plan. Suppose the guilty parties outnumber you?"

"Here's the part you should go for," I said. "The cops'll be in on this one."

Annie took my face in both hands and kissed me on the lips.

When she was finished, she said, "You've seen the light."

"I was seeing stars for a minute there," I said. "You want to practise your kissing technique some more?"

"Give me details," Annie said, ignoring my question. "Where's the room you're collecting everybody together? And who's everybody? And how about the police? Is that who you were phoning at the ungodly hour?"

A horn honked three times from outside the house. Annie walked across to the window and looked out.

She said, "First cab driver who actually gets out of his car and rings the doorbell, I'm gonna give him a fifty per cent tip."

"Only if he holds the car door open for you."

"Come on, I'm not asking the moon."

I watched Annie gather up her notes for the morning's radio show. And did my best to keep the edges of guilt and relief off my face. She'd asked too many questions I wasn't ready to answer yet. Saved by the honk of a horn. Annie hoisted her bag, and I followed her down the stairs.

"I'll be on the tear all day," she said, talking to me over her shoulder. "The radio program, two movie screenings, a press conference."

"The interview with good old Day-Lewis."

"Of whom you're no longer jealous."

"Switched my angst to Ted Koppel," I said. "But, look, have I told you about me and Sonia Braga?"

Annie stopped at the bottom of the stairs.

"What's that got to do with anything?" she said. "If it's my opinion you want, I think Sonia Braga's in the top five of the world's sexiest women."

"I think you just stole my thunder."

Annie opened the front door, and we stepped on to the porch.

"I'll phone you between screenings and things, here and at your office," she said. "When we connect, tell me what's happening. Okay?"

"I might be hard to reach myself."

Annie looked at her cab and back to me.

She said, "Just so I know, Crang, no bullshit, whatever you're cooking up, promise me absolutely the police are going to be present and accounted for."

"Cross my heart."

Annie brushed her cheek with mine.

"If all else fails," she said, "if I can't reach you, here's the fallback position—meet me at the Belair any time after eleven tonight."

"Agreed," I said.

Annie brushed my other cheek with her other cheek, and crossed the sidewalk to the cab. I watched as the driver performed a screeching U-turn and barrelled north on Beverley. Annie's arm was waving from the window.

Before she was out of sight, a car pulled into the space at the curb that the cab had vacated. It was a small-sized black Mercedes. Cam Charles stepped out from behind the wheel, and walked briskly around the car and up the three stone steps to my porch.

"An opening question, Cam," I said, pointing at the Mercedes. "Sun Myung Moon give you that thing?"

"Don't be absurd."

"Just wondering." I was still wearing my maroon dressing gown. "Come on up. It's fantastic timing you dropped by. I've got a little assignment for you."

"The shoe's on the other foot, Crang." Cam didn't give the impression he intended to come in off the porch. "It's I who am bringing you a word of advice."

"Just a quick stop on the way to the office?"

"Your phone was busy for forty minutes when I tried earlier," Cam said. His voice sounded put out. "And I need to bring you up to date before you make a complete hash of things."

"Could we just take my déshabillé upstairs and have the discussion?"

Cam trailed after me up to the living room. His eyes darted around the place. I couldn't tell whether he found it wanting.

Cam said, "Trevor intends to have Stuffy Kernohan invite you to his office for questioning about the Fenk murder."

"You can beat Trev to the punch," I said. "That's the assignment I'm talking about."

We were still standing in the middle of the living room.

"We might as well sit," Cam said. He chose the sofa. Recognized quality when he was next to it. I stayed on my feet and spoke first.

"You get to your pal Stuffy," I said. "Tell him this. Tell him to organize a police raid for tonight on a booze can—I'll give you the address—and tell him he'll come up big."

Cam took a long time crossing his legs. He had on a glen plaid suit that put my Cy Mann to shame. Even when my Cy Mann was dry cleaned.

"In the first place, Crang," Cam said, "raiding a so-called booze can isn't in the line of duty for a homicide detective like Stuffy."

"I bet he'll think so if you tell him he can scoop up Fenk's killer in the process."

"Will he? Arrest the person who strangled Raymond Fenk?"

"Got my word on it."

Cam stared at me.

I said, "My unadorned guarantee isn't the standard you're looking for?"

"Hardly."

"Try this for size, Cam," I said. "A bunch of Vietnamese cocaine salesmen run the booze can. Fenk funnelled them a supply of coke from Los Angeles. Indirectly he did the funnelling. But something fouled up the transaction, and that made the Vietnamese very upset. After a while, they got even by putting the choke on Mr. Fenk."

I allowed time for Cam to absorb the first blizzard of facts. He managed it calmly. Didn't uncross his legs.

I said, "Stuffy gets in there fast enough, into the booze can, he'll find himself enough evidence against the coke people, no defence lawyer could get them off. Including you."

"Do I assume," Cam said, "that Trevor is involved in what you've just described?"

"In the cocaine end," I said. "And his involvement is as tight as . . ."

I stopped to root around for the appropriately expressive simile.

"As tight as a gnat's ass stretched over a rain barrel," Cam said, unsmiling. "Is that about it?"

"Terrific," I said. "Where'd you get the line?"

"From a prominent rock musician. A client."

"Yeah, well, that's how tight Trevor's in the cocaine business." Cam tapped his forefinger on his chin and looked thoughtful.

"Leaving aside Trevor for the moment," he said, "something you overlook, Crang, it would take the police days to mount the sort of raid you apparently have in mind."

"Put it to Kernohan this way," I said. "In one night's work, the cops nab a killer, cut off a cocaine dealer who's right up there with General Motors for organization, and close down a booze can, which I gather from the papers isn't a victory they've experienced lately. Or ever."

"Manpower, equipment, coordination," Cam said. "The preparation's monumental."

"This isn't just crime-busting, Cam," I said. "For the police, this is what's called a public-relations coup."

"I could perhaps sound Stuffy out," Cam said without much in the way of enthusiasm.

"Sounding out, Cam, I could look after that myself," I said. "From you, I'm asking for a different level altogether. Persuasion."

"See your point," Cam said. His voice was developing a purr.

The flattery I was laying on Cam, the ego-stroking, might get him partly around to my side. But I needed a more practical argument. A clincher.

"Damage control, Cam," I said. "That's the advantage in sending Stuffy in at the head of the troops."

"How so?"

"Trevor's in with the coke gang," I said. "No doubt about that. None, zip. *Nada.* So, okay, if he's busted by cops from the drug squad, as he's bound to be one of these days the way he's carrying on, it'll be messy. Names in the press, splashy trial, other criminal lawyers snickering behind their hands at your firm. You can anticipate what I mean, Cam, the public humiliation."

Cam showed no sign he was about to go into panic, but I knew his mind was all mine for the moment.

"But," I said, "suppose Stuffy Kernohan's calling the shots on this raid at the booze can that's going to produce the goods on Trevor, among other illegalities. Good old friendly, understanding, cooperative Stuffy. See where I'm going, Cam? Stuffy can play it any way you want with Trevor. Maybe just throw a scare into Trev. Tell him he's got a choice, deal cocaine and go to the slammer or practise law and stay on the street. You and Stuffy work out the approach in advance. However it goes down, you can avoid all those other nasty consequences. No snickering lawyers, no embarrassment in the public prints."

There wasn't a gap, a blink, a millisecond between the end of my pitch and Cam's next words.

"I'll speak to Stuffy," he said. "*Persuade* him."

"That's my boy, Cam."

"You can count on the raid," Cam said, his face firm and steely.

"Women find that sensual, Cam?" I said. "Your decisiveness?"

A sound like harrumph came from Cam's throat.

"Your point about Trevor is well taken," he said. "But what you've told me raises other questions."

"And I got answers, Cam. But how about later? Both of us have places to go, people to see, raids to synchronize."

"For example," Cam said, apparently not inclined to vacate the sofa yet, "if Raymond Fenk was involved with the cocaine gang at this booze can, isn't that going to reflect badly on my film festival?"

"Maybe it just presents another opportunity for you and Stuffy Kernohan to play ball."

"You understand what I mean when I say questions need to be answered?"

"All in good time," I said. "I'll brief you later tonight, post raid."

"Debrief."

"Meantime you put the sale on Stuffy."

I gave Cam the details. Location and layout of Big Bam's booze can. The optimum time for attack. Nature of resistance.

"Timing is all," I said. "Otherwise I could be left on the spot. That's as in, get the shit kicked out of me."

My warning didn't make a dent in Cam's sense of concern. He was still mulling over consequences closer to his own interest.

"I'm giving an after-theatre reception tonight," he said. "Come by and assure me everything went as arranged in the raid."

"Debrief you."

"At the Belair Café until one or so in the morning."

"The Belair? I was heading in that direction anyway."

"You might say I'm invading the other side's territory," Cam said, wearing a crooked little grin. "The Festival of Festivals people think the Belair's exclusively theirs."

Cam lifted himself off the sofa.

"One last piece of data," I said to him. "Where's Trevor apt to be this morning?"

"He has a ten-o'clock bail application at the College Park Courts," Cam said. "After that, I've no idea."

Cam left without asking why I was interested in Trevor's whereabouts, and I made a run for the kitchen radio. Too late. Or almost too late. Annie was winding up her movie review. She was discussing a baseball movie. The sportscaster, not missing a trick, jumped in to raise his own point about baseball films. Mentions of *The Natural* and *Bull Durham* and *Bang the Drum Slowly* whizzed by.

"The absolute low point in baseball movies," Annie said, sounding like someone with a lock on the very last word, "the scene that hit rock bottom for authenticity, was in *Fear Strikes Out.* Tony Perkins played Jimmy Piersall, and in one scene he tries to catch a fly ball with his wrists together."

Where did *that* come from? I went into the bedroom and got dressed. I knew for a certainty Annie had never seen the inside of a ball park, real-life or TV. I put on an elderly but still presentable tweed jacket, my grey flannels, a blue shirt, and a tie with maroon stripes. So where did Annie acquire the bit of expertise on Tony Perkins's lousy catching style? And how'd she blow it by so convincingly on the radio? I walked south on Beverley to my first appointment. It was a lesson to keep in mind, what Annie had done. If you sound authoritative, chances are you can talk your way through brick walls and other, more human obstacles.

28

THE CLERK BEHIND THE DESK at the King Edward said Mr. Gant was having breakfast in the Victoria Room. Couldn't miss him, the clerk said. The clerk had a smirk on his face. Most guys behind desks in expensive hotels wear smirks. Probably learn how in first-year Hotel Management.

My heels made echoing clacks on the marble floor of the King Eddie's lobby. It was a rich sound. Everything about the King Edward sounded, looked, and smelled rich. Darnell Gant must have been a fellow in the chips.

I stood at the entrance of the Victoria Room. The clerk was right. I couldn't have missed Mr. Gant. He was the only black guy in the room. Also the biggest. Most handsome. Best-dressed. The man couldn't be all perfect. Probably didn't know the Johnny Mercer lyrics to "Early Autumn".

"Mr. Gant's expecting me," I fibbed to the maître d'. He was another smirker.

Gant was at a table for four, and over the settings for the other three people he'd scattered newspapers. *Wall Street Journal. USA Today. Financial Post.* He was reading the business section of the *New York Times* early edition. He seemed only mildly curious to find me standing at his table.

"I'm Crang," I said.

"Oh yeah," Gant said. "The gentleman who's going into custody today."

He moved some newspapers out of the way and motioned me to sit down. He was eating eggs Benedict.

"That'd be Trevor Dalgleish talking," I said.

"Only man I know in Toronto," Gant said. "You want some breakfast? Very good with the eggs Benedict here."

"Anything on the menu got a lot of fruit?"

"Compote they call it."

"That and coffee."

Gant had the waiter at our table with a flick of his hand. If I were the waiter, I'd have hustled too. Gant looked like he began life as a large piece of granite, and some sculptor very long on imagination devoted a decade or so to chiselling away at it. His build was powerful, not weightlifter powerful, more like athletic, born-to-it powerful. He had black hair in tight little curls, a high forehead, an aquiline nose, full lips, and a chin with a dimple in it. The combination was pleasing, especially, I'd wager, to the ladies. He had on a tan suit that looked Rodeo Drive expensive. He knew how to eat eggs Benedict without dripping yolk.

I said, "I expect Trevor's given you a rundown on me."

"A lawyer and a loose cannon."

"Those were his words?"

"Some of them," Gant said. "The rest were about how you're shielding the man who killed Ray Fenk. Sorry to hear about that."

"Sorry about me shielding the guy Trevor says killed Fenk?"

"No," Gant said. "About who the killer is. Dave Goddard. Always loved the way he plays tenor. Sounds like Stan Getz in the old days."

"He does," I said. "But, this is the real goods, none of that about Dave counts. He didn't do anything to Fenk except try to avoid him."

The waiter set down the compote in front of me. It had eight or nine fruits. All fresh. I started on the blueberries.

"Another thing," I said, "I know the last place you heard Dave play."

Gant looked at me, not much more curious than he appeared when I first showed up at his table.

"Culver City," I said. "Alley Cat Bistro, club in a shopping mall next to a shoe store."

"Not bad," Gant said, and went back to the eggs and other rich stuff.

"What I'm going to do," I said, "I'm going to tell you a story, and when I get to a part that isn't accurate, *if* I get to a part that isn't accurate, you say stop."

Gant poured himself more coffee from the silver pot on the table and got rearranged in his chair.

"Fenk dealt cocaine," I said. "That's when he wasn't cranking out movies that don't qualify for Oscars. You were a partner, associate, aide, something or other, in the coke line. He struck a deal with Trevor Dalgleish to peddle twenty-four kilos of the normal goods. The two of them, Fenk and Trevor, probably made their first connection when Trevor went shopping in California for movies to show up here at the Alternate Film Festival. My guess is Trevor got on to *Hell's Barrio*, and that took him naturally to Fenk. From there, one thing led to another. Movies to drugs. Fenk must have allowed as how he sold cocaine, and Trevor must have come back with, well, now, isn't that a coincidence, he happened to be in a cocaine-buying mood."

Gant's only reactions, as I talked, were to raise and lower his coffee cup and adjust his smile of irony.

"When it came to shipping the stuff up here, the cocaine," I said, "Fenk got this fiendishly clever notion. He stuck the cocaine in cans of film. And the thing was, he had a lot of cans to choose from because, apart from *Hell's Barrio*, he was the California contact man, no doubt by appointment from Trevor, for the five other movies from down Hollywood way. No difficulty for him to pack the coke in with the movies and ship them on to Toronto. But for some reason or other he didn't want to risk putting the coke in the cans that held his own film. I doubt the reasons were artistic. Probably nerves. He already had two coke convictions, and on the off chance the cops or customs people, anyone in authority, got to the coke before Trevor, Fenk didn't want to be roped in as the owner of the film and of the cans that held it. So he came up with the idea of making Dave Goddard the unwitting deliveryman of the four kilos of coke that weren't in the other people's film cans."

"Stop," Gant said.

He had his right hand in the air.

"That was my idea," he said. "The coke in Dave Goddard's saxophone case. Pretty inspired, you agree?"

"I suppose, if it didn't involve Dave," I said. "He's had enough trouble coping with the world, he didn't need that."

"Maybe," Gant said. He fiddled with his empty coffee cup. "But the idea worked as an alternative to the film cans. I knew Goddard was going from the Alley Cat to Toronto. Read it in *DownBeat*. And it was a snap to switch his old case for the new case. Four kilos in the lining, he'd never notice."

"Then Fenk started screwing up at this end."

"The man could be irrational," Gant said. "But I didn't expect he'd get into some kind of fight with Goddard, and Goddard'd strangle the dumb SOB."

"Dave didn't. That's the message I'm trying to get across."

"I hear you," Gant said, not at all irritable, but maybe not believing me either.

With all the chatter, I'd still polished off the fruit dish. Very tasty. Marvellous what money can do. I went for the coffeepot. It was empty. The waiter was over with a fresh pot in a blink.

"All the rest I told you was on the money?" I said to Gant. "The story I just spun?"

"What'd you call me? Ray's *aide*?" Gant looked pained. "Not me, not for a guy like Ray Fenk. I got other irons in the fire, but, yeah, I gave Ray a hand now and then when the job shaped up profitable."

"Well, this job's gone kind of awry."

"Awry?" Gant said. "Man's been murdered. You call that *awry*?"

"The violence may not be over," I said. "Reason is Trevor's customer up here is still short the four kilos from Dave Goddard's case, and he's not a man to hesitate doing damage to anybody between him and the cocaine."

"Who you suppose's got the four kilos?"

"Who else?" I said. "Trevor."

"Wrong."

"How's that?"

"I got 'em."

That brought me up short, and my face probably showed it.

"Well, now, Mr. Gant," I said, "you *are* a crackerjack."

Gant was doing more hand-flicking for service.

When the waiter came on the fly, Gant said to him, "What I taste right now is a Bloody Mary."

"That's a disappointment, sir," the waiter said. "The bar isn't open."

Gant looked at me.

"The law," I said. "Funny laws up here."

"Two serious guys like us?" Gant said. "Having a serious discussion? Can't have a serious drink?"

"Welcome to town," I said.

Gant asked the waiter again for a Bloody Mary, but, he said, hold the vodka.

"Crang, you're looking like my idea of a man got some smarts," Gant said to me. "Listen up to this. Tomorrow night, I'm meeting important folks in Beverly Hills. That means tonight, tomorrow morning latest, I'm gone from here. I need to get this whoo-rah about the four K tidied up quick, as in immediately. You want to help? *Expedite*? For a fee?"

"What's the matter with the guy you've been using up till now? Trevor?"

"Last Saturday," Gant said, "I got a message on my answering machine. Ray Fenk called. Said something's not right with our Toronto contact. Said he was stashing the last four K of coke, Fenk was, and I should phone him back at his hotel. Sunday I called, and I got the cops on the other end. Took a few minutes of fencing, but the cops finally told me Ray's dead."

"I hate those things."

"What? Cops?" Gant said. "Necessary to society's smooth functioning."

"Not cops," I said. "Answering machines I hate."

Gant got his Virgin Mary.

"Let me get a few things straight," I said. "How'd you put your hands on the cocaine so fast? You've only been here, what, day and a half?"

"Crang, here's a lesson you should keep in mind on things to hate and not hate," Gant said. "It was all on the answering machine. Ray said he'd reserve a hotel room for me and leave the package of coke at the desk. Man did me all right on the hotel, give him credit. I like the King Edward just fine."

"So the coke wasn't in Fenk's briefcase?"

"What briefcase?"

"The one whoever killed him probably took out of his hotel room."

"You just lost me."

"Never mind. If you've got the coke, it may not have much bearing on who did what at the Silverdore."

Gant was admiring his Virgin Mary.

"Funny thing," he said. "This tastes like it oughta taste, but later on I'm not gonna feel as good as I oughta feel."

"Have I got this part right?" I said. "Trevor doesn't know the four K are in your safekeeping?"

"Hasn't got any bulletins on that from me," Gant said. "And isn't about to."

"Trevor must be in a bit of a pet."

"Man's very, very angry. Wants his coke. Doesn't know where to look."

"See, something you may not be aware of, Mr. Gant," I said. "Trevor's already in pocket the money he was fronted by his buyer.

That'd be the gentleman with the penchant for violence I mentioned earlier, and what he's looking for from Trevor is the money back or delivery of the drugs."

"Way I look at Trevor Dalgleish's problems," Gant said, "Ray Fenk's message told me, where Trevor's concerned, watch out. Ray didn't say what went wrong. But I'm taking Ray's advice, advice of a dead man. I'm watching out for Trevor. Let him look after his own little quarrel with the bad guys."

"How about yourself?" I said. "You got any hesitation doing your own deal with these people? The bad guys?"

Gant took a moment to twirl the suggestion around his mental apparatus, which I was beginning to assess as formidable.

"Sell the four kilograms direct to Trevor's customer?" he said. "Let the customer stay on his own to recover the money he's fronted Trevor?"

I nodded, and felt pleasantly optimistic about the course the conversation was steering.

"And," Gant said, "a cute incidental, I keep the money Trevor's already paid Fenk and me for the original purchase."

"Sell the same goods twice."

"And hit American Airlines back to L.A. tonight."

"Well, no, early flight tomorrow."

Gant showed impatience for the first time.

"The customer's buying, I'm selling," he said. "Why not you and I get the goods outa my room upstairs and catch a cab right now wherever this man conducts his trade? Allow me to get on back to civilization and order my Bloodies any hour I please?"

I shook my head.

"Can't be helped," I said.

Gant wasn't ready to give in.

"Explain it," he said.

"Eleven o'clock tonight," I said. "You bring the, um, product to a booze can."

"I hear you clear? A *booze can*?"

"It's a place, people buy drinks all night, dance, sniff coke, that kind of thing."

"At home," Gant said, "in Los Angeles, we call that a nightclub. Or a restaurant."

"Well, you know, different country, different customs, different laws."

Gant looked at the remains of his Virgin Mary.

"Sunday night," he said, "not one damn store'd sell me a six-pack."

"Some laws we got up here," I said, "I make a living defending people against them."

"Growth industry, the picture I'm getting."

"All right," I said, "we're on for tonight?"

"Best offer I've had," Gant said. "Who'm I doing trade with? Who's this mean boss at the booze can?"

"A Vietnamese name of Big Bam."

"Oh, man, *no*." Gant let out a deep laugh that attracted long looks from neighbouring tables. He'd already been drawing a share of glances, especially from a fantastically sultry red-haired woman in a green silk dress.

"Oh, man," Gant said. "Big *Bam*? What TV show these people watch?"

"Face to face," I said, "on his turf, if I were you, I wouldn't mock the guy's name."

"Touchy, is he?"

"Got a whole gang of henchmen."

"Well, I got a whole gang of coke I imagine'll put him in a receptive mood."

"Just don't kid around."

"Eleven tonight, and what else? Run me down."

I gave Gant the drill. Told him the booze can's address. Said I'd arrange for someone on the steel door to take him through to Big Bam's office. And mentioned he could forget about a fee for me.

"What's this?" Gant said. He looked genuinely puzzled.

I said, "This is all part of the service to my client. And you're not my client."

"Lucky for one of us."

"Dave Goddard's my client."

"Sure," Gant said. "But if he didn't kill Ray, who did?"

"I think I know," I said. "But I'm hoping the truth'll come out in the wash."

"Out in the wash?" Gant said. "That a legal expression you Canadian lawyers favour?"

"Mostly," I said, "it's confined to my practice."

Gant decided on another Virgin Mary and made circling motions around the top of his empty glass. The waiter noticed.

Gant said, "Ray Fenk wasn't a guy you'd want to see married to your sister. Not *my* sister. But let's say I'd be intrigued to know who murdered him."

"Almost guarantee it," I said. "Before you leave the country."

"Glad of that."

I didn't know whether Gant meant he'd be glad to learn the killer's identity or glad to leave the country. He sipped at his new Virgin Mary, and I tried to think of ways to make my departure politely. I had everything I needed from Gant, much more than I expected, and there seemed no need to stick around for social reasons.

"You looking to cut out, Crang?" Gant asked.

"Got an errand to run, now you bring it up."

"Good," Gant said. "I might see if that red-headed lady in the nice green dress got anything in mind besides staring."

I shook Gant's hand and walked out of the Victoria Room and across the lobby. I could have left by the side door, but I wanted to hear my heels clack on the marble floor one more time.

29

SOMEBODY HAD RECENTLY thrown up on the carpet in the waiting room at the College Park courts. It didn't make much difference to the carpet. It was already a collage of stains, cigarette burns, and other suspect blemishes. But it made a difference to the air in the immediate vicinity. The air was of a spectacular ripeness, and everybody waiting for business in the courts had beat a retreat to the far end of the corridor. I walked past the crowd and through the waiting room to the bail court. I managed not to inhale the whole way.

By some quirk of custom—or maybe somebody from the Ontario Attorney General's office actually arranged it this way—all women who are being held in custody in Toronto have their bail hearings at the Provincial Courts in the College Park Building. Men come up for bail in the courts down at Old City Hall. The College Park Building used to be beautiful. It's at the corner of College and Yonge, and when I was younger, it was the uptown branch of Eaton's department store, and had a gorgeous auditorium. I once heard Dizzy Gillespie's big band play there. When Eaton's sold off the building, various merchants of a cut-rate sort took over part of it, and the provincial government took over the rest for its courts. Now it was a place where people threw up in the waiting rooms.

I sat down at the back of the bail court. The time wasn't much after ten, and the hearing must have just got under way. Trevor Dalgleish was on his feet and talking to the judge. His voice, forget the tenor pitch and the middling Atlantic accent, had a resonance to it. A good balance of reason and passion. For a guy who dealt cocaine as a sideline, Trevor was an impressive counsel.

Trevor's client was standing in the prisoners' box. She was thin, blonde, freckled, and had a defiant look. The judge was a woman, and so was the crown attorney. The crown attorney interrupted Trevor to say something about the blonde being a terrorist. Trevor said that was inflammatory, and the judge agreed with him. Trevor talked for ten uninterrupted minutes, and I began to catch the gist of things. The defiant blonde had been nabbed with a crate of Uzi submachine guns in her apartment. The armament was intended for some Nicaraguans. But one fact nobody mentioned was which Nicaraguans. Sandinistas? Or Contras? Turned out it didn't much matter. The judge refused to grant bail whichever side the blonde was on. She'd have to stay in the slammer until her trial came up.

Trevor's back was to me through the twenty minutes of the hearing. But when he walked over to say a few consoling words to his client, he noticed me. I seemed to distract him. He was talking to the client, but his eyes kept wandering to me. The defiant blonde finally turned to see what was behind her. I smiled and waved to her. She smiled back. With the smile, she looked less defiant. I hoped she was on the Sandinista side. Always thought they were the good guys.

Trevor marched down the centre aisle of the courtroom.

He said to me, "You're either dumber than I thought, Crang, or you've got a load of gall."

"A third alternative, Trev," I said. "I'm here as a bearer of glad tidings."

The judge called another bail application, and the lawyers collected themselves to make their arguments.

"If we have to talk," Trevor said, "let's do it in the waiting room."

"Wouldn't recommend that."

When we got out of the courtroom and into the ripeness, Trevor said, "This is disgusting."

"Buy you a coffee downstairs," I said. "Or you want smelling salts?"

We took a table in a speedy-service place on the ground floor. The seats were bright yellow and made of slippery stuff that made you think you'd slide on to the floor any minute. Probably part of the speedy service. Keep the customers on edge.

Trevor said, "My first call, when I get back to the office, this might interest you to know, Crang, is to the homicide squad."

"Might have trouble there, Trev," I said. "Stuffy Kernohan's tied up today."

"What're you talking about?"

I skated past the question.

"The real subject we got to talk about," I said, "is your troubles with Big Bam."

"No, you don't, Crang." Trevor looked like he was about to huff and puff. "The real subject is you, Ray Fenk, and some Dixieland musician named Goddard."

"Get it off your chest, Trev," I said. "But one clarification. Dave plays bebop. Not Dixieland. *Yechh.*"

"Ray Fenk was strangled with this musician's saxophone strap," Trevor said. "His name was stamped on it. Stuffy told us that, Cam and me. What I don't believe Stuffy is aware of yet, but what I made it my business to find out, is how intimately you're connected to Goddard."

"Big deal, Trev. I practically told you at the Eglinton Theatre the other night Dave Goddard was my client."

"He's more than your client."

"Well, let's see. At a guess, I'd say you've been working the phones. Talked to Abner Chase, and, who else, Dave's brother Ralph?"

"And Harp Manley," Trevor said. "And my conclusion from adding up all the bits and pieces about your clearly close relationship with Goddard is that you know what he's guilty of and where he's presently hiding himself."

"Accessory after the fact?" I said. "That's the charge you think the cops should arrest me on? Accessory after the fact of Fenk's murder?"

"As a lawyer, an officer of the court," Trevor said, "it's my duty to report knowledge I hold concerning a crime. Particularly murder."

Trevor's palaver was fretting at my nerves. He was breaking new frontiers in pomposity. But I had to let him unload before he'd settle down long enough for me to get in my innings.

"Want to hear something funny, Trev?" I said. "In court upstairs, you sounded good. Convincing. Very controlled. Down here, out in the real world, you got a tendency to bluster."

"Enough," Trevor said and started to stand up. He had trouble with the slippery seat.

I said, "You heard the name I invoked at the beginning of this conflab? Big Bam?"

"An associate of some clients of mine," Trevor said. He was still riding on the pomposity.

"Here's another name for you," I said. "Darnell Gant."

Trevor said, "If you're trying to make things seem more than they are, Crang, you can just forget it. Darnell Gant was a friend of Ray Fenk's from Los Angeles. Naturally he's grieved by his friend's murder."

"Cutting through the bull," I said, "Big Bam is a cocaine retailer in Toronto. Fenk, with occasional assistance from Darnell Gant, was a cocaine wholesaler in California. And you're the entrepreneur who played both sides to your own nifty profit. How much profit, I don't know. Two thousand bucks per kilo maybe?"

Trevor held a steady gaze on me. He was probably balancing a pair of conflicting inclinations. Should he carry his righteous innocence all the way? Or give in to curiosity about what I might really know?

I said, "Just like you, Trev, I've done some homework. One difference though."

Trevor waited a bit before he asked, "What's the difference?"

I said, "I'm not running off to Stuffy Kernohan and the other cops with my parcel of information."

"It's all preposterous," Trevor said. His voice had tailed off in the pomposity content.

"Here's the good news, Trev, the glad tidings," I said. "I got a handle on the missing four kilograms you're so worried about."

Trevor kept his silence. It must have been driving him nuts.

"The four K that were supposed to be in one of the film cans for *Hell's Barrio* but weren't," I said. "Want me to keep going?"

"As long as you're talking hypothetically," Trevor said.

"Okay," I said. "You made a deal to sell twenty-four kilos of cocaine to Big Bam. We'll call it hypothetical for the moment. That's on your selling side. On your buying side, you struck an arrangement with Raymond Fenk in California to take twenty-four K off his hands. Now comes the shipment part. Twenty kilos were tucked in the cans of five of the movies Fenk sent up to the Alternate Film Festival. Probably for each movie, Fenk added an extra can and stuffed it with coke instead of film. It was all done just like Fenk told you it'd be. Except the *Hell's Barrio* film cans were empty. You know why? 'Course you don't. Because Fenk and Gant switched the four K from the film cans to Dave Goddard's saxophone case. The lining in the case."

Trevor's face flushed medium red.

"Light starting to go on, Trev?" I said.

"You and this Goddard've got the cocaine," Trevor said. His voice had gone raspy.

"I thought we were talking hypothetically."

"You son of a *bitch*."

"*I'm* a son of a bitch?" I said. "You're the guy who was talking a minute ago about having me locked up. Accessory after the fact and all."

"How much do you want?" Trevor asked.

"Money? Now I know we've left hypothetical behind."

Trevor's hands were making clenching movements.

I said, "What I don't get, Trev, is why you haven't made peace with Big Bam the easy way. Just give him back the money he paid you up front for the missing four K. Apologize. Tell him it was a deal that happened not to pan out. He seems to be an understanding guy.

223

Potentially anyway. How come you're annoying him this way? Not returning Truong's calls? Avoiding the guys?"

Trevor said, still raspy, "The money had been *spent*. This is none of your business, Crang, but I apparently have to deal with you. The money I earned from the deal, *all* the money, was on the way out the instant I received it. I have very heavy financial obligations."

"Sure, I get it, the high lifestyle," I said. "But, jeez, how long'd you think you could steer clear of Big Bam and his minions?"

"I don't need to discuss this, Crang."

"Just wondering."

"As long as it took to get together enough money to repay him. Or to find that damned four kilograms."

"And now here I am with the four K."

"Here you are," Trevor said. His voice had lost most of the rasp, and his skin colour was closer to normal. No more fist-clenching either. Trevor was a guy with a temper that's usually called hair-trigger.

He said, "Let me repeat my question, Crang. How much do you and Goddard want for the cocaine?"

"Not a sou, Trev."

Trevor took a moment to adjust to the answer.

"What," he said, "is your intention?"

"My game? My angle? My edge? My—"

Trevor interrupted.

"Get the *fuck* to the answer," he said. His temper was making a return engagement.

"All you have to do," I said, "is show up at Big Bam's place around eleven tonight, the booze can over by Western Hospital, and I'll make sure the four kilograms are on the premises."

"Just like that."

"I'll be there too."

"How wonderful of you." Trevor was displaying his talent for sarcasm. "You're telling me I should walk into the place of business of a man who has reason to be angry with me, all on your word you'll rectify the situation. *Your* word."

"I already told Big Bam you'd be coming."

"Lord, Crang." Trevor wasn't showing anger or sarcasm any more. Closer to helpless resignation. "You really have invited yourself into my life, haven't you."

"Circumstances invited me," I said. "But, coast on this, Trev, I'm the only guy can ease your woes."

"*If* you're telling the truth about the four kilograms."

"Check out the reasoning," I said. "How else would I know about the stuff being hidden in the lining of Dave's saxophone case? You didn't have that information, right? If Fenk'd told you, you wouldn't be in your current pickle. And Darnell Gant arrived up here after the fact, after the four kilos were gone from the saxophone case."

Trevor went into a deep-think look. Maybe I'd fed him too much. The part about Gant might be skimming close to the danger zone. I couldn't be absolutely sure big Darnell hadn't told Trevor anything about the shipment arrangements for the four kilos. Was I getting too risky? Probably not. No, *definitely* not. Trevor had been genuinely surprised when I told him about the coke in the saxophone case, and Gant seemed to be giving me the straight goods when he said he didn't trust Trevor and hadn't uttered a word to him about the coke in the case.

I said, "I'm not just your best bet, Trev. I'm your only bet."

"What do you get out of this?" Trevor's question was in the spirit of a tough cross-examiner.

"You don't believe it's the generosity of my spirit?"

"Look at my face, Crang. I'm not laughing."

"In the long run," I said, "what I'm doing ought to help save my client. In the short run, too, with any luck."

"And perhaps there's more," Trevor said. "In exchange for returning the four kilos, you expect me to keep silent about your connections with this musician."

"Hadn't crossed my mind, Trev," I said. "Anyway, the master of homicide you and Cam keep talking about, the Stuffer, he should be able to put me and Dave together. Eventually he should, if it matters."

Trevor let that one lie.

I said, "What is it, Trev? In or out on the gathering at Big Bam's?"

"As you say, my range of options is limited."

"Let's call it eleven o'clock."

Trevor nodded in an abstract kind of way, and his teeth were clenched. Not his hands this time, his teeth.

"At the booze can," I said.

Another of the same nods. Also the same clench of teeth. I couldn't tell whether Trevor was working toward another release of temper or just woolgathering.

I said, "You don't have other pressing engagements tonight?"

"Crang," Trevor said, "if you're horsing around with me, if you don't deliver the four kilograms, if you put me in a worse jam with Big Bam, if *anything* goes wrong, I'm going to come down on you from a great height."

"Incredible, Trev," I said. "The way you said all that without unclenching your teeth."

Trevor stood up. The slippery seat didn't hamper him this time.

"The first thing," he said, "I'll rip out your tongue."

Trevor started to walk away. I stopped him.

"That client of yours upstairs," I said, "the blonde with the freckles and the Uzis, she doing it for the Sandinistas or the Contras?"

"Neither," Trevor said. "There's a third force building down there."

Trevor left the speedy-service place.

A third force? Did Ollie North know about this?

30

I **STEERED CLEAR** of people for the rest of the daylight hours. Not just Cam Charles and Darnell Gant and Big Bam and everybody connected to the whole gruesome Fenk case, but people in general. Mankind. I went down to the waterfront and took a ferry across Toronto harbour to Centre Island.

In July and August the island is jammed with tourists, sun worshippers, and anyone else looking for a quick escape from the city. By early September the traffic slopes off, and on this day I shared the place with a small and manageable bunch of other strays. I walked all the way across the island to the Lake Ontario side, sat on a bench, and looked out at the waves.

Trevor shouldn't be let off the hook. The argument I used on Cam was mostly bull. Necessary, but bull. Get Stuffy Kernohan to lead the raid on Big Bam's place and he'd be in position to grease Trevor's way out of his jackpot. That worked as an argument to Cam. Show him why it was in his best interests to have Stuffy on the job. That was *his* best interests. I was thinking of *my* best interests. I needed the cops' help at the big confrontation that night.

But allow Trevor to take a walk? No way. I had to cook up something that'd send him down the tubes with Big Bam and company. Not nail Trevor for Fenk's murder. Just for his cocaine offenses. It must have been Big Bam who did the murder. Or ordered it done. I wasn't clear on how to prove Bam was responsible, despite all the assurances I fed Cam about his certain guilt, but there was bound to be some way of pinning the killing on Bam. Maybe getting one of the underlings to spill the beans. Cut some kind of deal. Let it all come out in the wash. Out in the wash? Darnell Gant was right. It was a feeble approach.

A hot-dog stand was open near the island's ferry docks. I bought two dogs and a soda water, and carried them back to my bench. No nutrition, but out in the air, the sun, the breeze off the lake, the lunch tasted good in a sinful sort of way.

What about Darnell Gant? He was a needed part of the charade I was staging at Bam's place. Gant would show up with the four kilos of coke, and that'd stir Bam and Trevor into a revelatory exchange of views and insults and other spicy things. That was Gant's role.

But what else about Darnell Gant? Well, he seemed a nice guy for a dope dealer. And he had other irons in the fire, he said, Beverly Hills irons. I wouldn't worry about him. A guy with his muscle and wit could take care of himself in a pinch. Even in a police raid. On my list of matters to be resolved, Gant didn't figure. My main concern was to get Fenk's murderer under wraps, thereby freeing Dave Goddard of any suspicion in the dirty deed. Gant wasn't in Toronto when Fenk took his last breath. That put him in the clear. My inclination was to leave Gant on his own. Fenk's last breath? That must have been an ugly sight.

Towards three, the sun got hotter. I took off my jacket, bunched it into a pillow, and stretched out on the bench. Two hours later, the late-afternoon chill woke me out of a drowse. I unbunched my jacket and road the ferry back to the city.

At home, the phone didn't ring. No call from Annie. On the other hand, I only stayed around long enough to change into jeans, a blue work shirt, grey wool sweater, and my Rockport Walkers. Also long enough for one vodka on the rocks. Just right to steel the resolve, but not to fuzz the brain.

I dawdled the ten or twelve blocks to the booze can's neighbour-hood, picked up a container of take-out chow mein, and settled in to reconnoitre. From the outside, Big Bam's place looked like any other homely warehouse. The double steel door with the peephole was on the side of the building. To get to it, people would have to pass through the gate in the chain-link fence and walk down an alley that was about ten feet wide. That was on the east side of the building. On the west, there was another ten-foot gap between the building and a second warehouse that was the same height. The neighbouring warehouse was equally homely. And definitely empty. Unless it was another booze can with even better security than Big Bam's place.

My reconnoitring kept me in a lane next to a house across the street. The house was painted in a shade close to chartreuse. Over at Bam's, all was quiet until ten o'clock when two guys came out through the steel door and took up position at the gate in the chain-link fence. I didn't recognize the two guys, but I recognized their style in shirts, worn outside the pants, hanging loose. Yo, guys, I know what you got under there. Maybe, though, if these guys were doormen or greeters or bouncers, they were packing something else besides walkie-talkies. Weapons maybe. Something to keep interlopers at bay. That wouldn't be my worry. Might be a concern for Stuffy and his cops.

Five minutes went by, uneventful, before a car stopped at the gate. It was big and American, probably a Lincoln, and the driver waited while three people got out. A man and two women, mid-thirties, dressed to party. One woman had on a satiny red dress that would stop traffic. So would her figure. Buxom and hippy.

"Want me to order you a drink?" the guy with the two women called to the guy at the wheel of the Lincoln. "What? Scotch?"

The answer was muffled.

"I'll be on the dance floor, honey," the woman in red shouted to the guy in the car.

Ooh, ooh, her on the dance floor. That I had to check out.

The Lincoln pulled away, presumably to find a parking spot, and the two guards on the gate swung it open and let the happy threesome through.

"We the first?" the guy in the group asked.

One of the guards nodded his head.

"I'm gonna get in there and *shake*," Red Dress said with a little yip in her voice.

Go to it, big gal.

The three frisked down the alley to the steel door. They turned in profile to me, and I couldn't monitor exactly what was going on. But, at a guess, I'd have said someone was examining them through the peephole. It didn't take long. The three seemed to be regulars. There was a quick splash of light as the door opened, and the guy and two women disappeared into the booze can. The quick splash of light disappeared too.

Thirty seconds later, another couple arrived, both in silks and leathers. Then a party of six, likewise chic. Did nobody ugly or shabby patronize the joint? Then a guy alone, probably the Lincoln's driver and Red Dress's honey back from parking the car. Then an erect, silver-haired gent who could have passed himself off as any country's president except he was escorting two girls who could have passed themselves off as Lolitas. Then a group, all guys, who had haircuts like Leonard Cohen's. Then a grey stretch limo with a TV aerial on the back. The limo released too many people for me to catch in a fast count. All I knew for sure was that the last person out of the back seat had on a clown getup. Just come from a masquerade? Maybe going to a masquerade.

The flood was on. People streamed in, all of them with the looks of a prime-time crowd. The gate's guardians gave the arrivals a close once-over and turned away no one. Neither did the guy on duty at the peephole. In fifteen minutes, by a rough estimate. I clocked about sixty men and women into Big Bam's booze can.

Time for me to join them.

31

THE TWO LADS on the gate patted me down. That hadn't happened to anyone else. Must have been my jeans. And the voice that went with the eyes at the peephole asked my name. I answered truthfully. The peephole snapped shut, and twenty seconds went by before the steel door pulled open. A guy inside ran a metal detector over me.

"What's this about?" I asked. The guy might have been one of the lookouts from the afternoon at the Pits.

"It's about seeing if you got a gun. A knife," the guy said. "You never been here before."

"Big Bam's expecting me."

"I know," the searcher said, stepping back. "Have a nice night."

"I'll try."

I was shouting. The music from the giant speakers in the corners poured out at high volume. It was music that was heavy on repetition. Lot of bass guitar. Synthesizers. Overdubbing. It pounded through the huge space.

The busty dame in the red dress didn't mind the racket. She was on the midnight-blue dance floor shaking her formidable person. Her partner was the guy in the clown costume. They didn't have the floor to themselves. Eight or nine other couples were doing whatever was current and frantic in disco land. Did dances have names any more? What happened to the Twist? And was it necessarily a guy in the clown outfit? Did Red Dress care? Not from the expression on her face. Ecstatic.

There was room for another three hundred celebrants in the booze can, but the early arrivals were making enough whoopee to give the place a Hieronymous Bosch flavour. Half of the crowd was bellied up to the long bar, and behind it a dozen bartenders, all young guys, darted among the bottles. "Drinks six dollars!" signs over the bar read. "Cash only!" I had the distinct feeling not even Karl Malden could use plastic at Big Bam's.

I laid out six bucks for a vodka, and watched a woman in a tight spangled dress at a table near the bar. She was wearing one earring in the shape of a miniature Eiffel Tower. She leaned over the table, put a small straw in her nostril, and sniffed up a thin line of white powder from a small mirror. As she sniffed, the Eiffel Tower bobbed softly on the table top.

A black woman in a long white fur coat came through the steel door.

"Maisie!" some guy screeched at her.

The two rushed into each other's arms. The guy was one of the Leonard Cohen haircuts. The other haircuts were right behind him. They fell on Maisie.

Old-home week at Big Bam's.

The comings at the steel door—no goings—were regular and brisk. And the body count in the room rose steadily. So did the noise and the temperature. I was ready for a more settled ambience. I deposited my empty glass on a table next to a man's Gucci handbag, and pushed through the throng to the far end of the bar, where I knew I'd find the door into Big Bam's inner sanctum.

The door was in a pool of darkness, and I didn't see Tran until he straight-armed me in the chest.

"No one allowed in here," he said, tough, peremptory.

"Hey, Tran, loosen up," I said. "Remember me? Guy that cracked open a couple of Sprites with you the other afternoon?"

"Oh yeah, you."

It wasn't in a class with the embrace the haircuts gave Maisie, but it was an acknowledgement. Tran was dressed the same way he was the day before, same short-sleeved white shirt hanging outside the trousers. Same muscles too. He raised his arm in a gesture that told me it was permitted to proceed through Bam's door.

I opened it and caught the full blast of the Big Bam bonhomie.

"All *right*," he said, standing up from his chair. "Crang, my man, let's get *down*."

He reached across the desk and gave me a complicated handshake. I fumbled it. Truong stayed seated at his desk. He didn't look like he wanted to get down with me.

"Love your outfit," I said to Big Bam. He had on something in one piece, a jumpsuit maybe, dark blue, with lots of pockets and zippers.

"You don't get this off the rack," Bam said, looking down in admiration at his own stylish self. "Made to damn measure."

He rubbed his hands together and moved around the desk.

"Gotta have us a taste," he said to me. "Owner's prices."

"Long as you're joining me, pal," I said, striving to come up to the spirit of the occasion.

"Russian again?"

"Or Polish."

Bam left on the drinks run. With the door shut, the office was satisfyingly quiet after the roar of the room outside. And it was cooler. Truong, behind his desk, eyes on me, was on the frigid side himself. Or was it just a higher level of inscrutability?

"What's happening, Mr. Crang?" he said.

"Beginning to talk like your boss, Truong," I said. "'What's *happening*?'"

"I haven't liked the sense of you," he said.

"I think Bam would phrase that 'bad vibrations.'"

"You give me the impression of a man practising concealment," Truong said. The guy was single-minded. Also accurate.

"Well, I have my little secrets," I said. "Don't we all?"

Truong came quickly out of his chair. He took two steps to the old iron safe in the corner, and began to spin the combination dials.

"Was it something I said?" I asked.

Truong didn't answer. He opened the safe door and removed two long, narrow leather something or others. Truong tugged his shirt outside his trousers and buckled one of the leather things around his waist. It was a money belt, a belt with small buttoned pockets for holding bills. Truong buckled the second belt above the first and tucked in his shirt. He shut the safe door, and reset the combination.

"Can hardly tell there's anything under there," I said. "Under your shirt."

Nothing from Truong. I might as well not have been in the room. He was examining the top of his desk. It was the usual jumble of documents and record books. Truong picked up his pocket calculator and put it in an obvious spot. In his pocket. That was all he picked up. He adjusted his shirt, walked past me, and went out the door.

I got up from my chair and went around Truong's desk. It wasn't the desk I cared about. Or the safe. It was the window behind the desk, the window that wasn't painted over. I eased back the black blind an inch or two and peeked out. The window looked into the street. I could see the two men on the gate. I could see two swell-looking couples strolling toward the gate. I couldn't see anything else. No cops. No vehicles that might be unmarked police cars. Good. It was too early for the raid. I still had a lot to get done in the booze can. A lot to get done? I had *everything* to get done. All I'd accomplished so far was watch Truong go through an act that looked like he was taking it on the lam.

Big Bam returned. He was balancing three glasses in his two hands. Behind him, the boom and thump of good times trailed into the office. Bam closed the door. Relative silence again.

"Where's Truong?" Bam asked.

"Think he's gone to make a bank deposit," I said.

Bam laughed. I didn't think he took me seriously. He settled in his chair with a Scotch. I had my vodka. Truong's soft drink sat fizzing among the papers on his desk.

"Basically," Big Bam said, lifting his glass, "we're getting it on for some business here, you and me, Crang, but nobody said we can't party at the same time."

"Business simultaneous with pleasure."

"I can relate to that."

"About the cocaine," I said. "The four kilos. They're on the way with a third party."

"Anybody I know?"

"No, but you're gonna love Darnell."

"I'm gonna love the delivery," Big Bam said. "After, I may love Darnell."

"Delivery's always tricky."

"*Tell* me about it."

"For instance," I said. "The cans over there"—I waved a hand in the direction of the film cans beside the safe—"when Trevor brought you the coke inside them, that was crafty of him. Very original form of delivery."

"Cute, yeah," Bam said. He looked at the film cans. "Not so cute when the other cans we had to swipe came up empty."

"Well, not empty," I said. "*Hell's Barrio* was in there."

"When I said empty," Bam said, "I'm talking coke, the four K I was short from Trevor. All the damn film in there doesn't count."

"What'd you do with it? The film?"

"Still inside the cans."

"Admirers of Ray Fenk's movies will be relieved you didn't destroy it."

"Who's Ray Fenk?"

"The man you took the film cans from."

"Didn't take them from a guy," Bam said. "We took them from a theatre."

"The Eglinton?"

"Movie place up the north end," Bam said. "Nice place. I could get it on for a theatre like that."

I congratulated Bam on his taste. But what I was thinking about was his apparent forgetfulness when it came to Raymond Fenk. He couldn't remember a guy he bumped off?

"This Ray Fenk," I said, "he was the man Trevor worked with on the cans, the California end. Fenk put the coke in the cans in Los Angeles. Trevor passed them on to you. You took the coke out."

"Except for the four kilos."

"Right," I said. "But that's who Ray Fenk is."

"Guy in Los Angeles."

"No. *From* Los Angeles. He's up here now."

"What're we talking about, Crang?"

That was what I was beginning to wonder.

"Maybe," I said, "about why the four kilos didn't reach you when they were supposed to."

"I might be interested in that," Bam said. "But basically not *very* interested as long as you're going to produce them any minute now."

"I am, I am," I said. "But, see, Fenk put those last four kilograms in Dave Goddard's saxophone case. Dave's a jazz musician. From Toronto. And happened to be in Los Angeles. At the time Trevor's contact was putting together the shipment. That'd be Fenk."

I stopped. Big Bam was looking at me as if he had spotted an unidentified, unwelcome, and unnecessary object.

"I never was a vodka man myself," he said. "What do they put in that stuff you're drinking anyway?"

Bam smiled at me to show he was kidding, but he was also making the point that my story had so far recorded at zero for him.

"That's the abridged version," I said. "What I just told you."

"Crazy about it, man," Bam said. "But I don't think I got the time of night for the whole story."

"You knew about the cans?" I asked, persisting. "You knew that's how Trevor was getting the coke to Toronto?"

"Right on," Bam agreed, though sounding a trifle impatient. "Trevor told me the movies the coke was in. Six of them? Whatever, it didn't matter, 'cause he brought the cans over here himself, the cans that had the coke inside."

"Except for *Hell's Barrio*."

"I just told you, Crang," Bam said, close to getting really fed up. "We had to go to that theatre. Break into the damn place Sunday morning and steal the cans ourselves. Waste of a good break-in, it turned out."

"Sunday afternoon? This was after you couldn't get satisfaction from Fenk the day before?"

"What'd I want satisfaction from a guy I never heard of? Trevor's my man on this deal. I couldn't get anywhere with *him*. Couldn't get him to answer the damn phone."

"Yeah, but—Saturday afternoon at the Silverdore Hotel, ah . . ." My voice trailed off.

"What went down Saturday afternoon at the Silverdore?" Big Bam asked.

"Fenk got strangled."

"No shit."

Someone stepped into the room behind me. It was Tran. He spoke to Big Bam in Vietnamese. I tuned them out. Was Bam having me on? Just pretending he didn't know about Fenk's murder? But the way Bam was talking, he didn't know who Fenk *was*. If it was true, if I'd fingered the wrong party for Fenk's murder, where did that leave me? Up to my eyeballs in trouble was where. Tran and Bam finished their chat, and Tran stepped back out the door.

"Your deliveryman's arrived," Bam said to me.

"Darnell Gant?"

"With a woman."

"She's not part of the package."

"Trevor's on the scene too," Bam said. "Outside."

32

BIG BAM'S OFFICE was a squeeze for five people, particularly when two of the five, Darnell Gant and Trevor Dalgleish, were the far side of giant-size. The woman was no shrimp either. She happened to be the sultry redhead from the Victoria Room. Under the green dress she had a full figure, and in her high heels she made a tall and generous parcel.

"Gentlemen," Gant said, his arm around the redhead's waist, "let me present Dale."

Bam slipped easily into his mine-host posture. He held Dale's hand briefly and gallantly in his. Gave Gant some variation on a soul brother's shake. And clapped Trevor on the back.

Trevor was acting wary. I moved around to Truong's empty chair. That put some distance and a desk between me and Trevor. Whatever was going to happen in the room wasn't likely to improve his mood or his opinion of me.

Big Bam organized Tran into bringing in two more chairs, and everybody settled down. Dale held a large patent leather purse in her lap, and crossed her legs fetchingly. Tran returned to his post outside the door.

"Where are my manners?" Bam said. He gave himself a mock bap on the forehead. "Drinks for my new guests. What's you people's pleasure?"

"Tell you what, Mr. Bam," Gant said. "First, we talk a little bargain. Second, we celebrate over a big drink."

"Suits me," Bam said, and smiled at everyone, looking for the room's consensus.

"Swell," I said.

Dale radiated delight. She was about thirty, and seemed pleased as punch at what was going on around her. Or maybe the little-girl expression was permanent with her. Her eyes were the same colour as the emerald dress she wore.

"Don't let me impose, Bam," Trevor said, doing his best to project the level-headed side of his personality. "But my impression was that Crang here is going to remedy a certain misunderstanding between yourself and myself."

"Can it, Trevor," Gant said. "The floor's mine."

"I must insist on being heard," Trevor said, appealing to Bam. The flush was staging a full-bloom return to his cheeks. "Surely I have priority over Gant."

"Night's young, Trevor," Bam said. "Why not we see where our new visitor with the lovely companion is coming from."

"From Los Angeles, as a matter of fact," I said.

"Same as the other guy you were rapping about?" Bam asked me.

"Fenk."

"This time," Gant said, "I'm representing only me, and Mr. Bam, I got some eighty-per-cent-pure stuff might be right up your alley."

"How well you read me," Bam said.

"Four K of the best," Gant said.

He turned in his chair to Dale.

"Let's have the goodies, sweetheart," he said.

Dale opened the big patent leather purse and withdrew four thin packages wrapped in plain brown paper.

Trevor shot to his feet.

"That's *my* cocaine!" he shouted, giving a fine rendition of Mount Vesuvius in eruption.

"Cocaine?" Dale said. "Oh my goodness, Darnell, is *that* what I've been carrying?"

Dale sounded shocked but still retained her starry-eyed expression.

"That," Trevor repeated, "is *my* goddamned cocaine."

"Sit down, Trevor," Bam said. "I'm the chair, and I'm still recognizing Mr. Gant."

Trevor sat down. He didn't look happy about it, and his eyes stuck with the packages of cocaine. His eyes had opened almost as wide as Dale's.

"I'll pitch it fast and fair, Mr. Bam," Gant said, tossing the packages on to Bam's desk. "Trevor told us down in L.A. you were paying him ten grand a kilo. I can live with the same number if that's still on the table. Ten?"

"Zowie," I said.

Gant looked at me.

"What's with you?" he asked. "*Zowie?*"

I said, "I think you just got Trevor in the soup."

"I fronted Trevor twelve thousand a kilo," Bam said to Gant. "If he told you ten, he was running a number."

Big Bam smiled the smile of no menace. He gave the impression he was enjoying the soap opera unfolding in front of him.

I said to Gant, "How much did Trevor pay you guys, you and Fenk, for the coke?"

"Eight thousand per K," Gant answered. "Said his profit was two grand on every K."

"All right." Trevor looked like a guy who'd been holding his breath for a long time. "So I used a small business ploy with you," he said to Gant. "What did it matter? Eight thousand was a fair price anyway."

"When did Ray Fenk catch on?" Gant asked Trevor.

"It's ancient history," Trevor said. He'd developed his tic with the fists. Clenching and unclenching.

"Yeah," I said. "Ancient for Fenk as in dead history."

"Just stop right there, Crang," Trevor shot at me. "All of this is the product of your insufferable meddling."

"Boys, boys," Bam said, tapping his hand on the desk for order, but smiling, getting a kick out of the events in his office.

"You want to answer my question, Trevor?" Gant said. "Or you want a kick in the scrotum?"

"That's no choice at all," I said.

"When did Fenk realize I was getting twelve and not ten?" Trevor said, trying for a haughty tone and halfway succeeding. "That should be obvious. It was after he'd handed over the twenty kilograms in the movie cans, but before he did anything about the last four kilos, the ones nobody told me were shipped in the bloody saxophone case."

"That's what Fenk meant by his message on your answering machine," I said to Gant. "He must have found out Trevor was giving you the gears on the price."

"If you must know," Trevor said, "it was I who told Fenk about the difference in price."

"Not too bright of you, Trev," I said. "Letting it slip out that way."

"It didn't slip out, you fool." Trevor was mounting another head of steam. "I was trying to strike a new arrangement with Fenk to get those four kilos. I *told* him what my true price was from Bam. I *told* him I'd pay more. I *told* him I'd go to nine instead of eight. Nine *thousand*."

"For the last four kilograms?" I asked.

"Crang, you heinous prick," Trevor said, spittle flying from his mouth, "will you for God's sake keep out of this."

"First insufferable. Now heinous. You got a thesaurus of nasty adjectives?"

Darnell Gant had lost interest in Trevor.

"Well, Mr. Bam," he said to Big Bam, "we reached an agreement?"

"All you just heard," Bam said, "you still like ten thousand?"

"Got a plane to catch."

"The deal's done," Bam said.

"Wait," Trevor said.

"One formality," Bam said, ignoring Trevor. "I need to bring in my man that does the testing. Have him verify purity."

"Wait," Trevor said, a little louder.

"Wouldn't have it any other way," Gant said to Bam.

"Wait a damn minute," Trevor said, back on his feet and at close to a shout.

"Trevor," Bam said, "you are disturbing my space, and I can't relate to that."

"I don't give a flying fuck about your space." Trevor's face was crimson, and he had the shakes in the arm that was pointing full-length at Bam. "I've put too much money and effort into getting that cocaine to lose it now. I went through hell for those four damned kilos. First, that idiot Fenk didn't put them in the film cans he was supposed to. Then they weren't in the lining of that stupid saxophone case. Then—"

"Hold it," I interrupted Trevor. "How'd you know they weren't in the lining?"

"Because the lining was *ripped*, you complete moron."

"Yeah, but how'd you know that?"

Trevor tromped over my question. The guy was on the rampage.

"*Then*," he said, speaking to Big Bam, "the cocaine wasn't in Fenk's briefcase. *Then* Crang said he had it. *Now*, for God's sake, it's on your desk, and you're buying it from Gant. But I've *already* paid for it. Paid Fenk and Gant. So, let me hear you answer *that*."

"It's simple, Trevor," Big Bam said. "I'm cutting a little agreement with my new man here, Mr. Darnell Gant, and you can bring me another four K. Do that, or pay me back the forty-eight thousand. Take your pick."

"You bastard," Trevor said. His voice sounded like it was coming through a strainer.

"Trevor," I said, "about the ripped lining in the saxophone case."

"Shut up," Trevor said, low and hoarse. "You've already done me enough damage."

"What *about* the ripped lining?" Gant asked me, getting interested again in the Trevor angle. "And what happened to that sax case?"

"I got the case," I said. "Or rather Dave Goddard's got it. I gave it back to him. But my point is the only way Trevor could know it was ripped is if he saw it in Ray Fenk's hotel room."

"Crang," Trevor said, "how many times do I have to tell you to butt out?"

"For that matter," I said, "the only way Trevor could know about the briefcase and the cocaine not being in it is if he took it from Fenk on Saturday afternoon."

"This is getting rich," Gant said.

"It certainly is, Darnell," Dale with the green dress and the wide green eyes piped up. "But why is it getting rich, Darnell?"

"And," I went on, "the only way Trevor could have taken the brief-case from Fenk is if he killed Fenk."

Everybody in the room stared at Trevor.

"Crang's indulging in fantasy," Trevor said.

"Not me, Trev," I said. "I was there."

"You were where?" Gant asked.

"In Fenk's hotel room," I said. "That's how I know about the ripped lining in the case. That's how I *got* the flipping case. And, not only that, a few minutes before I went into the room, I saw Fenk with the briefcase Trevor's talking about. Fenk was practically married to that briefcase, and later, after Fenk got himself strangled, it was gone."

"Ray Fenk's hotel room . . ." Trevor said, and stopped.

I said, "It wasn't empty, Trev, if that's what you were going to say."

"Have you skipped a couple steps or what?" Gant asked me. "How could you be in the hotel room when Ray was getting killed and nobody saw you?"

"I was hiding in the closet."

"Oh, man," Gant said. "That's too ridiculous not to be true."

"In the closet?" Dale said.

"While somebody was strangling Fenk," I said.

"How horrible for you," Dale said, big green eyes all round.

"And it wasn't just any old somebody who was doing the stran-gling," I said. I knew I was on the right track. At last. "It had to be Trev.

He must have come back to the room with Fenk to haggle some more over the four kilos. But Fenk probably wouldn't go along with the raised price Trevor was offering, nine grand a kilo instead of the original eight. Trevor saw that the cocaine had already been taken out of the lining of Dave Goddard's case, and he must have figured it was in the briefcase. He got into a rumble with Fenk. Applied the saxophone strap a little too tightly to Fenk's neck. And scrammed out of the hotel with the briefcase."

Everybody stared at Trevor again.

"Preposterous," he said. His voice had sunk so low it was on the brink of vanishing.

No one spoke for a moment.

"Bottom line, Trevor," Big Bam said, breaking the silence, "it had to have been you that iced the man."

"You're lucky I didn't much like Ray Fenk," Gant said to Trevor. "Otherwise I might've had to get even."

I said, "I think I just solved a murder."

"It was awfully clever of you," Dale said.

The phone on Bam's desk rang.

33

WHOEVER was on the other end of Big Bam's line did all the talking. And not much of it. Bam listened for ten seconds before he hung up. He got out of his chair and peeled back the black blind a couple of inches the way I'd done earlier.

"Aw shit," he said.

I knew what he must have been seeing in the street.

Tran opened the door.

"Cops," he said to Big Bam.

"*Tell* me about it," Bam said.

"*Police*?!" Trevor burst out. His voice was back to explosion level.

"Oh my," Dale said.

"Damn," Gant said. "What kind of dumb-ass timing is that?"

Bam went back to his desk.

"Take them ten minutes to get through the steel," he said. He didn't look rattled. He looked collected.

I took his place at the black blind. Six or seven yellow police cars jammed the perimeter of the street, and behind them, reaching as far back as I could make out from the window, there seemed to be another dozen cars and big yellow vans. Cops swarmed outside the chain-link fence, a regiment of them. The ones who caught my fancy were the four guys hoisting a long battering ram. Bam was probably right about the ten minutes. It'd take that much time for the guys swinging the battering ram to flatten the steel door with the peephole in it. Besides the ram, the cops were packing plenty of other miscellaneous hardware and martial aids. One policeman carried a buzz saw. Another was wielding a crowbar. And a third was barely restraining a dog snarling at the end of a stout leash. Good old reliable Stuffy Kernohan, a cop equipped for every form of opposition.

"What in hell's happening down there, Crang?" Trevor asked.

"Right out of *Full Metal Jacket*, Trev," I said. "Total assault."

Bam's two guards at the front had disappeared, but they'd locked the gate with a thick chain and padlock. A cop was working on the chain with a metal-cutter. The cop had on a black crash helmet with a yellow visor. So did the other cops pressing up to the gate behind him. And all of them were bearing weapons. Automatic pistols. Rifles. Long billy clubs. One guy had a loud hailer in his hand. Probably in charge of the play-by-play.

In the office, Big Bam was talking calmly to Tran in Vietnamese. What he was saying had the ring of instructions, but there was no rush to it, no panic. Trevor, standing and rubbing his hands, had changed colours. Flushed red to milk white. And Darnell Gant was holding green-eyed Dale's hand.

"What happens," Gant asked Dale, "if I say goodbye to the coke, leave it right there on Mr. Bam's desk, and get myself arrested like all the other ordinary citizens out on the dance floor?"

"Why ask Dale?" I asked Gant.

"Woman's a lawyer."

"She *is*?" I said to Gant.

"You *are*?" I said to Dale.

"I only do commercial work, leasebacks mostly," Dale said, apologetic. "I've forgotten everything I was ever taught about criminal law."

"Leasebacks?" I said. "Who're you with?"

"McIntosh, Brown & Crabtree."

"I didn't mean to sound skeptical," I said. "But you don't look like a lawyer."

"Watch it, man," Gant said.

"I think I just sounded sexist," I said to Dale.

"Will you people get off that subject," Trevor said. "That's the police outside. We have an emergency on our hands."

"Your hands gonna carry most of the weight, Trevor," Gant said.

Dale was on her feet.

"Darnell," she said. "Maybe you better do something."

Gant stayed in his chair, giving a very good impersonation of a man with all the time in the world. He was still holding Dale's hand, but he was speaking to me.

"So what's the answer, Crang?" he said. "The question I asked Dale."

"Found-ins," I said. "That's what the civilians caught in the booze can are going to be charged as."

"Found-ins," Dale said. "*Now* I remember."

"Found in what?" Gant asked.

"Premises not licensed to sell alcohol," I said. "Hundred-dollar fine."

"No jail time?"

"You'll be on American Airlines tomorrow."

Gant got up and put his arm around Dale's waist. They made a handsome couple.

"Coke's all yours, Mr. Bam," Gant said.

"Bottom line, Mr. Gant," Bam said. "I like the way you cut your losses."

Gant ushered Dale to the door.

"Let's boogie, baby," he said to her.

Dale leaned around Gant's shoulder and gave a little wave to the rest of us in the room.

"Nice to have met you all," she said.

Gant opened the door, and the sound of rock 'n' roll and people partying blasted into the room. Under the happy blare there was another, more ominous noise. It was the faint bong of the battering ram smacking the steel door. The guests in the booze can hadn't cottoned on to the raid yet, but in a few minutes they were going to be joined by the guys in the black visors. Gant shut the door behind him.

I said, "Well, Bam, maybe I'll just truck on out of here too."

"You stick around, my man," Bam said. He was wearing his non-menacing smile, but there was a snap in his voice.

"You really want me getting under foot?" I said. "I know you've got things to do."

"Stay," Bam said, and motioned to Tran, who moved up beside me. I couldn't help noticing that Tran had a gun in his hand. It was a tiny gun, almost a toy, but I imagined it fired real bullets.

Bam got down on his knees in front of the old iron safe and spun the combination dials.

"Is there another way out of here?" Trevor asked Bam's back.

"I'm a businessman, Trevor," Bam said. "You think I don't know about contingency planning?"

Bam kept on spinning, and the other three of us, me, Trevor, and Tran, watched him. The atmosphere in the room had tensed right up.

"Can you believe where Dale works, Trev?" I said, making chatter to fill in the unsettling quiet. "McIntosh, Brown & Crabtree's gotta be the stuffiest law firm in the city."

"You expect me to gossip at a time like this?" Trevor said.

"I'm amazed they'd hire a woman," I said. "Never mind someone like Dale. Drop-dead beautiful."

"Shut *up*," Trevor said.

Bam pulled open the safe door. He lifted out an armful of money belts, and dumped them on his desk.

"Hold on," he said. "Supposed to be eleven."

"Two belts missing," I said. "Right?"

"Right."

"I think Truong's treating them as his very own pension plan."

Bam shook his head. It was an admiring shake.

"That fox," Bam said. "The man's a born survivor."

He handed three of the belts to Tran. Tran lifted his shirt and began buckling the belts around his waist. Three were as many belts as his waist could accommodate.

"World War III happens," Bam said, "Truong'll come out laughing, the kind of survivor he is."

Bam tossed three more belts to me.

"Get into these, Crang," he said.

"I'm honoured, Bam, but, look, I'm just an observer here."

"Do like I ask," Bam said, the snap back in his voice. "How else you think I'm gonna get the money out of here?"

Trevor stepped forward.

"Not you, Trevor," Bam said. "You're travelling light."

The belts fit snugly under my shirt and sweater. Bam unzipped his jumpsuit from the top and strapped on the last three money belts. He zipped up again. Darnell Gant's cocaine was still on Bam's desk. He picked it up and tucked it into one of the myriad of pockets. Bam wasn't through packing. He reached into the safe, and took out a pistol. It didn't look like a toy. It was black and had a long barrel. Bam dropped it in another zippered pocket.

"'Kay," he said. "All systems are go."

"Lead on, Bam," I said.

Lead on? Was I nuts? The cops were a few yards and fewer minutes away. Rescue was at hand. I'd got done what I came to do. Uncover Fenk's murderer. It was Trevor. Maybe the case against him was short on hard evidence, but I had plenty to hand the police. And I could let Stuffy and his troops take care of Big Bam and his cocaine corporation. No reason for me to linger in Bam's company. That was the message from my brain. But the two guns, Tran's toy and Bam's howitzer, said otherwise. At least for the moment.

Tran opened the office door. At the same instant the cops' battering ram burst open the steel door across the room. Some of the dancers kept on shaking and shimmying, and some of the drinkers kept on bending their elbows. They were too absorbed or too drunk or too stoned to take note of the cops and the helmets and guns and clubs, the buzz saw, the crowbar, and the snarling dog that were in their midst. The other patrons, the people who were caught in the vanguard of the police rush, sent up a hullabaloo of screams and cries and hollers. And, over the top of the din, the cop on the loud hailer had a repeated announcement:

"This is a raid!" he kept on broadcasting. "This is a raid!"

"No kidding," I said to myself.

Outside Bam's office, the four of us were temporarily secure in the darkness along the wall. Bam poked me in the back and pointed to the right. It was too noisy in the huge room, too thick with clamour, for communication of the verbal sort. Bam was sticking to sign language. His sign said to follow Tran along the wall.

I did as I was told, and after a dozen steps in the gloom, I bumped against Tran. He'd stopped. He was stretching in the air to his full height, which wasn't much, and pulling at a set of metal stairs. They were bolted to the wall, a kind of narrow indoor fire escape. The stairs were movable at the bottom, and Tran heaved them down to chest level. He swung himself on to the first step and scrambled into the darkness above. His move was so adroit that I got the feeling he had rehearsed the trip up the metal steps many times before.

Bam gave me another poke. I grabbed the bottom step and made a fluttery upwards leap. Not deft, but not bad for a guy who hadn't rehearsed. I scampered after Tran. Under my feet, the iron steps swayed and quivered. Were the damn things going to hold? No time for foolish questions. I kept moving, one foot in front of the other. To the rear, the steps developed a ferocious shiver. Must have been Trevor and his bulk climbing aboard. Feet, I begged, do your stuff.

Up ahead, six or seven steps ahead, a door opened. Tran, his back to me, was climbing through it. I could see his body outlined against the sky and stars. Tran disappeared. The door must open on to the roof. Brilliant conclusion, Crang. I took a fast look down below. Not one of my better ideas. The floor of the booze can was a long drop away, four storeys, and my stomach went instantly queasy. I stumbled up the last steps and through the door. Big Bam was on my heels, and a couple of seconds after him, Trevor crashed on to the roof. Tran slammed shut the door.

"More fun than a scavenger hunt, Bam," I said. I seemed to be short on breath.

We were at the back of the building and on the west side. The police raid was concentrated at the front and the east side, and it reached our ears as the sound of distant tumult. But it wouldn't be more than five minutes before the raiders wised up to the metal stairs and investigated the roof.

"What's our next step?" Trevor asked Bam. Trevor was in full supply of breath. For all his heft, he kept in sound aerobic shape.

"Basically it's not a step," Bam said. "More like a running broad jump."

Bam was pointing at the roof of the building next door, the warehouse to the west that was separated from the booze can by an alley.

"Always loved that roof-to-roof trick in *Arabian Nights*, Bam," I said. "But it's got to be ten feet across there. Not my best distance."

"Eleven feet," Bam said. "And you'll have help."

"What? A catapult?"

"You won't fail me, Crang," Bam said. "I got an investment in you."

"The money belts?"

"Hundred grand in each belt."

I patted my waist.

"Never been so intimate with such large numbers."

Tran stood at the edge of our roof. He looked across the alley, turned himself one hundred and eighty degrees, and walked back ten precise paces. He stopped and faced around to the building next door. He started to run. He had immaculate form. Graceful and muscular. He ran to the roof's edge and took off. Sailed up and over the alley. When he came down, he was a safe three feet beyond the edge of the other roof.

"Bravo," Bam said.

"Kid's got style like Baryshnikov," I said. "But that's the catch. My style's more like Curly, Larry, and Moe."

"Watch," Bam said. "We practised this a hundred times. Trust me, it's fail-safe."

He lined himself on the running path Tran had followed, ten exact steps from the edge of the building. Across the alley, Tran and his muscles were crouched at the side of the other roof. His arms were reaching out in front of him, and his feet were propped behind a small, tin-covered elevation that ran along the roof's edge. Bam and Tran looked like they were prepping for a tryout with the Flying Wallendas.

Bam ran down the line toward the alley. His form wasn't in Tran's league, but he was getting the job done. He hit the end of the roof and flew through the air. Both of his arms and both legs were stretched forward. The legs landed on the tin, and as they touched down, Tran grabbed him by the arms. Tran gave a backwards yank, and the two of them, Bam and Tran, were locked together in a dancing embrace on the building's roof.

Bam pulled out of the waltz, and called back to Trevor and me.

"See?" he said. "No sweat."

"Easy for you to say, Bam," I answered. "But Trevor and I haven't practised a hundred times."

"Shake it up, Crang," Bam said.

"Not even one time."

"Are you a coward as well as stupid?" Trevor said to me. He was practically spitting contempt.

"You know what, Trev?" I said. "I can hardly wait to see you in chains."

Trevor stepped past me to the launching path.

"Uh-uh, Trevor," Bam shouted. "Crang comes next."

"I don't mind bringing up the rear," I said.

"I mind," Bam said.

He unzipped one of his pockets and produced the black gun with the long barrel.

"See what you mean," I said.

So much for that possibility. If Trevor had jumped the roofs first, I could have beat it back down the metal stairs and alerted Stuffy Kernohan to Big Bam's great escape.

"Hold your fire," I called to Bam.

"Something else I practise," Bam said. "Target shooting."

"I'm coming. I'm coming."

I stood at the point ten feet from the roof's edge. No sense delaying. It was like plunging into cold water. Get the pain over in a hurry. Except in this case there wouldn't be time for pain. It was either a safe leap into Tran's brawny arms or a quick drop into the alley.

I sucked in my breath and took off on the run. It was marvellous how fear concentrated the brain. I wasn't conscious of anything around me, not Trevor at the side, not the stars above, not the alley below. All I saw were Tran's arms ahead. I hurtled through the open space, willing myself to clear the distance. Whatever I looked like didn't count. Probably I looked frantic and absurd. No matter. It was getting there that counted.

And I got there. In fact, I got too far. I slammed through Tran's waiting arms, and the two of us hit the roof. The fall didn't hurt either of us—Tran because his layers of muscle protected him, and me because my landing was broken by those same layers of muscle.

Tran pushed me off and took up position to receive Trevor.

"How many points for my technique?" I asked Bam. The blood was pumping through me at a ferocious rate.

"Only two scores for this event," Bam said. "Perfect ten or a dive in the alley."

On the other building, Trevor was into his takeoff sprint. He rumbled down the track, reached the roof's edge, and got airborne. He was up and aloft, halfway between the roof of the booze can and the roof of the building that might represent a getaway. He looked, in that instant, splendidly confident. His jump was athletic—his feet tucked together, his body in the shape of a compact question mark, his arms reaching forward, and his hands ready to lock with Tran's.

In that moment, with Trevor at the midpoint between rooftops, Tran turned his back on Trevor and stepped away from the side of the building.

Trevor's face lost its look of confidence. His body thrashed in the air. The tuck of his feet, the compact question mark, the outreaching arms all dissolved in a confusion of windmilling limbs. There was no one, no Tran, to catch Trevor and pull him to safety. And Trevor's eyes could see his fate.

"*Noooo!*" I screamed.

No one heard me because Trevor was screaming the same word much louder.

"*NOOOOO!*" Trevor screamed.

I jumped forward, past Tran, and grabbed for Trevor.

His hands slapped the top of the tin and bounced off without gripping. His right hand brushed mine and flew away, clutching nothing.

Trevor was still airborne. And dropping. And screaming.

He screamed all the way to the bottom of the alley. He screamed until he hit. I didn't hear him land. I only heard the scream.

"No," I said, much quieter.

No one heard it either.

Not Trevor.

And not Big Bam or Tran. They were running across the roof to a door in the building like the door we'd come out of on the booze can building.

"You guys!" I called after them.

Both stopped.

"Hustle that money on over here," Bam called back.

I leaned over the edge of the building. Trevor was down there.

He looked like a bundle of thrown-away clothes. And he seemed to have landed face first. It was going to be tough on the person who found Trevor. The person was going to find a splat of a corpse.

I trotted over the roof to Tran and Big Bam. Bam had a key and was putting it in the lock to the door.

"You planned that," I said to him. "That fall Trevor took."

"What do you care?" Bam said. He swung open the door. "The bastard stiffed me and knocked off the other guy."

"Fenk."

"Never remember the name," Bam said. He said it airily.

"You didn't have to kill Trevor," I said. "Not like *that*."

Big Bam gave his largest grin.

He said, "I thought it had an inventive touch, as executions go."

The guy was loony. Or totally gone in amorality. Didn't matter which. I was still in his company, his and Tran's. Tran, the designated executioner. And what of an inventive nature did they have in store for me?

Past the open door, the stairway was in deep blackness. Bam took a small flashlight from another of his pockets. He might be loony or amoral, but he was one step ahead in every crisis. The light shone our way on the stairs, and we raced down four flights. At the bottom, Bam produced a key that unlocked the door. Keys, flashlights, guns. For his next trick, Bam might pull a Honda out of that damned jumpsuit.

The door opened on to another alley. It was on the west side of the empty warehouse, as far away from the booze can and the cops as we could get. The alley was unlighted, but across it I could make out a row of backyards. They belonged to houses that ran about a half-block to a main street that had fairly heavy nighttime traffic. The street was Bathurst, and I wished I was on it. Any place but the alley with Bam and Tran.

"Wheel the Porsche up here," Bam ordered Tran.

Tran beat it down the alley in the direction away from the street, and disappeared around the corner of the warehouse.

"Well," I said, "guess you want the money belts."

My voice had a tremor in it that was new to me.

Bam said, "What say you and me get into some brainstorming?"

"Right here? Can't it wait till we're comfy in somebody's conference room? That be better?"

"Indulge me."

"Tell you what," I said. "Why not I deposit the three hundred grand with you, and we call it a night? Been great, Bam, but, tell you the truth, I got a late date with some hot stuff."

I lifted my sweater and tugged at my shirt.

"For instance," Bam said, "coincidence."

"You go right on, Bam, free think, whatever," I said. "I'll just un-buckle here."

"One day, Crang, you come into my place," Bam said. "Next night, the cops come down on it."

"Oh," I said. "That kind of coincidence."

I stopped fiddling with my shirt and sweater and left the money belts around my waist. Better to focus on a more pressing issue. Saving my own hide.

"You're speculating," I said to Bam, "is there any connection between my visit and the raid?"

"If there is," Bam said, "I'm basically gonna have to take steps."

When Big Bam talked steps, he meant baseball bats or guns or dropping people from tall buildings.

"Your suspicion," I said, buying time for reflection on my predicament, "cuts me to the quick, Bam."

Big Bam was standing with his back to the street. He held the flashlight in his right hand, and the black pistol was zipped in one of his jumpsuit's many pockets. It'd take him three, four seconds to draw it. The distance from Bam to the street was about thirty yards. There were cop cars on the street, but Bam'd pick me off before I got close to them. Back of me, in the other direction, it was no more than ten yards to the alley behind the warehouse. That was my logical route, go back, not forward, and count on making it around the corner of the building before Bam assumed his target-practice position.

"Bottom line, Crang," Bam said, "you call in the cops?"

"Know this old saying, Bam? All good things must come to an end? Your booze can? Your cocaine trade? Your freedom?"

Bam looked briefly mystified.

I popped him with a short, straight right on the point of his Turhan Bey chin.

It was no knockout blow, but punchy enough to topple Bam over backwards.

I spun around, and took it on the Carl Lewis down the alley.

34

WHAT I HAD IN MIND, my intention, was to circle the warehouse at top speed and maintain velocity until I reached the booze can. Search out Stuffy Kernohan and seek asylum. Claim refugee status. Anything to evade Big Bam's clutches. Not to mention his black gun. I skittered around the corner of the warehouse, and I came bang up against Tran. There went that intention.

Tran was behind the wheel of the red Porsche convertible, top down, and he was gunning on a line that would catch me about knee level. He was twenty yards away, and he hadn't turned on the headlights. Probably to avoid the cops' notice. The turned-off lights might work to my advantage. Make it harder for Big Bam to pot me with a shot from his gun. Too dark in the alley for accurate marksmanship. I reversed directions and bolted for the fence into the neighbouring backyard. Could I outrun a Porsche? Maybe over the short haul. It was ten yards to the fence.

I caught a glimpse of Big Bam out of the corner of my eye. He was on his feet, but was his gun in hand? I couldn't tell. I was two yards from the fence. The Porsche's bumper touched the back of my jeans. Just touched. Tran must have been braking. He didn't want to hit the fence. He was probably wrestling with a dilemma. Bang into me and the fence? Or stop short of both? With the first, he'd nail me, but put a dent in Bam's expensive car. With the second, he'd let me get away, for the moment anyway, but preserve the car. He chose in favour of the Porsche's integrity. He braked. The fence was a little more than waist high. I dove into it and flipped over, head first, feet in the air, bum thumping the ground. I landed in somebody's rhubarb patch.

"Leave the lights off," I heard Bam say to Tran. Bam's voice was an urgent whisper.

I kept low in the rhubarb, and scrambled through the dark toward the next fence. My bum hurt, but it wasn't impeding progress. The only trouble was noise. I was making a lot of it. Bam and Tran might not be able to see me, but they sure as hell could hear me.

"You're going nowhere, Crang," Bam called. His voice was still urgent.

I reached the second fence, and flattened myself on the ground at the base of it. Time was on my side. Or so I figured. With all the cops in the area, Bam couldn't afford to dally. When the police finished processing the mob in the booze can and came up short on guys in the boss's office, they'd spread their net wider. I hugged the earth down among the rhubarb plants.

Bam and Tran were leaning over the fence on the alley. I could see their heads and shoulders in outline. Bam had the gun in his right hand, the small flashlight in his left. He switched on the flashlight's beam and flicked it around the yard. Ha, I got another break. The beam wasn't strong enough to carry all the way to my fence. Bam switched off the flashlight, and he and Tran backed away from their fence, out of my sight.

I stayed prone. Or was it supine? Flat anyway. And the next sound I heard was the Porsche driving away. It was going south, away from the warehouse, down the alley in the opposite direction from the street where the cop cars and vans were jammed up. Had I out-waited Bam and Tran? I stood up.

And saw Tran hurtling the fence from the alley. I hadn't out-waited the guys. They'd outsmarted me. I put my hands on top of the second fence and swung over. At least I had a lead on Tran. I was one backyard ahead of him, but he owned an edge in speed. He wasn't bad at high jumping either.

The next backyard was all grass. I made swift time through it, and cleared the next fence. There looked to be five or six more yards before I reached Bathurst Street. Bathurst Street? Omigawd, that was probably where Bam was headed in the Porsche. The guys were putting on a pincher move.

I didn't look back, but I seemed to be holding my advantage over Tran. Crang in front by the length of a backyard. The yards were varied. One was all flagstone. Another showed the devotion of a fanatical gardener. I caught the fragrances of herbs as I whizzed by. Sage. Basil. Lavender. And in the second-last yard before Bathurst, five people were winding down over the remains of a barbecue. A table was cluttered with wine bottles and half-filled glasses. Nobody paid attention to me scurrying through the party. Maybe they'd invite Tran to stop for a drink. If it was Sprite, he'd accept.

I got over the last fence, and came down on the sidewalk. Bathurst Street. No sign of the red Porsche. I ran north to the intersection of Bathurst and the side street. Tran's feet flopped to the sidewalk behind me. I looked over my shoulder. Tran was over the last fence too, but he was on his knees. Must have turned an ankle. Yet another break for me.

A streetcar was stopped at the intersection, and three people were climbing aboard. Not my first choice in getaway vehicles, but it was no time to act particular. I swung on to the first step, and the driver closed the doors. Tran was still limping up the sidewalk.

"Fare, please," the driver said to me.

"Wouldn't happen to have change for a five hundred?"

"Why, sure," the driver said. "Long as you don't mind 499 singles."

The driver was a joker. I counted out the right change from my pocket, and dropped it in the fare box.

The car was about a quarter full, mostly with women who looked like they worked at the Western Hospital up the street. I went straight through to the back of the car, and watched out the window for Big Bam's Porsche.

The streetcar travelled north. It stopped at College Street. No appearance by the Porsche. The streetcar pulled up to the Harbord stop, and when I checked out the back window, I was looking down on Big Bam's grinning countenance.

Bam was in the Porsche's driver's seat. Tran sat beside him. The top was still down, all the better for me to appreciate the Porsche's fine appointments. Shiny red upholstery. Tape deck. Cellular phone. And Bam with a smug expression.

At Bloor, the streetcar steered into the station that marked the end of the line. Bam couldn't follow in the Porsche. The station, surrounded by fences and gates, was for streetcars only. That didn't mean the pair of them, Bam and Tran, wouldn't come after me on foot.

I was first off the streetcar, and ran across the concourse and down two flights of stairs to the subway platform. No trains were in the station. I was on the eastbound side. So were another dozen people. None of them was Bam or ban.

In two minutes a train pulled in. I boarded a car near the middle, and hung at the door watching for pursuers. I saw one. Tran. He came storming down the stairs, the limp all gone, and squeezed on to the train just as the conductor was blowing his whistle and closing the doors. The train rattled out of the Bloor station. Tran was in a car two up from mine. Did he know where I was? Had to. He'd probably been holding back, waiting to see if I stayed on the train or jumped back on the platform.

I sat in a seat under a poster advertising Druxy's Deli. Eccch. My idea of a long, dull evening was watching a ball game on TV, beer in one hand, pastrami on rye in the other. The train rolled in to the Spadina station. I popped my head out the door. Tran was on the move. He bobbed out of the car he was on, and before the train started up again, he bobbed back into the car next to mine. Not only did he know where I was, he was sneaking closer to me and my car.

At the next station, St. George, I copied Tran's stunt. When the train stopped, I darted from my car and into the next car down the line. I glanced back. Tran had moved up. He was in the car I'd just deserted. Wily devil.

The train reached the next station, and I bailed out for good. It was the Bay station, and there were two routes that led up to the street. One of them, the biggest and busiest, was down at the east end of the platform. I couldn't take that route. Tran was between it and me. I lit out down the west end of the platform to the other, much smaller exit. And I could hear the light flap of Tran's shoes at my rear.

The Bay station at the west end was spick and span, done in white tile, free of graffiti and other defacing. My bathroom should be so impeccable. I reached the stairs and took them two at a time. At the top, there was one turnstile for exit. And there was no attendant at that late hour on duty in the booth. And nobody else in sight except Tran. I could sense him getting closer. In no time, he'd be breathing down my neck. Except he wouldn't breathe on my neck. He'd give it a karate chop.

The exit turnstile was a bizarre arrangement of metal bars. Three sets of two-feet-long horizontal bars were attached to a central vertical pole that ran floor to ceiling. The bars formed three little cage-like enclosures that you got in and pushed through to the outside lobby. I shoved forward in the first enclosure, and when I was on the other side, in the small lobby, I turned and waited for Tran.

He rushed into the next enclosure. I paused a half-second, and with Tran inside the cage I grabbed one of the sets of horizontal bars and pushed back. The enclosure stopped turning, and Tran, caught off balance, pitched forward. His forehead slammed into the bars. I yanked the cage toward me. Tran's head whiplashed, and the back of it banked off the set of bars behind him.

Tran stumbled out of the cage, shaky and dazed. I fired a low right hand into his stomach, stepped to the side, and clipped him with a left hook high on his cheek. They were picture punches, the kind you see in boxing highlight movies. Not bad, even if I was up against an opponent who'd already been blitzed by two sets of metal bars.

Tran lay flat on the station floor. Out cold? I dragged him to the corner of the lobby and rolled him over. Yeah, out cold. I ripped off his white shirt, tore it in two, and tied his wrists and ankles. Tran was packing two pieces of equipment on his belt. A walkie-talkie and the little pop-gun. I left the walkie-talkie, and stuck the pistol in the small of my back under my sweater. The walkie-talkie? Had Tran used it to keep Big Bam up to date on my peregrinations? I'd better watch my rear. And flank. And front.

There was a pay phone in the corner of the lobby. I dialled 911.

"That raid tonight on the booze can near College and Spadina," I said to the woman cop who answered. "One of the guys who ran the place is waiting to be picked up at the west exit of the Bay subway station."

"Sir," the woman said, "I have no record of a raid at College and Spadina."

"Okay, try this one," I said. "The body of the man in the alley next to the booze can, the guy in the subway is responsible for that killing."

"You been drinking, sir?"

"My last shot," I said. "This guy here at the subway station, he's lying on the floor with his shirt off, and it's going to be a disgraceful sight for people using the facility."

"I have a car on the way, sir."

I walked up the steps of the exit to the street. The street was Cumberland. On the south side, there was a small parkette and a big parking lot. The north side was chockablock with smart shops and restaurants. La Belle Boutique. A place that specialized in Cuban cigars. Jacques's Omelettes. Esthetics of Lara. Wonder what Lara did when she wasn't losing at spelling bees. There were no-parking signs along Cumberland, but the north curb was lined with cars. BMWs. Audis. Jaguars. A Rolls-Royce. Ferraris. The owners of the pricey automobiles were undoubtedly taking their pleasure in the restaurant at the end of the block, the place I was headed for.

The Belair Café.

35

MIDNIGHT, and the Belair was peaking. At the bar, the smart set stood four deep, and in the restaurant, the floor was so thick with table-hoppers that it took me a couple of minutes to pick out Cam Charles and Annie. They were sitting opposite each other at two single tables that had been pushed together. Empty glasses and plates were strewn across the other two places at the table, but the chairs were empty. Probably the only empties in the room.

I plunked down in the seat beside Annie.

"Honey," Annie said, glad to see me, but concerned too. "You look frazzled."

Cam didn't care how I looked.

"Too bad you didn't come earlier, Crang," he said. "Daniel Day-Lewis just left."

"That would've rounded out my evening just about right," I said.

Cam said, "Annie and I had a fascinating chat with him."

Annie was still giving me her worried attention.

"Apart from frazzled," she said, "you look kind of chunky around the waist."

"I got three hundred thousand reasons for that," I said. "Tell you later."

"You smell funny," Annie said. "What is that? Rhubarb?"

The waiter came by, and I asked for a double vodka on the rocks.

"I bring good news, Cam," I said. "And bad news. And really bad news."

Cam flicked his eyes at Annie.

"Don't worry about Annie," I said to him. "She knows all the past history."

"And I'm discreet," Annie said.

"But you're press," Cam said to her.

"Only way I'll report on this story," Annie said, "is if it gets made into a movie."

"Could happen," I said.

Cam's face arranged itself into his stern expression.

"Let's have your report, Crang," he said.

"The good news," I said, "is Trevor won't stand trial."

"Thank heaven for that," Cam said.

"The bad news is he killed a man," I said. "And the really bad news is someone else killed him."

It might have been the first moment in his career when words failed to spring to Cam Charles's lips.

Annie spoke before Cam recovered his wits and vocabulary.

"Who did he kill?" she asked me.

"Fenk."

"No." Cam had found a word.

"Yeah," I said. "Probably nothing premeditated. I think his coke dealing must have been driving him a little crazy, trying to keep the turnover going, earn the money to pay the bills for the grand way he lived. And when Fenk crossed him on the last part of a deal the two of them had going, Trevor's temper went past the boil. He took everything out on Fenk. Frustration, rage, all the stuff that was knocking his judgment and balance loose."

"No," Cam said. He was sticking to the one word he had under control.

"That's my analysis anyway," I said. "But I think the homicide people, your mate Stuffy Kernohan, they'll put it together the same general way."

"So who killed Trevor?" Annie asked. "And when and how?"

"How, I don't think you want to hear," I said. "Trevor's body isn't going to be a pretty picture. It happened an hour ago, and the two guys who did it—killed Trevor—are from the cocaine bunch he was selling to. A thug name of Tran, and the coke boss and booze can proprietor, guy who goes by the handle of Big Bam."

Cam cleared his throat.

"Does Stuffy have the two in custody?" he asked me.

"Cops should have their mitts on Tran any time now," I said. "But Big Bam is somewhere loose in his Porsche."

"You mean he's likely to be leaving the city?" Cam said. "Trying to run from the police?"

"Not immediately," I said. "Right this minute, he's hunting for me."

"You?" Annie said. "Why you?"

I lifted up my sweater and shirt.

"What is the world are those?" Annie said, looking at my waist.

Cam stood out of his chair to see over the table.

"Why are you wearing money belts, Crang?" he asked.

"Big Bam's idea," I said. "He'll have done some serious rethinking on that one in the last hour."

Cam sat down and retreated into silence. If I knew my Cam, his brain was ticking over, conjuring up ways to put daylight between his law firm and the Trevor Dalgleish fiasco. Or tragedy. I tucked my shirt in with one hand. Just one hand because Annie was holding the other. The waiter with my double vodka arrived at the table.

And so, right behind the waiter, did Big Bam.

"Oh, wow," I said.

Cam and Annie looked up at Big Bam. They had the same first reaction to him. They started to smile a greeting. Why not? Bam was a presentable guy with his matinee-idol face and his ritzy blue jumpsuit. But the smile on Bam wiped the smiles off Cam and Annie. Bam's was a cold smile. Menacing. At last, the kind of smile I'd been waiting for.

I took a gulp of vodka.

"Annie and Cam," I said, "like you to meet Ng Thai. Also known in cocaine and booze can circles as Big Bam."

Cam's system must have adjusted to shocks. He wasn't struck speechless this time.

"You have your nerve," he said to Big Bam. "At this moment, the police want you for a number of crimes."

Bam sat down beside Cam. Bam and Cam? What was this? A 1960s folk duo? Or a couple of characters from *Sesame Street*? Bam folded his hands matter-of-factly on the tablecloth.

"Do I need to know you?" he asked Cam.

"My name," Cam said, majestically, "is Cameron Charles."

"Hey, right on, Trevor's boss," Bam said. "Heard good things about you."

"Crang says you killed Trevor," Cam said.

"Crang's a regular little tattletale," Bam said, looking at me. Then, back to Cam, "But what hasn't gone down yet, the police haven't talked to Crang. Heard his fairy story. Maybe they never will."

"What are you suggesting?" Cam asked.

Cam had regained his regular take-charge self. While he talked and kept Big Bam's attention, I held the vodka in my left hand, disengaged my right from Annie, and let it slide down my backside. Everything about my moves said Mr. Casual. Or I hoped that was how Bam would see it. I dipped the hand into the small of my back and eased Tran's little pistol out of my belt. Annie didn't notice. She was intent on Big Bam. And Bam was listening to Cam Charles's pontifications. I leaned forward, and held the gun under the table.

"Let me check you into this piece of info," Bam interrupted Cam. "Crang over there's carrying three hundred thousand dollars. What's that say about him? Anybody going to believe a man with three hundred thousand that's not his own when he accuses another man of murder?"

"Is that what's in those money belts, Crang?" Cam asked, turning the hard look on me. "Three hundred thousand dollars?"

Annie's head swivelled to me.

"Straighten these guys out, sweetie," she said.

"What's your play, Bam?" I said. "You want your money back? Or you think you can leave it around my waist, and that'll discredit me when I tell the cops how you and Tran let Trevor drop four storeys? Or maybe you got a plan to have it both ways?"

Did I sound tough? Well, maybe not Humphrey Bogart, but I was giving Bam stuff to chew on. Keep him occupied.

"Dropped him four storeys?" Annie said. "They can't get away with *that.*"

"Tran already hasn't," I said. "I've sort of taken him out of commission."

"Some kind of troublemaker, Crang," Bam said.

"I'll agree to that much," Cam said.

"Nice, Cam," I said. "Really appreciate your support."

"I've lost track of the truth," Cam said. "That's the long and the short of it."

"The long of it is Trevor went face first from the top of a building," I said. "The short of it is the guy sitting beside you orchestrated the fall."

"Where you at, Crang?" Bam said. Could eyes look menacing? Bam's seemed to. Must have caught it from his smile. Bam said, "You about to hand over the money *and* me to the cops?"

"You got it, Big Bam," I said. "Catch my drift?"

"Catch this, asshole," Bam said. "I still got that gun in my pocket, and it says you and those money belts are gonna walk out the door of this restaurant with me."

"Surprise, surprise, Bam," I said. "You got a gun in your pocket, but I got one in my hand, and right this minute it's under the table pointed at the middle of that jumpsuit of yours."

"A gun?" Annie said.

"Just a minute, Crang," Cam said.

"Don't fuck with me, Crang," Bam said. He had the tough sound down pat, less Humphrey Bogart and more somebody from *The*

Godfather. "You were clean when you came into my booze can tonight, and there's no place since then you could've picked up a weapon."

"Tran's gun," I said. "You don't believe me, phone the cops at 52 Division. They'll tell you they took in Tran minus his gun."

Nobody spoke for five seconds.

"Great idea now that it occurs to me," I said. "Phoning the cops. Why not you do it, Cam?"

Cam stayed put in his chair.

Bam said, "Okay, maybe you got Tran's gun under there. But no way you got the nerve to shoot me."

Big Bam was closer to the truth than he knew. Or maybe he did know. I'd never fired a gun in my life, not even an itsy-bitsy handgun like Tran's. But there was always a first time.

"Try me," I said to Bam. My voice still didn't exactly ring with authority, not even like the guy who played the weakling in *The Godfather.* John Cazale?

But it was apparently enough to make Big Bam shift gears. When he spoke again, he turned smooth and oily.

"Listen, Crang, my man," he said. "You just relax up now. What I'm gonna do, I'm gonna remove the piece from my pocket at the front here. Keep it below the tablecloth. No fuss or muss for anyone. And you're gonna slip me the money belts under the table, you with me?"

I didn't answer.

"And after that," Bam went on, slick as grease, "I'll take my leave of you folks. Let you enjoy the evening. Drink your aperitifs. Sit tight. All that. You hear what I'm saying?"

What should I say? "No dice" would be dramatic. But did I want drama? Something neutral would be better. Delay for a time. Somebody might come to my rescue.

Big Bam showed signs he didn't have time and wasn't inclined to delay. He unfolded his hands on top of the table, and dropped the right one into his lap. I knew what that meant. He was going into the jumpsuit for his gun.

I'd run out of choices.

I was down to one.

I shot Big Bam.

The noise I made, the noise of Tran's gun, wasn't louder than the squibby pop of a small firecracker, and the hubbub of the packed room cancelled out the tiny sound. Bam may not have heard the shot, but the evidence seemed to be he felt it. He went over the left side of his chair toward Cam's lap. He didn't topple out of the chair. It looked more like he'd dropped to grab at something down below.

"What happened?" Annie asked me.

"Shot the bad guy," I said.

Bam, bent over and out of my sight, was muttering in Vietnamese, and sprinkling the mutters with little whimpers.

"Where'd I get him, Cam?" I said.

Cam wore an expression of horrified distaste. He was pushing at Bam, whose slumped weight was dislodging Cam from his own chair.

"I think he's been hit in the foot," Cam said.

"Nice shooting, sweetie," Annie said. "Put the guy on the disabled list."

"There's no blood down there," Cam said.

I said, "Beats me the damned bullet even got through his shoe."

Bam groaned something in Vietnamese from under the table.

"Cameron," a deep voice broke in.

None of us saw the man approach our table. He was tall and slim, and had wavy grey hair and a spiffy three-piece brown suit.

"Why, Stuffy," Cam said, coming out of his chair. He moved so abruptly that the moaning Bam slumped against Cam's thighs.

Stuffy? This gentleman was Detective Stuffy Kernohan? But he was supposed to be short, round, and red-faced. At least in my mind. In real life, he looked like a brain surgeon.

"I've a painful duty, Cam," Kernohan said.

"It's all right, Stuffy." Cam put a hand on Kernohan's shoulder. "I already know. Trevor's dead."

"That sad news travelled quickly," Kernohan said. He had two men behind him who looked like real cops. Lumpy guys with no necks and polyester suits.

"This man here may be responsible for Trevor's death," Cam said, trying to pry Big Bam off his legs.

"Who is he?" Kernohan asked.

Cam turned to me, and Kernohan followed his glance.

"Ng Thai," I said. "But you'll recognize him as Big Bam, the master of revels at the booze can you raided tonight."

The two lumpy guys squeezed past their boss and pulled Big Bam up by his shoulders. Bam let out another groan.

"Don't be a baby, Bam," I said. "It's only your foot."

"And where did you belong in all of this?" Kernohan asked me.

"He's the lawyer I told you about," Cam answered.

"Crang?" Kernohan said.

"In person," I said.

"We expected to meet you inside the booze can."

"Well, something came up, and I had to stay undercover. Underground too, come to that."

Our waiter pushed between Kernohan and the other two cops.

"Will you gentlemen be ordering?" he asked.

"I'll have another double vodka," I said. "What're you drinking, Annie?"

"*Crang*," Cam said, reproving.

"White wine, please," Annie spoke up.

Bam whimpered.

"What's the matter with him?" Kernohan asked.

I brought my right hand from under the table, and dropped Tran's gun on the cloth. The two lumpy cops made quick moves inside their suit jackets.

"Never mind," Kernohan told them.

"I had to wing Bam with this thing," I said. "Or, wait, you call it *wing* when you get a guy in the foot?"

"Never mind, Crang," Cam said.

"Anyway," I said, "the popgun belongs to a guy named Nghiep Tran. He works for Bam. If you check, you should find Tran's already been nabbed by your fellas at the subway station down the street from here."

One of the lumps took a handkerchief out of his pocket and picked up Tran's gun with it.

"You guys want a real mean six-shooter," I said, "unzip the front pocket on Big Bam's jumpsuit."

The second lump went into the handkerchief number and took charge of Bam's gun.

"You seem to know a great deal about all of this," Kernohan said to me.

"Happy to share it with you," I said. "But maybe your first order of business is getting Bam out of here and patched up."

Bam moaned on cue.

"Stop acting like a wimp, Bam," I said. "It's just a little ping in the foot."

"You come too, Crang," Kernohan said. "I want to hear how this man killed Trevor Dalgleish."

"Ten minutes, Stuffy," I said. "Annie and I've got drinks on the way."

Kernohan stiffened, and the two cops in polyester looked like they were itching to cuff me or something else fierce.

Cam stepped in.

"Perhaps we can leave Crang for the moment, Stuffy," he said. "You and I might profitably exchange a few thoughts."

"Before the press gets wind of tonight's events," I said.

"I'll speak to you about silence later," Cam said to me.

"And about a fee?" I said.

Cam latched on to Kernohan's elbow, and steered him between the tables toward the door. Kernohan didn't seem to object. The two cops hoisted Big Bam under the arms, and escorted him in the same direction. Bam was hopping on one foot.

The waiter returned with our drinks.

"Are these charged to the Charles party?" he asked.

"And give yourself a generous tip," I said. "Twenty-five per cent."

The waiter gushed his thanks and left.

"What a hero," Annie said to me.

"Hard part's up ahead," I said, going for a modest tone. "Stuffy'll keep me explaining all night."

"Poor baby."

"Do this for me, honeybun," I said. "Guy in the phone book named Ralph Goddard. Call him and get his summer cottage number. That's where Dave Goddard is. Phone Dave and tell him it's all clear to come home."

"The jazz musician," Annie said. "Everything that's happened tonight, I forgot he was the point of the whole exercise."

"Dave's not enraptured with the ornithology up where he is."

I took a long, comforting pull on my vodka.

"That was incredible marksmanship," Annie said. "Shooting blind like that, under the table, and you got the man in the foot."

"Not so incredible," I said. "I was aiming at his knee."